THE Ugly TREE

Cayla & Ashleyn,
Enjoy! Hope you
love the story!
Tamara Lyon
10/23/10

Tamara Lyon

Comfort PUBLISHING

Copyright ©2010 by Tamara Schmidt
Library of Congress Control Number: 2010927847

The Ugly Tree

All rights reserved. The author guarantees all contents are original and do not infringe upon the legal rights of any other person or work. No part of this book may be used or reproduced, stored in a retrieval system or transmitted in any form or by any means without prior written permission of the publisher, except in the case of brief quotations embodied in critical articles and reviews.

For information, address Comfort Publishing, P.O. Box 6265, Concord, NC 28027. The views expressed in this book are not necessarily those of the publisher.

First printing

Book cover design by Colin Kernes

ISBN: 9781935361527
Published by Comfort Publishing, LLC
www.comfortpublishing.com

Printed in the United States of America

This book is dedicated to Nanny, my very own Grandma Betty.

Prologue

On the night that I was born, the circle of life sucker punched my family in the face. Grandma Betty stepped up to the plate, and out of her iron will to make lemonade out of lemons, she named me Cane, claiming it was because I was as sweet as sugar.

There are two problems with my name. First, there isn't really a thing about me that's sweet. Second, I've read the Bible. The spelling of a name doesn't mean anything, and you can't convince me otherwise.

Before I had even come out of the womb I had broken the sixth commandment, more than once, and was in dire need of absolution by the time they wiped the birth matter off of me. When I sit in Grace Lutheran Church with Grandma Betty, I'm always on the lookout for God, but I've failed to find Him. Maybe it's because of what I did that God chooses to ignore me when I'm in church. "Come out, come out wherever you are," I say to Him, but He keeps on hiding.

Wooden pews and rote prayers don't offer much comfort, but I've found a place that has. Every Sunday evening after Grandma Betty goes to bed, I tie a rope to a limb on the oak tree outside my bedroom window, climb down, and run to the forest preserve on the other side of town. Just inside the split rail fence that borders the back of the property is a daunting hill that overlooks railroad tracks, cornfields, and one turbulent and defiant stream that floods every spring.

A solitary maple punctuates the knoll. Unattractive but brawny, it was struck by lightning on the night I was born, during the storm that ruthlessly destroyed our lives. An inspiring portrait of life and death, only half of the tree lives. It defies death every time it sprouts a leaf, grows a limb, and slowly but steadily inches its way upward, taking its dead half along for the ride.

Part One
June 1992

Bygones

"You better get up sweetheart. You have to leave for work in a half hour." Grandma Betty pulls the cord on the vertical blinds letting in sunlight and showing me that she means business. "It's a beautiful day," she chirps.

Groaning I sit up, decide against it, and then collapse back onto my bed. Hopefully she didn't come armed with a water pistol. It takes a lot to get me going in the morning, and she has resorted to some ingenious tactics lately. My eyes are lined with a brittle crust, sealed shut at the edges. Rubbing it away, I attempt to look outside, but everything is blurry.

"I packed your lunch and put it in your backpack. It's going to be hot today. I can just smell the sun, can't you?"

Grandma Betty turns her head and sniffs the air suspiciously. "I swear, the dandelions are sizzling outside, and it's not even eight-o-clock."

Allow me to introduce my grandmother: the bloodhound. The woman can smell everything; I've told her more than once that the police force needs a good tracker. She laughs at this suggestion, but I'm convinced she could solve crimes by following her nose. Toucan Sam doesn't have a thing on her.

"Don't expect me home for dinner; I have to work late. Connie called in sick again. I don't mind," she says breezily. "We could always use the extra money."

My grandmother was born to pick up the slack. It's her nature to run her life and everyone else's.

By the time I've finished shoveling scrambled eggs and Lucky Charms down my throat, Grandma Betty has everything I need lined up in a neat little row by the back door. If I would let her, she would sew name tags on the inside of my clothing, strap an ID bracelet to my wrist, and happily put my hair in pigtails. I put an end to this nonsense in the fourth grade.

"Now remember, tonight you have to swing by the library and return books. I stacked them in the hallway on the table, five of them I think."

"I know."

"Dinner shouldn't be a problem. I whipped up a casserole; it's in the fridge. There are directions written on top. Preheat the oven and put it in for an hour. Make sure you eat some vegetables, too."

Her thoughtfulness brings out the worst in me, and I know that I will bake that casserole tonight and then dump the serving I'm supposed to eat in the garbage disposal and grind it up. I should get it over with and tell her that her casseroles suck and that I am tired of her treating me like a baby, but I don't want to upset her. So, what do I do? I waste her hard work and hurt her feelings without her knowledge.

"Bye, sugar Cane." Grandma kisses my cheek. Her skin smells of Ivory soap and yarn; it's silky and cool against mine.

"Bye," I say in return, stifling a yawn. I scrub my dishes and set them to dry in the drain board.

"You behave yourself today," she winks at me and wags a finger playfully. Then she's out the door.

What would it be like if I wasn't the perfect kid, if those silly warnings I got on a daily basis were given because I was constantly getting into trouble? Being good tires me out, and I've been so good for all of my life I'm not even sure how to go about being bad. I don't know how to find trouble; it eludes me. Do you have to have a membership to be a delinquent?

Well, I'm not completely innocent. There's always my secretive warfare with Mikayla, my neighbor and nemesis for four years running. When it comes to plotting against her, my imagination takes a nosedive into the deep abyss of evil. If Grandma Betty only knew the things I've done.

Slinging my backpack over my shoulder, I head outside. My means of transportation are pathetic given that I am a hop, skip, and two months away from turning sixteen. While most kids my age have graduated to riding in their older friends' cars or driving their own, I still ride my 1976 royal blue Huffy bicycle, christened Smurfette, due to my childhood obsession with the cartoon, The Smurfs. Complete with a banana seat and frayed wicker basket on the front that's roomy enough to accommodate my backpack, it's practical and comfortable. Even though I'm short, five foot three and a quarter, I outgrew the bike years ago. I have the seat up as far as it will go, but it still looks like I bike-jacked a little kid. Since it's my biggest source of misery, I should wise up and stop riding it. I've heard it all.

"Nice dildo seat."

"She skipped the candy and stole the baby's bike instead."

"Watch out, it's the retard motorcade."

Or the simple and eloquent, "Nice ride, freak."

A miser at heart with money piling up in my bank account, I could replace it. But, I'm attached to Smurfette for nostalgic reasons. I can't let go of things very easily. There's plenty of proof under my bed at home, a stockpile of items that Grandma Betty, honorary president of the organization police, is just dying to be rid of.

Dumping my backpack in the wicker basket, I maneuver Smurfette onto the road. The streets are deserted this morning, not that I expected a traffic jam. Savage, Illinois, the place I've called home my whole life is a bucolic farming town about an hour and forty five minutes northwest of Chicago that hosts a colony of five thousand inhabitants. The only wild thing about Savage is its name, the origin of which no one can agree upon. One theory is that when the land was first settled it was terribly uncooperative and ran rampant with coyotes. Others swear it had something to do with a group of unfriendly Native Americans; this presumption is no longer referenced in this new age of political correctness. I don't care how this place earned its name, but it would be cool if something major happened to give credence to the name Savage. However, in a town with one stoplight, you can't raise the bar too high.

Monday through Friday I work at Schaeffer Acres, a prestigious dairy farm, now under the ownership of Samson Schaeffer. Thanks to eighty years of blood, sweat, and tears, this family business is worth millions. Schaeffer Dairy stores are located throughout northern Illinois; they deliver and sell milk and delicious, artery-clogging ice cream to the masses.

At the farm, I don't necessarily work with the livestock, and that's just fine with me. Shoveling cow manure, yanking on teats, and scrubbing down the living quarters of those beasts isn't my idea of a party. I like to think of myself as the resident landscape architect, but, if I'm being honest, I have to admit it's a fancy name for a groundskeeper. I'm about as low as you can get on the job totem pole.

I'm subjected to a variety of odd jobs that generally include prettying up the place. There's not much glory in it, but I don't mind the work.

Manual labor, although tedious at times, is something my agile, wiry body is good at. While most girls my age prefer to have jobs in air-conditioned clothing stores, I can't be confined. Walls make me claustrophobic, and whenever I'm indoors for too long, I start sprinting through the house, doing jumping jacks, or walking up and down the stairs. During the winter, Grandma Betty gets fed up with my antics and drives me down to the YMCA in Clinton, a large town thirty miles away, and makes me swim laps in the pool to get rid of the "ants in my pants." I thought I would have outgrown this, Grandma Betty told me I would, but puberty only made the problem worse. A couple of years ago, I joined cross-country and track, and since then, there have been fewer emergency trips to the YMCA.

Given my job at the farm, I'm outside from late spring through early fall, and during these months I rarely have "ants in my pants." My body and mind are too busy getting drunk off the summer cocktail: mix warm weather, cerulean skies, and one engorged sun, and the combination is heady. Despite my faithful application of thirty plus sunscreen every morning to prevent blistering sunburns, I'm sure that the exposure to all these rays of light will catch up to me in thirty years and make my face as unattractive as a wrung-out dishrag. However, the penetrating warmth of the ultraviolet rays, the way it sometimes feels like someone is holding a magnifying glass against my skin, is a pleasure I can't deny myself. When I go home at night, I put my nose against my arm and inhale the sweet, burnt odor the sun has left on me and study the small freckles that have pushed their way to the surface and clustered together like miniscule raisins.

While I enjoy my job, the days are made long because of Samson's wife, Jenny Ryanne. Samson hands me the paycheck every two weeks, but I know who wears the pants in the family and in the dairy business. Samson might as well walk around in his boxers. Jenny Ryanne is the one who decrees my every action. Given the woman's obese figure, penchant for glittery clothing, and habit of wearing raspberry colored lipstick on oversized, clown lips that look like they've been pumped full of collagen, I privately refer to her as Jelly Roll. Really, at some point the woman must have taken lessons from a hemorrhoid; rarely do ten minutes go by before she's on my butt about something. A perfectionist with the heart of a dictator, no one can please her. She white gloves everything that goes on at the farm. Her obsessive compulsiveness has paid off; last year the Schaeffer homestead had a full spread in Country

Life and Farming magazine that spanned seven pages. Every one of those pages is laminated, matted, framed, and hung on the wall in the dining room of the Schaeffer's immaculate and historic three-story, renovated farm house.

When I bike the three miles to their farm every morning, I study other properties in the area that are comparable in size, and they look like normal farms: peeling paint, crooked siding, a fine grit hanging in the air, dust covering the windows, discarded machinery in foot-high grass, driveways with deep rivets from the spring thaw, and an odor of animal feces and mud. Not the Schaeffer farm; it's an anomaly. It boasts barns in a deep cherry hue, crisp concrete drives that connect all the buildings, beautiful cedar fencing that is fanatically sealed each summer, surfaces (including the grass) that look like they're scrubbed nightly. The windows reflect an obscene amount of light, and if I'm not wearing my sunglasses and accidentally look at those shiny panes of glass, my retinas feel like they're burning. Even the cow manure smells perfumed. I can't explain it.

Jelly Roll is always on my case, but she doesn't hound me because I'm lazy. Usually she has to find more work for me to do because I'm too efficient. It's my theory that she hates me because of history and genetics. She went to high school with my dad and, according to my grandmother, had been shamefully in love with him. My dad was never interested—thank God for that. When my mother came along in college, no one else ever stood a chance. Since Jelly Roll always gets what she wants, I'm sure this is still a sore spot for her. Bygones are never bygones, especially seeing as how I am the carbon copy of my mother, from her dark auburn hair to her hazel eyes. You don't just inherit looks from your parents; you inherit enemies.

All of Jelly Roll's bitterness has been transferred to me. She tries to cover it up, but that only makes it uglier. Whenever she looks at me her mouth wiggles its way into this zigzag smirk, and when she manages a smile, it's a smidge short of a sneer. Some of the things she says to me are downright mean, but she goes about it in a backhanded way. So that if push came to shove and I ever made an objection or an accusation, she could tell me I was reading into things. Yesterday, while I was shoveling mulch into a wheelbarrow, she stood with her arms crossed and flexed her toes on one foot; her flip-flop banged against her calloused heel.

She said, "You're really thin, it's a good thing you've got those muscles to give you some definition, and a good thing you've got that hair to help you look feminine. Your hair is what sets you apart. When you get all the mulch down, I want you to level it out with your hands."

The translated version: "You look like a skinny boy, and I hate the color of your hair. For your punishment I want you to bend over for hours and get splinters in your hands and knees while you make my landscaping look perfect."

In a world where there were no consequences, I would have fired back, "You're so fat, it's a good thing you wear flip-flops all the time, because I don't think you could bend over to tie your shoes. Why don't you get your fat butt down here and spread this mulch yourself."

Plenty of times I have had to plant the heel of my left foot on the tips of my right toes to stop myself from saying something that would get me fired. They pay ridiculously well for me to jeopardize my position by opening my big mouth.

Despite Jelly Roll's heartache over my dad, she must have moved on, because she married rich Samson Schaeffer, who just so happened to have been my father's best friend. How's that for a twist of fate? She produced what I think is a shameful amount of children given the fact that she isn't Catholic and we live in a world where over-population is the talk of the times. I go to school with her eight kids, and since she had them consecutively, most separated by only a year or two, they span all of the grade levels. They all have J names. Normally, this kind of stunt would make life insufferable for the kids who would endure endless teasing, but the Schaeffers have money and influence, apparently making them untouchable. From oldest to youngest: Jeremy, Joshua, Jordon, James, Jocelyn Ryanne, Jonathon, Jonas, and the youngest, who loves to show you his boogers and then eat them, Jade.

You would think the Schaeffers have enough help on the farm with the children, but the oldest four boys spend the summer playing baseball, attending basketball camp, riding their four-wheelers, and going on long camping retreats. The only girl, Jocelyn Ryanne, is a miniature Jelly Roll with much less ambition than her older counterpart. She devotes her time to the television where she watches movies on the VCR. When she does move, it's to the refrigerator to get a Coke or to the freezer for a bowl of Chunky Cow Pie, the best-selling flavor of Schaeffer ice cream. The younger boys play in their tree fort that is a replica of the house and dedicate the rest of their free time to swimming in the super-sized family pool, outfitted with a slide, waterfall, and diving board. Not once have I seen any of the kids help with any chores, at least not for more than a few minutes, lending credence to the silver-spoon theory. I guess that's why they hired me when I was only eleven.

As I bike down the driveway, I hear the hiss of the air compressor being turned off and the scream of James' new dirt bike. Jelly Roll, wearing a white cotton shirt that's sprayed with silver glitter, walks out the side door with a clipboard in her hand. I reach down and adjust my kickstand, tightening the screw that holds it in place with my fingers. Neither of us looks at each other until we have to. I stand slowly.

"Good morning," I say politely, my fingers finding my back pockets and hanging there.

Jelly Roll never has time for small talk.

"I've got quite a few things on here today. Start at the top and make your way down. I expect the grass to be cut diagonally one way and then the other. Be sure to cut it twice, because Samson likes the look of baseball fields. Don't get sloppy around the trees like you usually do, but don't hit them either. I had James put air in the riding mower tires. Everything should be ready. There's extra gas in the barn if you need it. Also, Samson's nephew is here for the summer. He's going to be learning the ropes. When you're ready, he'll help you dig the trenches out back for the new sprinkler system we're having installed; you'll find him in the cow barn."

"What are we supposed to do with all the dirt we dig up?"

She purses her fat lips and looks at me like I'm speaking a foreign language. "Leave it in a pile, but make sure it's on the other side of the fence in the field. We can put it back after the system is installed and seed it. If you have time after the trenches are dug, I want you to power wash all the driveways and scrub the mud out of the seams with a brush."

Jelly Roll hands me the list, I briefly scan it and know I won't have time to piss my pants let alone power wash the miles of concrete. I suppose I should be thankful that she's letting me use the power washer and not making me get down on my hands and knees and lick it clean.

"What's his name?" I ask as she's walking away.

"Whose name?" she asks impatiently, pinning the clipboard against her meaty thigh.

"Mom, I want to go to the store now!" Jocelyn screeches from the front porch. She swings her mother's purse from her hand. "Hurry up!"

Jade is standing next to his sister, holding up a prize of a booger for me to inspect. I inwardly sigh, pushing all the air out of my lungs. "Your nephew's name," I clarify.

"Justice," she answers.

Of course it would have to be a J name. When she's busy ushering her children toward their oversized luxury van, I snicker and head toward the equipment barn to retrieve the riding mower.

Samson is on the opposite side of the barn. He waves to me, and I wave back. This is the usual sum of our communication. Appropriately named, Samson is a giant of a man with hands the size of dinner plates. When he waves, I swear I can feel a breeze. Six feet, six inches and solid muscle from years of physical labor, he's a force to be reckoned with. If not for his infectious grin and chipped front tooth, two qualities that make him accessible, he would be intimidating. When I first started working here, I deluded myself into believing that we would forge a strong friendship and have long, heart-to-heart conversations about my father. I've since learned that Samson rarely speaks, probably because he's married to a tyrant who won't keep her trap shut. Even though Samson has never said a word about my father to me, I think he wants to. There have been times when I've caught him looking at me, his expression one of disbelieving grief, the kind of look you would have if you were standing over a casket or seeing the ghost of someone you loved. It makes the hairs on the back of my neck prickle and fills me with a hollow sadness.

I hop on the riding mower and power up the engine, driving out of the barn slowly. Although I don't really enjoy sitting for three and half hours, the typical time it takes to cut the two acres of manicured Schaeffer lawn, it gives me time to do the three things I love most: listen to music on my Walkman, study my Trivial Pursuit cards, and scheme against Mikayla.

Once I get the first pass cut and make sure the lines are straight, I relax and pull out the stack of Trivial Pursuit cards from the back pocket of my jeans. I devote hours to memorizing absurd facts. While I love fiction, nonfiction bores me to tears, and I consider trivia games my stab at higher education. Today, I'm sticking with my strong suit, the art and literature category.

What is the literary term for a play on words?
Pun. Jelly Roll anyone?
What did the old woman in the shoe give her children to eat?
Broth. Grandma Betty's favorite ingredient; she adds chicken broth to everything, including her casseroles.
Who wore the coat of many colors?
Joseph. *Duh.* That's Sunday school fodder. If I didn't know that, it's unlikely that I would be allowed through the church doors.
What magazine paid Ernest Hemingway $15 a word to write

a bullfighting article?

I have no clue. I flip the card over. *Sports Illustrated.* I didn't even know that magazine had been around that long. As for Hemingway, I don't know what all the fuss is about. Literature elitists would stone me to death for saying this, but I think his writing is mediocre and most likely produced under the influence.

Don't drink and write, Ernest, but he went ahead and did it anyway.

Who was Helen of Troy's Trojan lover?

Paris. I know many of the famous lovers in literature and history: Romeo and Juliet, Cleopatra and Mark Antony, Cyrano and Roxane, Tristan and Isolde. Anything memorable has to do with love.

What word is used in Hawaii as both a greeting and a farewell?

Aloha.

I'm totally kicking butt today!

When I'm finished cutting the grass one way and then the other, I meander over to the livestock barn to meet this Justice boy. During my three hour tour on the mower I've already made a pile of assumptions. I expect that he's my age or younger, and since he's related to this family, he's spoiled, rude, and arrogant. If he's like the older Schaeffer boys, he actively participates in flatulence contests, rating on both sound and smell. Or maybe he's more like the miniature Jelly Roll, so fat he can barely move, and his parents sent him to the farm instead of fat camp.

I round the corner, and he's standing there, towering over me at six feet. I'm not one of those girls who swoon over guys. The walls in my room aren't plastered with handsome men but instead feature famous quotations, pictures of nature, and one R.E.M. poster. Yet, here I am depleted of oxygen like an asthmatic and in danger of keeling over.

When I look at him more closely, I think of those Stetson ads on television, the ones that feature the cowboy up on the stallion. He could be straight from the Wild West; then again, a costume change, a shave, some hair gel, and he could be a ringer for a young Superman. He possesses all the superhero qualities: the strong jaw, the piercingly blue bedroom eyes, and even the cleft in the chin. However, his imperfections, the slightly crooked nose and stubble that is sparse in some places and thick in others and dimples that appear to be slightly uneven, are the things that make him breathtakingly beautiful. I need a shovel to scoop my jaw off the ground.

"You must be the illustrious Cane." He extends his hand. "Nice to meet you," he adds.

As I put my hand in his, I can feel my pulse everywhere, in the tips of my toes, in my lower abdomen just under the waistband of my jeans, and in the base of my neck.

"Hi…um, so I guess we have to dig a trench for a new sprinkling system?"

"That's the plan." Justice turns and loads shovels and spades into a tractor cart. "It's in one of the fields near the rear of the property. I've already outlined the area with some landscaping paint. Are you up for this? I could do it myself."

"It's not a problem." For once, Jelly Roll has done me a favor, and right now, I love her.

"Why don't you hop in back, and I'll drive us out there."

I want to suggest that I could ride up front with him, that we could make room on the seat, but I don't.

"Sure." Feeling my disappointment in my shoulders, I climb in back and hold on to the metal sides of the cart. I don't know how to interpret Justice's expressions. When he smiled at me before he turned around, his lips were rigid. Was it a smile or a grimace? Is he annoyed? I wonder if I'm something he has to put up with, and I can't handle this thought. I don't want to be the kid, but in his eyes, that's what I am, isn't it?

During the bumpy drive to the back field, I assess myself and try to see what Justice must see, a scrawny girl with long, messy auburn hair whose pale skin is dotted with a million freckles. Move over stars in the sky, I've got constellations right on my body. While I love to think that people notice my almond-shaped eyes that can go from gray to olive to cobalt depending on my mood or oddly enough on the weather, they're probably overlooked because of those annoying brown spots.

At one time I had appreciated my freckles. In grade school they served as a form of entertainment; my friends and I used them to play connect the dots. With a little ink and some ingenuity, we were able to make all kinds of shapes and objects. Our game irritated the teachers. What could they do, take our pens and pencils away, erase my freckles?

After Justice turns off the tractor, we unload all the materials in the type of silence that as it goes on is harder to break. I would like to think that this uncomfortable feeling is sexual tension, but let's get real. He probably wouldn't touch me with a ten-foot pole. Justice is probably worried that I'll slow him down, so he's trying to think of a way to get rid of me and do this himself. Actually, this is my only advantage right now, my only weapon. If there's one thing I can do, it's amaze boys with my strength. I'm determined to impress Justice, and that means I can't focus on his now shirtless, tanned body and those horrifyingly delectable muscles. The boys in school, even the athletic ones, don't have the kind of muscles that Justice has, which leads me to believe that he isn't a teenager and so far out of my league I would need to be shot out of a cannon to reach him.

Thanks to my superhuman strength, I do succeed in getting noticed.

"To be honest, I thought you were going to slow me down out here," Justice pauses and leans on the end of the spade.

Hah! I was right.

"But, it looks like I'm the one slowing you down. You're strong," he falters on this comment.

"Don't you want to add the 'for a girl' part?"

He laughs and yanks the spade out of the ground. "I wasn't going to say that."

"I've heard it before."

"I don't know what I was expecting, but I'm impressed."

A small victory. I grin smugly. "I'm used to this kind of thing. I've been working here for four years."

"It shows."

"Yeah, my biceps are bigger than yours." Even though this is a complete exaggeration, I stop and flex my muscles for him.

He raises an eyebrow skeptically. "I think something is wrong with your vision."

Thankfully my face is already pink from the hot sun, so I don't think he notices my startling blush. My face turns red on a dime, and the color refuses to stay in the lines like a normal person. It spreads all the way up into my hairline, keeps going, and lands on the nape of my neck. At least my hair covers that part.

"What are your stats?"

"What?" I toss a large mound of dirt onto the pile, and half of it slips off the shovel and lands in the plush, weed-free grass. Crap. I wouldn't put it past Jelly Roll to make me use tweezers to clean up all the loose soil.

"You know, name, age, occupation, background, hobbies. That sort of thing. Get that out of the way and small talk isn't necessary anymore. Future discussions will actually mean something since they won't be steeped in formalities."

The best thing about Justice is that he isn't like any other boy I have ever met. For one thing, he has a vocabulary; he knows how to say more than 'cool', 'dude', 'whatever', or 'yeah, sure.' Since he is already making reference to future discussions, I allow myself to hope that he's interested in speaking to me after today.

"Oh, stats." I scrunch up my nose and push the shovel into the earth, then jump on it with all of my ninety-nine pounds trying to get it in further. While doing this, I consider lying about my age, but I'm pretty sure my nearly flat chest and Huffy bicycle would make it impossible for me to tell him that I'm eighteen. Inwardly, I curse myself for wearing my sports bra and not getting rid of Smurfette four years ago. "I'm Cane, but you already know that. I'm almost sixteen."

"Almost?" he asks, amused.

"In two months."

"Oh." He smiles.

God, I should have just rounded up. That's like saying I'm fifteen and a half, something that only a kid would do. I'm such an idiot. "Background? I'm not really sure I have one. I've lived in the area my whole life. I spend way too much time reading, probably because we don't have cable. I enjoy trivia games, sports, and being outdoors."

In a nutshell, I'm lame. I should have told him I was a teen model and that I frequently traveled to exotic locations for photo shoots but that I've decided to take time off to write my autobiography.

"What kind of trivia games?"

"Mostly Trivial Pursuit. I love to memorize facts that no one else knows."

Justice considers this for a moment. "Huh," he says. "Is that what you were doing earlier, on the mower? I saw some cards in your hands. You were pretty focused on studying them."

I couldn't believe he had been watching me! Had I done anything embarrassing? Had I scratched my armpit? Had I half-stood and picked the underwear out of my butt? I did that sometimes. In my defense, my butt got hot and sweaty sitting on that vinyl seat after an hour. "Um, yeah, I just like to bring them with me for distraction."

"What kind of sports do you like?"

"I'm on the track and cross-country teams in school. I also play volleyball and basketball, but not professionally."

Justice laughs and quickly appraises me. I blush fiercely, again, and turn away, because this time he probably does notice.

"You're a good runner?" he asks.

"The best. Well, not the best. There's this one girl with legs that are about as tall as I am. Her name is Shannon. She's the best. I'm in slot number two."

"That isn't bad."

I scoff. "No one ever remembers second place. It's the blue ribbons that mean something."

"I don't know if I would necessarily agree with that."

Justice and I have dug about twenty feet, maybe more, and my arms are aching. I forcefully suck in my cheeks, something I do whenever I am in pain. Although the guppy look isn't attractive, the only alternative is taking a break, and I'm not stopping until he does.

"What are your stats?" I need to know as much information about him as I can.

"Justice Price, twenty-one, full time college student."

Five years and a couple of months isn't a gap, just an inconvenience! I inwardly celebrate.

"I grew up just north of Clinton, in Hampton. I'm a sports junkie, basketball in particular, and I played varsity ball all four years in high school. I'm sensitive to the second best thing since I was second best on the basketball team, and I would like to think that people remember me."

"Where do you go to college?"

"U of I. I'm majoring in history and business, two opposite ends of the spectrum, but I want to keep my options open for career moves just in case the family business doesn't stick. I'm getting my feet wet this summer, and Samson was nice enough to let me live here for free, not to mention he doubled the wage I was making as a bank teller."

"You worked in a bank?" I couldn't picture Justice counting money all day; I could see him in a newsroom as a hunky reporter, but that's my Superman fantasy getting the best of me. "I can't stand being cooped up inside. I wouldn't have lasted a day in that bank."

Justice lowers his voice. "I lasted a week. It was just too quiet in that place. I can't tell you how many times I had the uncontrollable urge to scream."

I laugh and pull my hair back at the same time, fixing it into a pony tail with a rubber band that I had around my wrist. "I don't blame you. I hate being inside too, which is why I've worked here for so long."

Justice pushes his dark eyebrows together, and his ocean blue eyes meet mine. "Four years here, huh?" He whistles. "I'm surprised you keep coming back for more. She's not the easiest person to work for, is she?"

He glances in the distance.

The humor fades as I see Jelly Roll driving across the field on her pink golf cart. The unevenness of the terrain makes every ounce of her fat jiggle. Even from the considerable distance I can tell she isn't happy about something. Her lips appear broken at the edges.

"Oh, God," I mutter under my breath.

"Hell hath no fury," Justice intones quietly.

Sensing impending doom, we keep our eyes focused on the dirt we are shoveling. She yells at me before the engine of the golf cart has been shut off and then leaps out of the golf cart, a surprisingly nimble move for her.

"What are you doing, Cane? This is absolutely the wrong depth, and the line is supposed to run east, west, not north, south. You have overheard me talking about the plans for this sprinkler system, you should know better."

Never mind that Justice took charge of this project and had drawn the lines earlier. But, I'm not about to throw a sexy man under the bus. "I'm sorry."

Justice steps in front me.

"Aunt Jenny, it's my fault. I painted these lines. Cane was just following my directions."

He's defending me! I hide my smile by wiping my mouth against my forearm.

Jelly Roll adjusts the strap of her swimming suit cover-up, that incidentally doesn't cover enough. "That doesn't mean she couldn't have spoken up." She sighs and straightens her sunglasses that are coated with a thick layer of sparkles just like her swimsuit underneath.

Barf, does she ever look disgusting. Wearing that outfit exposes a generous amount of skin. She looks like a bejeweled, roasted marshmallow.

"You're going to have to fill this back in. You'll have to get some grass seed too. Cane can show you where to find it. I want the line to run that way, parallel to the fence," she points at the fence with her sausage finger. "About two feet in front of it. Don't forget to water the seed after you are done. It's going to take some work to get a hose out here. I'll see what Samson can do about that."

When she gets back in her cart and stomps on the gas, Justice sighs and remarks, "That's the reason why I'm shocked that you've lasted this long. I don't think the woman does anything but critique all day long. Kudos to you for being able to put up with her. I'm only one day in, and I'm fed up with it."

"It helps if you call her Jelly Roll. Trust me, it makes you feel better about the situation you're in."

Justice laughs when I explain the derivative of the name, and for the remainder of the day he refers to his aunt as Jelly Roll and snickers every time he says it.

Being around Justice feels normal and natural, but in an elevated, thrilling way. It takes some concentrated effort to forget how handsome he is, but when I succeed, it's like I'm hanging out with my best friend. I don't feel weird or awkward like I do around the boys at school. We spend four hours together, minus a thirty minute lunch break, and the whole time I'm fishing for information. I've learned his favorite things, besides basketball, are water skiing and kayaking, but he hasn't done either in far too long. His mom, Samson's sister, is a pediatric nurse who isn't too involved with the family business, but he doesn't mention a thing about his father. I assume he isn't in the picture.

The juiciest material I got was that he recently ended a long-term relationship with a girl at school. He said he was glad for the break from all the drama. He was hoping that this summer would give him an opportunity to get his head on straight.

Personally, I don't think it's crooked at all; he seems fine to me. His situation is my providence. He's out here alone, single, and possibly wounded from a break-up. I have a chance, even if it is a snowball's chance in hell.

Throughout the day I'm witty, appropriately sarcastic, and sometimes flirtatious, not that I am an expert on this. Who knows; I'm probably making an ass of myself with my body language and giggles. When I run out of things to discuss, I test his knowledge of sports with my trivia questions and stump him when I ask him what sport FISA governs, which is auto racing. He claims that he doesn't know anything about that sport and that he doesn't particularly like cars. This is another attractive quality about him, considering the guys in high school make owning a sports car their number one priority in life.

At the end of the day, after we've put all the tools way and stand chugging water from our thermoses, I decide that I'm going to ask him to hang out with me. If I want to be an equal, I have to be confident but casual.

"Um," I say and rock onto my toes. "What are you doing tonight?"

"Beyond dinner, I have no idea. Samson invited me to the bar to meet some of his buddies. I might go."

"I'm going swimming, and I was wondering if you wanted to

join me."

"Oh," he says, his voice dipping low. He sets his water bottle down slowly and stares at the cedar fence that borders the oak tree on the corner of the property.

I follow his gaze to where I have dumped Smurfette, the bike that is currently defiling my reputation and subtracting years instead of adding them. I've spent all day building a bridge between us, and now I'm witnessing its destruction.

"Um. I'm not sure."

A few displaced crickets chirp in the barn behind us.

Justice rotates his foot and glances at the mud that is caked on the bottom of his boot. He smacks his heel down hard on the grass and it falls out of the treads.

"Are you going to swim here?" He glances over his shoulder at the Schaeffer's pristine, resort-like pool. Jade is sitting on the edge of the diving board, and for once his fingers are nowhere near his nose. Someone should take a picture.

"No way. I don't even think Jelly Roll would allow it. I go out to the gravel pit, off of County N; it's just past the forest preserve. There's a pond on the west side, and you don't have to worry about seaweed because it's deep. I'll probably get there about ten tonight. If you want, you can join me."

I don't give him the opportunity to say anything more. "Aloha." I pick up my backpack and head toward the road.

Aloha?

What the hell was that? There's a loose wire between my mouth and brain, and I wish I could hire someone to fix it. Thankfully, by the time I make it to the oak tree, Justice has gone somewhere. Embarrassed, I climb on Smurfette and furiously pedal home, trying to outrun my childhood. I don't know if I'm fast enough or if I can ever catch up to Justice, but maybe I won't have to. If he would turn around and meet me halfway, we could be together.

Peas in a Pod

Mikayla and I were born on the same night, August 19th, 1976. I think God was trying to make nice by giving me someone to take my brother's place. Although I don't remember the occasion, we met when the grass over my family's graves was beginning to thicken under the September sun.

A young couple with an infant had just moved into the grand, brick Georgian across the street from Grandma Betty. Being the socialite and neighborhood ambassador, Grandma Betty carried me in one arm and a plate of brownies in another and went over and rang their doorbell.

Annette, Mikayla's mom, answered the door with a wailing infant in her arms. Tearfully happy for the visit, she invited Grandma Betty into the house where they spent over an hour swapping condensed life stories. Annette had grown up on the west coast; a true California girl who loved the ocean, sun, and sand more than anything on earth, she had never expected to leave. Desperately homesick, there wasn't a thing she could do about it because her husband, Mitch Atwood, a pilot, had been hired by a major airline in Chicago, and his career was finally taking off, literally and figuratively. He was often gone, and Annette said it was lonely and difficult to adjust, especially with a newborn.

Although Grandma Betty hadn't been transplanted to another part of the country like Annette, her life had been uprooted and thrown into the wood chipper. Grandma Betty shared what had happened in our family, leaving out the gory details that she doesn't like to think about, the same ones that I obsess over. Their shared desperation and grief sealed the deal; fast friends were made.

It's no surprise that when I was three months old and Grandma Betty had to return to her management position at Hometown Drugs that she didn't have to pound the pavement to find a reliable babysitter for me. Annette jumped at the chance; she wanted Mikayla and me to grow up together.

I really don't have any childhood moments that don't include Mikayla. In fact, my very first memory, the first time I was even aware that I was a living, breathing creature we were sitting side-by-side, staring into the long mirror that was propped up in the corner of Annette's bedroom. I believe my experience was unique, in that I didn't just realize that I existed, that I was an arrangement of fascinating and beautiful things like limbs, eyes, hair, ears, lips, and teeth, but I was also acutely aware that the presence beside me was entirely separate. There were two reflections, not one.

How could this be? Weren't we the same person? I had assumed up until that moment, in that spongy, pre-cognizant phase of my life, that Mikayla and I had been the same person. The mirror snapped my theory in half. Upon discovering this, I burst into tears, because not only was it my first memory of being alive, but also my first memory of being alone.

Separate we were, but rarely were we apart. Grandma Betty and I became part of the Atwood family. They became everything that was taken away from me, and so I raised them up on a pedestal and made them my ideal. In them, I had a mother, a father, and a sister. What more did I need?

On many occasions when I was out with Annette, people assumed that she was my mother; sometimes they even told me I was beautiful just like her. When this happened, Annette never rushed to explain the history behind our relationship or deny ownership. She would simply bend down and plant a delicate kiss on my scalp. During those moments, I realized that I had become as much a part of Annette's heart as she had become of mine.

Naturally, our socializing went above and beyond the daycare arrangement. The lawn in front of both of our houses was worn in spots from our footprints. We didn't just share impromptu dinners, summer days swimming in the town pool, and nights spent around a bonfire roasting marshmallows and reducing life to the bare bones with stories and anecdotes, but we shared the important things that stick to your ribs and heart, the kinds of things that stay with you forever. Every milestone, every accomplishment was made with Mikayla by my side.

Mikayla and I learned our letters together and sang each other the alphabet song so frequently it would be ringing in my ears at night when Grandma tucked me into bed. When Annette gave birth to Mikayla's baby brother, Gabriel, Mitch drove both of us to the hospital. Pressing our faces against the nursery window, we stared at her little brother and secretly told each other we didn't think he was that great. When it was time for preschool to start, we clung to Annette's legs, Mikayla on the right, me on the left, and cried until the teacher had to pry us both off as Annette escaped. The following year we held hands as we waited for the kindergarten bus to arrive, our matching Strawberry Shortcake backpacks overflowing with school supplies. In first grade we both lost our first tooth on the same day, and Grandma Betty picked me up from Mikayla's house after work and said to Annette, "These two are certainly peas in a pod, aren't they?"

"I think they're more than that," Annette said, smiling and carefully putting my tooth in a small plastic bag to take home.

Our friendship went beyond the ordinary, and if I could try to put into words what it was like, I would say that our spirits were sewn together. I never really felt like a whole person unless Mikayla was by my side. Others took notice of our connection as well, especially when strange things happened for which there was no logical or scientific explanation.

The first time was when we were nine-years-old. Mikayla stayed home sick with strep throat. I visited her after school, holding onto a couple of text books and a story that I knew would make her laugh. Mrs. Parttyde, also known as Mrs. Farttyde, had been the substitute. The woman never had a chance; I mean, with a name like that, she was bound to be phonetically destroyed by a bunch of third graders who believed bodily functions to be the ultimate source of humor. That day her nickname grew legendary when Jason, the chubby and gregarious class clown, inflated a whoopee cushion and discretely hid it under a cardigan on Farttyde's chair. When she lowered her ample bottom to the chair and the sound erupted beneath her, the class nearly fell on the floor with laughter. Mikayla had the same reaction when I told her the story.

Nothing had gone wrong at our visit to suggest that something awful would happen to her that night, but at two the next morning, I woke up clutching my throat and a horrible fear flattened my stomach like a pancake. When I ran down the hallway to wake Grandma Betty my legs could barely support me.

"Wake up, wake up! Something's wrong with Mikayla!"

Grandma Betty reached for the lamp. "Honey, did you have a dream? Are you sick?"

"It's not a dream. I'm not sick! Something is wrong with Mikayla!"

"I know honey, she's sick, but I'm sure she's better now. Go back to bed."

"You don't understand! You've got to call their house now!"

Grandma sighed and swung her legs over the side of her bed. She sat there with her head lowered to her chest and rubbed her face with both her hands. "Cane," she said softly, her tone reassuring and flimsy, a sign that she wasn't really getting the message.

If I had to, I would run across the street. I just knew Mikayla couldn't breathe; my own windpipe constricted in response.

"We don't have time! Something is really wrong."

"Okay, okay," she said sleepily and picked up the old rotary phone on her nightstand and dialed the numbers. Luckily, they answered.

The sound of sirens filled our neighborhood mere minutes after that call. Mikayla had suffered a nearly fatal reaction to the antibiotics the doctor prescribed. Her temperature had spiked, her throat had started to swell shut, and in her feverish stupor, she hadn't been able to wake her parents. She spent a day in the hospital recovering, and not only did she receive balloons and flowers from everyone, but I did as well.

For days afterward, Grandma Betty, Annette, and Mitch walked around with goose bumps, rehashing the unusual chain of events. None of them could quite believe my clairvoyance. They chalked it up to divine intervention. They said it was a one time thing.

Only it wasn't. Mikayla and I became a medium for each other's trials and tribulations. I was sitting in church when I just knew that her golden retriever, Salem, whom we both loved more than anything in the world, had been run over by a car. Grandma Betty couldn't figure out why I had started crying and took me out of the sanctuary. When I told her what had happened, she took me home without a word. We buried Salem in the Atwood's backyard that night.

It wasn't always life and death. Mikayla had been visiting her grandmother in California when she told her mom that she wanted to go home because I had the chicken pox and was feeling lonely. Annette did some fact checking with Grandma Betty, and sure enough, I had just come down with the chicken pox and was lonely. The Atwoods didn't cut their vacation short, but I did receive several care packages that included gifts from Disney Land, Venice Beach, and Hollywood.

Mikayla and I accepted what we knew to be true, that our souls were conjoined twins, seamlessly sewn together. The adults in our lives, however, had a hard time coming to terms.

When I broke my arm falling out of a tree, an event that Mikayla had known about hours before I showed up at the Atwood's door wearing a cast, they were still trying to sweep things under the rug.

"It's a fluke," Mitch said. "Kids are like that. They can sense things. They'll grow out of it."

"I'm sure they will," added Grandma Betty. "It's a shame, though, that they're going to lose that connection."

"I'll be glad when they outgrow it. Anytime one of them is upset, I automatically assume something horrible has happened." Annette picked up a thin, black marker and signed my cast, her signature said, "To my second beautiful daughter, Cane. I love you."

The thing about a connection is that it can never be outgrown or broken. Relationships, however, can. The relationship I thought I could count on the most fell apart. It happened so quick that if I had closed my eyes, I might have missed it. There's misfortune and heartbreak in what happened, but if Mikayla and I could somehow stop hating each other and peel back the layers between us, we would find that we had been right next to each other all along, like two peas in a pod.

A Natural Disaster

In our garage there's a box filled with painting material. My grandmother, fickle when it comes to color, repaints the rooms in our house annually and sometimes seasonally. I swear that the square footage is shrinking; the layers of paint are probably thicker than the plaster. During these decorating whims, I assume the role of indentured servant. I've spent my fair share of nights and weekends with a roller in hand painting the walls colors like: Moonshine Yellow, Tang-a-Green, English Rose, Daredevil Red, and Candy-Cane Pink.

Opening the supply box, I remove a painting tarp and then proceed to mummify Smurfette, wrapping her securely inside the canvas. Under any other circumstance this would have been a monumental gesture, but after meeting Justice it's a necessary step in the right direction. Hefting the bike over my shoulder, I carry it to the store room and place it next to the boxes of things waiting to be sold at our annual July garage sale. When I have the opportunity, I'll have to buy a grown-up bike to replace Smurfette. For now I'll travel by foot, because I refuse to ride Grandma Betty's bike. It screams old lady. The seat on her brown and orange Schwinn is large enough to accommodate Jelly Roll's butt. Saying one last goodbye to Smurfette's corpse, I flick off the light.

Inside, I prepare dinner, following Grandma Betty's instructions that she took time to type and then tape to the top of the aluminum foil. After eating a portion of the casserole, which doesn't taste all that bad after I bathe it in a layer of ketchup, I go upstairs to my room.

My nervousness about tonight is ridiculous. I'm no pocket-protecting math geek who can spit out numbers like Rain Man, but I know the chances of Justice showing up tonight are less than one percent. Still, I'm hanging on to that one percent by the skin of my teeth; it's enough to make my stomach quiver. I've heard of butterflies, but what I'm feeling is an indigestible ball of nausea, fear, and excitement.

I hear Grandma downstairs. She calls up to me.

"You home?"

"Yes," I reply loudly.

"How was your day, sweetheart?"

I instantly smile, because I'm thinking about Justice's dimples.

"Fine," I say casually. "How about yours?" I ask loudly, giving her permission to relay the events of her day, something I know that she loves to do. She plods up the stairs and stands in her room, talking as she changes her clothes.

"Oh, you know, Frank came in, and he said to make sure I said 'hi' to you. He's fascinated about some storm we're supposed to have tonight, says it's going to be one for the record books, he's sure of it. You know how he is about stuff like that! It makes me nervous, but there's no stopping him. He bought some batteries for that high-tech equipment of his. I don't even know what half of those thing-a-ma-bobs are for even though he's tried to explain it to me so many times.

"Can you imagine filming storms and taking pictures? I told him that normal people stay in their houses and duck and cover if they need to. Play with fire and you're bound to get burned."

Grandma Betty makes a clucking noise. "He's going to get himself killed if you ask me. He worries me half to death.

"Then I find out the real reason Connie didn't come into work is because she was out on the town last night, having herself too good of a time at Savage Suds, partying it up like she didn't have a care in the world when I know that she's late on her rent. She's constantly telling me that she wants to turn things around for herself, but she's taking all her chances and throwing them out the window. I keep trying to tell her you only get so many opportunities to set things straight. It's a shame; I don't know if she'll ever learn responsibility. And how does it look that I'm the one who hired her! It's a travesty if you ask me, and another thing…"

Her lengthy monologue, comprised mainly of gripes, will last for ten minutes, maybe more. Wrapping things up with words is her therapy, and I'm the therapist. Lucky me. Thankfully, I'm never expected to respond. Tonight, I don't have the patience for it. I quietly get up and discreetly close my door, shutting out the sound of her chattering.

Since I still have to go to the library, I want to get everything prepared for tonight. Stripping off my clothes, I pull on my bikini, not the most practical for swimming, but I'm going to impress Justice if I have the opportunity. Then, due to my inverted chest (is it possible to be a negative A?), I cringe. The cups are far from running over, more like they've never been filled. My sporty navy two piece that resembles a sports bra and underwear is a better choice. Maybe I'll pack my bikini, just in case I decide on a costume change. I'm not sure where I would do this, but I'll figure that out later. I fold it up and put it in my backpack along with a couple of beach towels.

Grandma Betty approaches my room, and I rush to throw on a t-shirt and shorts over my swimsuit. I don't want her to have a clue about where I am going tonight.

She opens my door without knocking. "Was the casserole good?"

"Uh-huh," I respond apathetically.

"You didn't eat much," she comments, her forehead creased with concern.

"I don't have much of an appetite." This is the truth. My stomach, the gymnast, leaps back and forth inside of me.

"Honey," she plants her hands on her hips, screws up her nose and squints thoughtfully, "Did you reapply sunscreen? You probably got sun sick! You might even have a fever!"

More like love sick. "I'm fine."

"Want me to make you something special?"

"No, I don't want you to make anything else. Just leave me alone," I say crossly, my voice rising close to a shout. Why does she always have to be so accommodating? Her kindness wears on me, even demoralizes me. Why can't she get angry? Even perfect moms like Annette yell.

"Something happen at work?" she asks with concern.

I roll my eyes so far back I can see the divots in my brain. I needed to get out of this house about five minutes ago. "No, nothing happened! I'm fine. I'm just getting ready to run to the library."

"You're going to run? Why don't you take Smurfette?"

"I'm going to run," I enunciate each word through gritted teeth.

"Okay, okay. That's fine," she shakes her head and leaves my room, mumbling something about hormones and teenagers being the world's greatest mystery.

My plans for the evening change when I go to pull on my running shoes and my fingers make contact with shiny, sticky goop. Upon further investigation, I discover that the inside of every shoe I own is coated with a generous amount of Vaseline.

"Damn it!" I mutter under my breath.

I don't know why I'm surprised. Two weeks ago, to the day, I snuck into Mikayla's house and decorated her cheerleading uniform with a tube of toothpaste, squeezing the mint green gel in the pleats.

"Shit!" If I'm going to run to the library or to the gravel pit, I have to have at least one pair cleaned.

I manage to make it down to the kitchen unnoticed and retrieve a spoon and paper towels. In my bedroom, I get to work, and after an hour most everything is cleaned out. I take my Nike shoes downstairs and run them under hot tap water in the kitchen sink. Now thoroughly soaked, they need to be dried fast. I run down to the basement and toss them in the dryer, a move that elicits a comment from Grandma Betty who's sitting on the couch. Her knitting needles work away at each other like a set of miniature teeth eating up the yarn.

"Sounds like you're drying a herd of elephants down there."

I lean against the door frame. "Just my running shoes. I washed them."

"Your trip to the library is going to have to be postponed. There's a tornado watch until eleven tonight. You're not going anywhere."

The National Weather Service message streams across the bottom of the television screen, promising torrential rains, lightning, and the possibility of a tornado.

Pat Sajak smiles at the woman wearing hoop earrings that are bigger than my head. When the wheel lands on the five hundred dollar space, she claps like she's won the lottery.

"R, choose R!" shouts my Grandma Betty whose Wheel of Fortune addiction has made her scary good. "There are two of them in that phrase. If you don't know this one, you don't have a chance!"

The woman chooses B, and Grandma slaps her thighs.

"Oh, schlop," she exclaims, her delicate version of shit. "I honestly don't know where they find these people."

"It's not even raining outside," I lightly throw the comment out there. "I'll be fine."

Grandma Betty puts her knitting down and turns her nose into the air then breathes deeply. "No, I can smell the storm coming, and I don't think there's going to be much rain, but lots of lightning. And a tornado for sure. The air smells of sulfur, nasty cumulus clouds, and a faint trace of static. Can't you smell it?"

"I'm not part dog." I cross my arms.

"Very funny young lady," says Grandma. She shakes her head and resumes her critique of the game show.

"I'll be quick, I promise."

"You're not going anywhere."

Fine. I won't go to the library, but I'm not canceling my plans for later, no matter what.

There's a persistent and rhythmic knock at our front door that is clearly heard over the rattle of our window air conditioner. Grandma Betty pulls her glasses off and squints at the door. It doesn't require my psychic abilities to know who it is. She's come to gloat.

"I'm not home," I say adamantly and hurry to the kitchen just as Grandma Betty's opening the door.

"Hi, Grandma Betty. How are you this evening?"

"Mikayla! I don't see you around here near enough."

Like not at all, I'm thinking.

"How are you, dear? Come inside. It's just so hot out there!"

"Grandma Betty, I just had to come over to tell you that I am in awe of your flower garden out front. It looks absolutely stunning. What is it that you planted on the corner? The plant with the purple flowers? "

I stick my finger in my mouth. Gag. The thing about Mikayla is that not only is she beautiful, in the conventional perfect breasts, long legs, flawless skin, blue eyes, perfectly symmetrical face, long blonde hair kind of way, but she's also sickeningly kind and respectful to adults. So much so that she has everyone over twenty-one convinced of her sainthood. However, her peers view her in a more realistic light. When called for, she can be ruthless and manipulative, but she does it with such slight of hand, it's like watching a magic trick. Her talents have secured her popularity in high school. She's the *it girl*; everyone loves her. As for me, I just plain hate her.

"It's called Salvia, and I'm so happy that it's thriving this year. Frank was thinning out his garden last fall, and he gave me some. Anyway, I'm so glad you noticed! Not many people your age take an interest in landscaping."

This comment is a barb aimed at me. I refuse to help my grandmother with landscaping since she spends more time transplanting and rearranging than enjoying what she has.

"I think a manicured garden makes the house. My mom wishes she had your green thumb. She says so all the time, but she has to hire someone."

Oh, please. Mikayla's blowing so much smoke I can barely see through the smog.

"You be sure to tell your mom that I would be happy to help her if she ever decides to take up the hobby."

"Is Cane home by chance?"

"Of course, she's in the kitchen. You go on back."

She sold me out; I live with a traitor. As Mikayla enters the kitchen with a smug smile on her face, I grind my teeth. She raises her eyebrows and regards my bare feet with disdain. "Hey."

"What do you want?" I ask tersely.

"Just dropping by to see how things are."

"Fantastic."

"Have you gone running yet today?" She asks innocently and leans against the kitchen counter.

"Vaseline? Not the most creative." I notice how her toes are buffed and fresh from a pedicure; my toenails are pale and slightly misshapen from a botched trim. Self-conscious, I curl them.

"I'm here to warn you." She leans toward me and lowers her voice. "I've had enough of this petty shit."

"You started it." Technically, this isn't true. She started what led up to the war. I'm the one who threw down the gauntlet.

"Can't we move on? Haven't you ever heard of water under the bridge?"

"I've heard it, but I suggest you get a life jacket, because the current is still strong."

"Grow up, Cane."

When Mikayla gets angry, her thin face closes in on itself and becomes gaunt. Her blue eyes darken to a smoldering gray. Since I know her so well, I can push her buttons better than anyone, and what really pisses her off is passive aggressive sarcasm.

"You first," I say politely and follow up with a wink.

It works. She sucks in her lips so that her face becomes nothing but sharp cheekbones and wide eyes. Then, because Mikayla prides herself on not letting anyone get the best of her, she puffs herself back up and thinks of a witty response.

"I'm already there," she glances conceitedly at her chest and then stares at mine before meeting my eyes, "obviously you aren't."

"Why are you here? I don't recall extending an invitation."

"I'm here, because I'm tired of this grade school bullshit, and if you don't knock it off, I'll do something that you'll regret."

I gnaw thoughtfully on my thumbnail. "The toothpaste in your skirt was too much for you, wasn't it?"

Mikayla takes a step toward me with her hands on her hips, and her attitude is so similar to Jelly Roll that I start laughing.

"What's your problem?"

Spreading my hands out in front of me, I shrug. "I don't have a problem. You do. You started it."

"Why can't you just get over it already?"

I lower my voice to a rumbling growl. "Get the hell out of my house. Don't you have something to *do*? Like Nate, for instance?"

Nate, Mikayla's older boyfriend, a football god with a brand new red Mustang, reigns as Savage High's most popular boy. Not many people can see past his handsome face or through his charm, but I have x-ray vision. He's pond scum.

Narrowing her eyes at me, Mikayla reaches up and winds her long, blonde tresses around her hand and then flings her hair back over her shoulder. "At least I have a boyfriend."

"So do I," I claim vehemently. "I'm meeting him tonight." If Grandma Betty just heard this, I'll be subjected to an inquisition.

"Sure, what-ev-er. Just so you know, one more stunt and there'll be hell to pay."

"*The calm before the storm!*" Grandma Betty shouts the Wheel of Fortune phrase. "How can you not know that?"

"I'm shaking in my boots." I make a motion to go along with this.

Mikayla strides out of the room, her shapely tan legs moving gracefully. If only God hadn't been cruel and given me a pair of freckled sticks to carry myself around on.

"Bye, Grandma Betty. You have a lovely evening."

"Thanks for stopping by! You and Cane should chat more often. Stop over again."

"I will."

Angrily, I stomp up to my room, ignoring Grandma Betty when she asks how our visit went. Is she really that clueless? Doesn't she know that Mikayla and I stopped being friends four years ago? I mean, after all, she witnessed some of it.

After slamming my door, I decide to sift through some Trivial Pursuit cards and brainstorm about how to get back at Mikayla. My efforts are pointless.

Suddenly that drug commercial where they crack an egg and fry it in a pan makes complete sense, only I substitute one word. "This is your brain. This is your brain on Justice. Any questions?"

Holy crap, am I pathetic or what? All this energy wasted on a guy who probably thinks I ride to daycare after work on my Huffy bicycle.

I slide off my bed and go over to my window. Kneeling, I pry the dusty screen off and then crank the window open. Sticking my head out into the summer air, I rest my elbows on the sill that I painted only last month per Grandma's insistence, a color called Cotton Puff.

From the second floor, I have a clear view of our compact neighborhood that is just under two miles north of downtown Savage and can easily spy on any of the eight houses that line the southern portion of Scott Road, a gravel thoroughfare that wanders lazily through the countryside and ends up spilling onto County N. Beyond the thick of ancient hickory, maple, and oak trees that surround the houses, are corn fields spread so far it gives credence to the theory that the Earth is flat.

The storm that the forecasters have predicted is taking its sweet old time; it rattles the leaves on the tops of the trees and darkens the horizon. While I can't yet hear thunder, I do hear the familiar rumble of Nate's Mustang. He brakes hard right before Mikayla's driveway, and the back end swings out and sprays gravel onto our front lawn. What an ass! Mikayla bounds out her front door and practically leaps into his front seat. They're whispering something to each other, and then they both look up at my window. Despite the camouflage of limbs, they can see me.

Nate slowly backs out of the driveway, shifts gears, and before he takes off he shouts, "LOSER" in my direction.

For once, I agree. Slamming the screen back into place, I close the window and pray that Nate forgets to put the top up on his Mustang so that the rain will ruin his leather interior.

The rain seems imminent, given that the horizon is an ominous shade of violet, but I don't care. No matter the circumstances, I will go, even if it means running a few miles in the rain and dodging a few bolts of lightning. I have a follow through that sometimes annoys me.

The next three hours I waste on reading articles in Seventeen Magazine, a subscription that I study more religiously than the Bible. Over two years worth are safely tucked under my bed and serve as my reference library when I need information on femininity and on how to attract guys. There's no denying I need all the help I can get; most days I'm a walking natural disaster. Let's face it; Grandma Betty isn't the greatest source for current trends. God love her, but the woman favors polyester pants with elastic waistbands and views Aqua Net hairspray as trendy. Need I say more?

After studying photos and scanning articles, I'm successfully confused and annoyed. I'm supposed to: laugh at his jokes, ask him lots of questions, use coquettish body language, entertain him with a story, and let him see the best parts of my personality (like I even know what the best parts are.) Not only that, but it's advisable to wear a stylish outfit and have a natural face, opting for mascara, blush, and some lip gloss. It's doubtful this would do me any good since we're going swimming. If I wore mascara, I would end up with raccoon rings. Lip gloss, however, is an option. As for an outfit, the majority of my wardrobe is brand-less and all in shades of white and blue. My closet looks like it belongs to a United State's naval officer. About as inventive as I get is teal or black.

Grandma Betty walks into my room without knocking, and I shut my magazine and toss it under the bed like it contains illicit information.

"I'm off to bed sweetie," she randomly straightens my room, picking up pillows, folding clothes, and adjusting my R.E.M. poster. "You know, I really like the color of this trim. You did a good job painting."

Still bitter that I wasted an entire Saturday painting, I regard the trim with distaste.

Grandma Betty pulls a knitting needle from where it's perched on her ear and uses it to point to my walls. "I'm not sure about the walls, though. They said at the store that Mountain Ridge was a terra-cotta, but it's darker, looks more like watered down instant coffee, don't you think?"

"It's fine," I insist, fearful that she'll want to experiment again. I wish we had more money and she could play interior designer with fabrics and furniture instead of paint colors.

"I'm making another blanket for your room. I hope it matches. I should have held up the skein next to the wall before I started. You better get to bed. Get to sleep before the storm wakes you up."

The sky outside is clear and dotted with stars. "It's already passed. It stopped raining over an hour ago."

Grandma Betty bends at the waist and glances outside. "No, it's not finished. I can smell the electrical current. The air is braided with it! The weather man says there's another line coming, and that's the one that's causing concern. I'm sure we'll have to go down to the basement tonight. I expect to hear those sirens in an hour or so."

Privacy, I scream internally. I want privacy! When is she ever going to leave? Obviously, the sign on my door that says *Please Knock* doesn't mean a damn thing.

"You sure you're okay? You look flushed." She places the backs of her hands against my cheeks. I bat her away.

"I'm fine," I snap.

She grunts indignantly, but despite her frustration she bends down and gives me a kiss on the cheek.

I wait fifteen minutes, and when I see that she has turned off her bedside lamp, I prepare to make my getaway. I fish the rope out of my closet, the one that I use for midnight getaways, and untangle it. Opening my window, I tie it around the wide oak limb outside my window. I put on my backpack and look for my shoes. Crap! They're still in the dryer, which means I'll have to go out the back door. Risky, considering Grandma Betty has superhuman hearing to go along with that nose of hers. Undoing the rope, I coil it up and hide it in the back of my closet.

Thankfully, I make it to the basement undetected. When I'm finally outside, I wait under Grandma Betty's window to make sure that I don't see her light come on. I tiptoe across the lawn and walk on the side of the road until I'm confident she isn't going to come running out after me.

The night is a warm, black cape around my shoulders, and I drag it along for my run. My backpack bounces with each stride, and my pace, quick and effortless, allows me to reach the end of Scott Road in less than nine minutes. When I turn onto N, the shelter of the trees vanishes, revealing the night. The eerie green horizon pulses with amethyst lightning. It's not the storm I fear, but rather Justice's failure to accept my invitation. I'm not deluded by grandiose adolescent hopefulness like other kids my age. I'm well aware the odds aren't in my favor. Still, there's always that small chance…

By the time I reach the entrance to the gravel pit, I know I should turn around and go home. A rotten, instinctual lump has taken shape in the pit of my stomach, telling me something is wrong. But, I'm not one to back down.

Hiking to the far west end, I gingerly discard my backpack and sit down on the uneven pebbles that surround the shores of the pond. While I wait for Justice to disappoint me, I notice how active the fish are tonight. They leap in the air and flop frenetically under the surface. Just to the north, the storm has gathered itself together, puffed up its chest. Lightning flares brutally and thunder shakes the ground beneath me; the rain that begins to fall is anything but sure of itself. It's delicate, hesitant. Stripping off my outer layer and then even my swimsuit, I raise my arms, let me head fall back, and turn around faster and faster until I'm dizzy. Off balance, I dive naked into the silky, frigid water, swim half the length, and then back again. I emerge shivering and out of breath; my long hair creates a river that runs off my back and splashes onto the rocks beneath. Twisting the long strands, I wring out the water.

Then I hear what I think is an explosion in the distance, and my insides react with an overdose of adrenaline. The explosion turns into a long rumble, a shake of vicious thunder that doesn't go away. I see it even before the sirens begin to blare, a swirling mass of darkness so obscenely large and powerful it looks phony. It has already accumulated souvenirs. It rips away at the landscape, dislodges trees, and regurgitates what I believe to be a tricycle. I watch the darkness closing in on me, and its roar, not unlike that of a demon from the book of Revelation, crowds my ear drums until I feel them shake and pop.

Slipping into the water, the lowest point I can think of, I float on my back like a dead man and wait for the twister's wrath. I am calm, because I am Cane. I have been marked by God. He will spare me.

Headlines

Under my bed in a Ziploc bag, I store a newspaper article that outlines the pertinent details of my family's tragedy. For reasons that I can't explain, I've committed it to memory.

Whenever something horrible happens, I lock myself in my room and repeat this article verbatim, speaking it as if I'm a television news reporter with an authoritative and sympathetic inflection in my voice. Doing this reminds me that no matter how awful things are, they could be worse.

"Tragedy struck our small town last night, August 19th, when Savage resident Alex Kallevik, age twenty-five, and his wife, Mary Kallevik, age twenty-four, were killed in a car crash on County Road N. The driver of the other vehicle, Kevin Price, is in critical condition. The couple was on their way to Mercy General Hospital in nearby Clinton when the high speed crash occurred after the couple left their residence shortly after ten p.m.; Mary, forty weeks pregnant with twins, was in labor.

"Police chief, Frank Amundson, said the Kallevik's Chevy Nova was struck on the driver's side when Price failed to stop at an intersection, causing the Kallevik's car to spin and then flip.

"Emergency personnel pronounced Alex dead on the scene. Mary was rushed by ambulance to Mercy General where an emergency Cesarean section was performed. Due to the severity of Mary's injuries, she died during the procedure as did her infant son. The female infant, who has not yet been named, is in serious condition but expected to be released near the end of the week.

"Visitation for Alex, Mary, and their infant son, Craig, will be held on Friday in Savage at Grace Lutheran Church from noon until five pm.

The funeral will be on Saturday at noon, also at Grace Lutheran."

The story is more familiar to me than my parents themselves. Most times, I don't even think of them as my parents. They are Alex and Mary, the young couple who died in a car crash on County N. When they rushed my mother to the hospital, pulled me out, and cut the cord, is it possible that they severed my emotional attachment? What I want now, all these years later, is to be surgically reattached.

Genetics isn't tangible—it's not something you can touch or love. I wish my parents had something more to do with my past than DNA. I want a memory of my mother's voice. I want the sensation of my father's arms wrapped around me. Most of all, I want my brother by my side, someone who can understand what it's like to be me. Why can't I have any of this?

It's because of what I did. I'm the one with "ants in my pants." If only I had been more patient, I'm sure my mother wouldn't have gone into labor. However irrational this thought may be, damning evidence has taken physical form. When I was born, healthy but shaken, God tattooed my skin with a small but noticeable birthmark in the shape of a cross. With the texture of a scar, I can't help but notice it. An innocent swipe of my forehead and my fingers run over it. I read it like Braille, and I'm reminded. I've always wondered what mark God left on Cain's forehead. Was it just like mine?

Damaged Goods

The storm passed over me, pulling everything up, up, and away. The calm that had descended upon me minutes before and swallowed me whole now spits me out. I had known that God would save me, but what about Grandma Betty? Watching the erratic and ruthless path of the spiral storm, headed directly for our neighborhood and downtown Savage, I shake violently. The water around me ripples from my distress. Swimming clumsily to the shore, I dress as quickly as I can, the clothes sticking to my wet skin. Throwing my backpack on, I run and wonder why I can't feel my legs beneath me or my heart beating inside my chest.

It's raining steadily now, and I'm blinded by it. In my path I encounter various objects the tornado has regurgitated: a basketball, a pile of shingles, a mangled shoe, and a rusted antenna. I run, and then because it seems the distance has increased substantially, I sprint until every cell inside of me screams for oxygen. The nearer I get to Scott Road, the greater my guilt. Why did I leave my house tonight? I can't even remember. I've been shocked into a state of amnesia, and my head is thick with concussion symptoms. As I run over the uneven gravel on the side of County N, my ankle twists and I collapse in pain. Holding my Achilles' tendon, I remember the Vaseline, the rattle of the air conditioner, Mikayla's visit, Wheel of Fortune blaring in the background, and my grandmother yelling, "The calm before the storm!"

I think of the crash that my parents were in as I pass a flipped car with a For Sale sign in the window. A stunned cat crouches and then runs across my path at the sound of my footsteps. A car approaches and slows down; I move over. Turning, I see Frank's white Buick with shiny gold trim. He motions to me and then rolls down the window.

"Cane, what are you doing out?" he demands. "Grandma Betty has to be worried sick."

"I have to get home!" I say breathlessly, gulping in more rain than air.

"You bet you do! Now get in!" He leans over and opens the door for me.

I've barely closed the door when Frank takes off quickly, his tires squealing on the wet pavement.

"Seatbelt," he barks in drill sergeant fashion.

He watches me to make sure I obey.

"It was a bad one, the worst I've ever seen. I took pictures and filmed every last second." He swallows and nervously rubs the round bald spot on top of his head. "Stupidest move I've ever made. I'm lucky I made it."

Scattered on the floor and on the seats there are numerous video cameras and other electronic equipment. Frank Amundson, former chief of police and adrenaline addict, has traded his badge for the honorary title of town storm chaser. A stock market junkie and successful investor with a pension to boot, he has money that won't run out. He indulges himself with the latest and greatest gadgets.

"I - saw - it - go – right – over – me." I drag out the words like I'm trying them on for size. *Did it really happen*, I wonder to myself.

Frank rolls his lips inward until they disappear; his expression is inscrutable.

We turn onto Scott Road and immediately we're confronted by a snarl of limbs and branches. Frank swerves to avoid the mess, and the tires briefly slide off the gravel and hit the weedy shoulder; he brings the car to a quick stop, propelling us forward with such force that the seatbelt digs into my neck.

His hands grip the steering wheel, and his jaw is set in a hard line. He turns to look at me. "Why were you out in this?"

I try to swallow the hard knot in my throat, but it bobs right back up. "I don't know." Dazed, I look through the driving rain, and the headlights offer a distorted view of the terrain that has been sliced and diced. Who knew that something so round and billowy could be sharper than a razor?

"This isn't good," says Frank somberly. He runs his hands up to the top of the steering wheel and holds them there. "There are power lines down," he points to the side of the road. "I could get around the trees, but I'm not going to risk it. Let me radio in to the department and see what's going on."

Despite his retirement ten years prior, he still has a police radio on the dash of his car. He flips the switch, and instantly we hear chatter. Frank picks up the receiver and calls in. "Joe, you copy? This is Frank. I'm out here on Scott Road, just off N, and there appears to be power lines down."

"That's not all that's down, Chief."

Frank shakes his head miserably. "What does it look like out there?"

"Not good. Downtown is hit hard. The neighborhoods are in shambles."

"Casualties?"

Joe sighs. "Too soon to call. We've got the electric company and emergency personnel on their way from Clinton."

"Copy that. I'll be in touch. Over and out."

I'm shaking and have to hold my knees in place to keep them from knocking together. "We have to get to Grandma Betty."

"Yes, we do." Frank ducks his head so that he has a better view of the landscape. "We're going to have to turn around, go back to N, and take Main Street toward downtown and then get onto Scott by County H."

"It's going to take forever," I complain.

"We don't have a choice." Frank whips the car around and takes off quickly. The wet gravel and sludge shoot out from under his tires.

"I saw the tornado," I say reverently as if speaking of something other-worldly, which I'm sure it must have been. "I've never seen anything like it."

"It was something, wasn't it?" Frank turns to me and shakes his head in unabashed, horrified amazement.

His sadistic fascination with the tornado makes me uneasy.

"It looked fake, like something you would see in a movie." I divide my wet hair into two equal sections and begin to braid. When I'm nervous, I have to keep my fingers busy.

My knowledge of tornadoes is mostly from a weather trivia book that I checked out at the library.

How fast does the average tornado move? Thirty five miles per hour. **What direction do tornadoes rotate?** Counterclockwise. **What was the speed of the fastest tornado winds ever recorded? Where and when did this occur?** 286 miles per hour. Wichita Falls, Texas; April 2, 1958.

I swallow nervously, wondering what the winds were inside this tornado. If they had been faster, would they have lifted me out of the water?

"You think Grandma Betty is going to be okay?" My heart pounds so much it rattles my brain.

Frank doesn't hesitate. "Absolutely! She knows how to take care of herself."

For all his bravado, I don't believe him. There's something about the way the corner of his eye is twitching and the way he's concentrating on keeping his features in check that panics me. He's as worried as I am.

"I should have been at home," I whisper to the window.

I finish braiding the left side of my hair and turn my attention to the right. County N blurs by, and when Frank slows the car and turns right onto Main, the wide thoroughfare that heads south into downtown Savage, I'm reassured that everything is okay. The damage is insignificant. Snapped branches, vagrant garbage cans, and one mangled lawn chair seem to be the extent of the damage. As we continue into town, I relax. "It's not that bad, is it?"

"Not here." Frank's tone is optimistically cautious. "No."

Working my pointer fingers through my hair, I unravel both plaits at once and start over again, but when I spy downtown a few hundred feet ahead of us, I stop.

Frank rubs his jaw, reaches for the radio, but then glances at me and thinks better of it. "Let's go find Grandma Betty."

The piercing, jarring sounds of ambulance and fire truck sirens fill up the streets; the red and blue glow from their rotating lights illuminates what remains of the downtown. Many of the buildings that have been standing for more than one hundred years have been reduced to muddled, brick shells. It's hard to tell if the structures exploded or imploded. Maybe it was both. The bank, hardware store, and post office look like a tinker toy experiment gone awry. The framing is all that remains, and the boards hang awkwardly; not even an orthopedic carpenter could make them right.

Frank clears his throat to disguise a groan. "I'm sure it looks much worse than it is."

"How can you say that?" In disbelief, I scan the area.

A fleet of emergency vehicles parades into town trying to navigate streets that are nearly impassable because of the debris; the vehicles turn different directions in a divide and conquer formation. Frank pulls over to the curb, allowing a wide berth for all emergency vehicles to pass.

I look back at the buildings and for the first time notice the sidewalks, upon which some stunned Savage residents carefully wade through the wreckage. They huddle together in groups and frantically exchange information and reassurance with gestures and body language.

There's a sharp whistle in our direction, then a shout, and Frank lowers his window. Joe Radtke, the officer who Frank talked with earlier, jogs over to the curb. He leans on the car and lowers himself until his elbows stick out at right angles. He is about to say something to Frank when he spies me in the passenger seat.

"I picked her up on the north end of Scott," explains Frank hastily. "Any news?"

Joe looks at me one more time, "Um," he pauses uncomfortably and drums his thumbs against the car door. He continues guardedly. "The emergency teams from Clinton are here and so is the power company."

"Good." Frank reaches for a video camera that sits on the seat between us and pushes an eject button on the side. He extracts the tape and examines it before handing it to Joe. "I'm sure the news teams are on their way."

"We've gotten word they are. They're even coming from Chicago."

Frank jiggles the tape. "Can you see that they get this?"

"Sure."

Joe scans the area with his eyes. "You know, Frank, the weather service is saying it was somewhere between an F3 and F4."

"I'm not surprised," says Frank soberly.

Joe's radio beeps, and he pulls it off his belt. "I've got to go. Be careful."

Neither of them knows of my significant knowledge base when it comes to storms. The Fujita scale, a tornado damage scale, was developed in 1971 by T. Theodore Fujita of the University of Chicago. An F3 contains winds of 158 to 206 miles per hour and causes severe damage. Roofs and walls can be torn off houses. Trains can be overturned. Trees are pulled up by their roots, and cars can be lifted and tossed through the air. An F4 is bleaker, boasting winds of 207 to 260 miles per hour, and causes devastating damage. Houses are leveled; structures with weak foundations are blown away. Cars are thrown, and large missiles are produced.

This knowledge that has been handed over unceremoniously has ignited a frenzied fright, and my body goes from hot to cold and back again.

"Can we hurry?" My voice is a screech.

Frank pulls away from the curb. "Of course we can." He looks at me out of the corner of his eye. "Don't worry, she'll be okay."

Who are adults out to convince when they say things like this? Surely not me. I'm not blind or stupid. Does Frank think that I can't see the pickup truck that is coiled around a birch tree? If that isn't enough of a clue, how about the houses?

They're worse than the buildings; they're deflated. The storm came along, pulled the plug, and let the air out of them. But, there's no sense to what has occurred, because right next to the ones that have been destroyed there are others that are perfectly and arrogantly intact. The damage inflicted seems intentional, and it gives the tornado a humanistic quality, making its wrath highly personal.

Just off the town square on Washington Street, a narrow brick avenue with houses dating back to the Civil War, there's minimal damage for most of the block. The tornado must approve of these grand old homes and can't bear to see them destroyed. One house, a brick Georgian, has a few shattered windows; the wavy glass finally waved goodbye under the duress of the high winds. An old Queen Anne Victorian with a wraparound porch is missing its staple swing; the delicate white chains rock nothing but themselves. The roof of an understated Craftsman boasts a bald spot that spans ten feet or more.

A few blocks west of Washington, the houses are torn apart at the corners, and I cover my eyes with my hands. Spreading my fingers into the shape of a fan, I peek out again. This is what it must be like to live in a war-ravaged country or in a village in the Middle East after the bombs have fallen.

Emergency vehicles are parked at the end of the street. A Red Cross crew sets up camp, constructing tents and pulling boxes out of the back of a flat bed truck. At the end of the block, a reporter from Clinton stands with a microphone in her hands. In the air I hear the steady thump of helicopter blades.

Frank exhales heavily but says nothing; he focuses on maneuvering the car through streets that are a treacherous, narrow maze. More than once we have to turn around and start over, find another way.

When we finally approach County H, the road that feeds onto the south end of Scott, we encounter a road block. They're not allowing cars in or out, and I am ready to open the door and sprint. Frank turns and sees my hand on the handle. "Stay put, I'll get us through."

"Hey Wes," Frank greets the current police chief with a sedate smile. "Hell of a night. I need to get through, trying to get Cane home. We've got to check on Grandma Betty."

Chief Wesley Fitzgerald, a balding, portly man with a fondness for laying down the law and daring anyone to go against it, pinches the edges of his curly mustache and tugs downward. "Wish I could let you through, but we're keeping the roads open for emergency vehicles only."

"Wes, if I don't get through, Cane is going to go alone, and we can't have that happen."

Wes stands up taller, sticks out his stomach, and slides his chubby fingers under his waistband as he considers. Frank still has pull in this town, and Wes knows it.

"Fine, fine. Go in then. Radio if you need anything. We're sending some emergency crews out your way because..." he stops, and his eyes dart my way. He wipes his hand across his mouth, "I'm sure they're needed."

He's hiding something; I'm sure of it.

When the barricades are pulled away, I still have a desire to get out and run. I know I could get there faster, but I've already made too many mistakes tonight and can't risk another. Grandma Betty needs to know that I'm okay. I need to know that she is okay.

Having turned onto H, I have limited perspective of the devastation since the houses in this region are set back off the road, but I can see the storm has been merciless here as well. Smaller trees have been torn out of the ground, their root bulbs, similar to a colony of lifeless snakes, jut up into the air. A rundown ranch that has always been an eyesore has caved in; its roof is now in the formation of a sharp V. Frank turns onto Scott Road.

As we approach the houses, I can feel my heart beating in my fingertips and in my head but nowhere else. The miscellaneous rubble is unruly and substantial, and I can't see past it. Frank's window is still open and in the distance I hear shouts, and I can make out one of the voices. It's Mitch, Mikayla's father.

"She's got to be in there!" he yells.

Frank pulls over. "Let's get out and walk. Stay close by me now." He hands me a flashlight. We pick our way over the confusion of vegetation and garbage. Clothing, pictures, shattered pottery, and a smashed VCR with wires protruding are strewn across our path. I look down on what is beneath my feet because I don't have the courage to look ahead.

I hear a frantic voice, Mikayla's this time. "She's not in there! She's not! I know it!"

"She has to be."

"I'm telling you, she isn't!"

Finally, the path clears in front of Frank and me, and I lower the flashlight to my side and my fingers uncurl of their own accord. The flashlight makes a soft thud as it hits the ground. Franks places his hand on my shoulder. The landscape spread before me is something that can only be conjured up in a nightmare.

"She's tough," Frank says simply, but his voice catches on the words. "She'll be fine."

When I was little, I used to love it when Grandma Betty read the *Three Little Pigs* to me. It wasn't necessarily the story that I enjoyed, but it was the dramatic way Grandma Betty would pretend to huff and puff and blow the houses down. Now the big bad wolf had come and done that to my house. The front hangs together limply; the walls are severed and slashed in unusual places. I can't see the back of my house well enough to assess the damage, but it appears almost normal. I race toward our house, leaping over whatever is in my way like a professional hurdler.

Annette, Mikayla, and her younger brother Gabriel are in my front yard, standing guard over something. They turn and see me, and Mikayla says, "I told you she wasn't in there. I knew it."

Mitch, who has been navigating the mound that had been my house, carefully makes his way toward us. "Cane!" he shouts with relief.

"Cane!" Annette shouts. "Oh, my God! Sweetheart, where have you been?"

I can't answer them, for I see that Grandma Betty is lying at their feet covered in a blanket. Her face is bloodied; there's a wicked gash above her eye. The shallow movement of her chest is the only thing giving me hope.

"She's going to be okay," Annette grabs on to both of my hands. "Mitch got her out. I don't think she made it to the basement."

Because she was looking for me. The thought immobilizes me, and I hold tightly to Annette's hands.

Frank kneels next to Grandma Betty, and his upper lip twitches. He plants both of his hands on the ground, and I expect his voice to shake when he speaks. It doesn't. He's cool, calm, and collected.

"What's the situation?" he directs this question at Mitch.

"I've called the police. They're sending an ambulance. That was about ten minutes ago. They said they were going to be here soon."

Everyone looks in the distance for signs of the ambulance.

"Aren't the phone lines down?" asks Frank.

"Yes, but I have a cell phone; the airline requires it," explains

Mitch. "They said they would be here."

"Did they realize the urgency?"

"I tried to tell them," assures Mitch.

"They're not going to be able to get through, at least not all the way." Frank presses his shaking fingers against Grandma Betty's neck. "Her pulse is weak, breathing is shallow. This is urgent." When he pries open her eyelids with his fingertips, I look away. I can't face her unseeing stare.

"I'm running back to the car to radio Wes and tell them we need a chopper to take her right away. Cane, you stay here." Frank takes off in a flat run.

Releasing Annette's hands, I drop to the ground. My shins press into the wet soil. I flip my hands over and study my palms for signs of blood. This is my fault. My teeth knock against each other.

Annette issues a command. "Mikayla, go to my car and get the blanket in the trunk. Cane is cold."

I'm not cold; it's just that my blood isn't circulating. If fingers were pressed against my carotid, there would be nothing pushing back.

Crawling over to Grandma Betty, I wrap my hands around her arm and squeeze hard enough for her to wake up and say "Ouch, Cane! You stop that nonsense!" But, she doesn't react.

Across the street I hear the trunk slam shut. Annette moves closer to me, bends over, and talks to me in a small, soft voice. "Mikayla kept telling us you weren't in there, said she knew, just like when you were kids. You remember when you used to do that? That one night when you saved her life. I still think about that to this day. You two have something that can't be explained. That hasn't changed. I keep remembering you two as babies, and tonight, oh, I'm just so thankful-" Unable to finish the sentence, she starts crying.

Mikayla drapes a blanket around my shoulders.

Pushing aside the blanket that covers Grandma Betty, I clutch her pajama top. "When are they going to be here?"

"They'll be here soon," Mitch reassures and continues pacing. He impatiently scans the area.

When Frank returns, he and Mitch exchange information in low tones.

Sirens blare in the distance. Two young paramedics make their way through the rubble and inform us that air support is on the way. One of them quickly examines my grandmother; he takes her pulse, pries open her eyes again, and rubs her sternum.

A helicopter lands in a clearing in the neighbor's yard on a spot that hours earlier had been the sight of an elaborate swing set. Two nurses and doctor rush over and carefully lift Grandma Betty onto a flat board, securing her head between orange cushions. They say that I can come with. I crouch down and run behind them with Frank by my side.

"I'll meet you at the hospital as soon as I can," shouts Frank.

Right before they lift Grandma Betty away from us, Frank reaches out and puts both his palms flat against her cheeks. He says something to her, but it's too noisy to hear anything, and I'm no good at reading lips. The pilot pulls me up into the helicopter and shuts the door. Frank moves away, and as we take off he stays right where he is, looking as lost as I feel.

The motion of the doctor and the nurses on board are frantic; their hands move over my grandmother in a blur. Their efficiency is reassuring, and in less than ten seconds there is a mask on her face, an IV in her arm, and flat discs pressed against her bare chest.

I'm about to take a deep breath for the first time all night when one nurse shouts, "I don't have a heart beat!"

How many tornadoes, on average, hit the US every year? 800.
How many does it take to change your life forever? One.

Sticks and Stones

I can tell you where the unraveling began, where everything began to go wrong. You know what they say. There's a thin line between love and hate, and the spring before seventh grade, an eraser was taken to that line. What Mikayla did wasn't as bad as what she said; her words were the death certificate. That phrase, 'sticks and stones can break bones, but words can never hurt me,' is a bunch of crap. Words can do more than hurt, and when she said those things to me, my best friend, the person I trusted most in the world, it was a cleaver to my heart.

Mikayla and I didn't have any threats to our relationship until middle school, those dreaded three years when hormones start kicking in and no one can quite figure out where to go with them. These unruly brain chemicals were responsible for Mikayla's development; I watched her body change fast and pitied mine, which was stuck in neutral. She grew and grew, and I wondered if I would need a ladder to talk to her in high school. One day while we were changing into swimsuits, I grabbed a pair of her Guess jeans out of her drawer and held them against my body. They came up to the middle of my chest.

"I'm a midget," I proclaimed theatrically and cast her jeans aside.

"No you aren't! You're petite and cute."

"I hate cute," I said as I glanced at Mikayla and made more comparisons. My breast buds, barely discernable with a magnifying glass, were nothing compared to Mikayla's firm, round lumps, which were getting plenty of attention from the older boys at school who whistled, made comments, and asked her to "go out," (this being defined as an occasional conversation in the cafeteria, a nighttime phone call, and the distinct advantage of being able to hold her hand or, if they were daring, to kiss her).

It wasn't just the boys who worshipped her; the girls revered Mikayla like a goddess. They handed her notes that asked questions about boys and pleaded with her to hang out with them. When all of this started, we both laughed, but now that I have the advantage of hindsight, I realize we laughed for entirely different reasons. I laughed because it was ridiculous, and Mikayla laughed because she felt triumphant and powerful.

Then, one day in May near the very end of sixth grade, it happened. Mikayla achieved popularity; she wasn't just one of the popular girls in our glass, but THE popular girl in our class of one hundred and twenty students. I'm sure it had something to do with her charm, outgoing personality, and fashionable, expensive wardrobe (Mitch made more in one year as an American Airlines' pilot than Grandma Betty made in eight and could afford whatever Mikayla needed or wanted), but I'm also certain it was directly linked to her cup size, leg length, and hopelessly beautiful face. And while she still included me in everything, hence boosting my own popularity, I began to feel the slow amputation of myself from her life.

It was a given that I would accompany her wherever she went, and, at first, my position was envied. I mean, after all, I had been Mikayla's best friend as far back as any of us could remember. Everyone had always seen us as a unit, but as her popularity evolved, their envy turned to irritation. I told Mikayla it didn't take a genius to know that I wasn't welcome at the sleepovers and parties we went to since I was mostly whispered about behind Mikayla's back or ignored completely.

My insecurities were confirmed when I discovered a note making its rounds in the sixth grade class. It had been drafted by Brittany O'Malley, which I knew because of her signature style of handwriting that included miniscule hearts for the letter O and the tiny ladybugs over the letter I. Mikayla's new group, myself not included, was comprised of Brittany O (as everyone called her), Mikayla (the ringleader), Melissa, and Bridget. I referred to them as the BOMMB squad. The note, folded into a cube, read, "Do you like Cane? Please write **yes**, **no**, or **maybe** on the line below. Do you think she should be hanging out with us? Please write **yes**, **no**, or **maybe** on the line below."

Everyone in the BOMMB squad had written definitive NO'S that were capitalized, underlined, or written in bubble letters. Mikayla's handwriting was missing, so I assumed this was a covert operation. I confiscated the note and didn't say anything about it to Mikayla.

The afternoon following this incident I went to Mikayla's after school to study and discovered a slumber party invitation on her dresser. On the bottom it read, 'Please don't invite Cane. She's way weird.'

Mikayla walked into her bedroom and saw me reading it. "I'm not going to go."

"No, you should go." I cast it aside. "Just because they don't like me, doesn't mean that you shouldn't hang out with them."

I knew she was going to go when she wouldn't look me in the eye. "You'll always be my best friend, Cane," she said reassuringly, but her expression, one of joyful relief, upset me. Had I really been holding her back all this time?

I'm not sure of the exact chain of events at that slumber party, but after eavesdropping on conversations and dissecting rumors, I discovered there had been a grueling game of truth or dare. Mikayla had chosen dare. Apparently, she was dared to cut off three inches of my hair during school. She should have had the guts to tell those girls to **go screw themselves**, because that's what I would have done. Instead, given her innate need to dominate every situation, she took their dare and added to it, telling them she would cut off six inches.

I never saw it coming. If Mikayla had warned me, told me what was going to happen, I might have been a willing accomplice in the scheme since she was still my best friend, even if those girls were trying to pry us apart. But she used guerilla tactics and ambushed me during a snore-worthy math lecture on pre-algebra. I remember hearing the sliding of metal against metal that sounded just like the pair of rickety old scissors that Mr. Siebert kept on his desk. Drowsy from the drone of Siebert's voice and the buzzing of the fluorescent lights, I couldn't quite figure out what was happening even with the cutting noise and the gentle tug on my head. Only when I tentatively reached back and felt my t-shirt instead of my hair did I realize what had happened.

When I turned around and saw Mikayla's hands holding at least eight inches of my auburn hair that I believed to be my only beautiful attribute at the awkward age of twelve, the inside of my chest gave way beneath her betrayal. She had disowned me, and so I would do the same.

I didn't give any of the BOMMB squad the benefit of seeing me react at all. I went through the rest of the day as if nothing had happened, but the rest of the class, including the members of the BOMMB squad, could not stop talking about it. When people asked me how I felt or what I was going to do in retaliation, I merely shrugged my shoulders and said it wasn't that big of a deal. When Mikayla tried to talk to me several times, I told her we would discuss it later and then walked as far away from her as I could. My carefree attitude about the prank made me a hero that day, but on the inside I was a miserable and broken Humpty-Dumpty.

It was Grandma Betty who put me back together again. She listened for more than an hour as I told her the story and then ranted about the BOMMB squad and what had been happening to Mikayla and me. When I finished, she took me to a posh salon in Clinton where they fashioned the hack job on my hair into a fashionable and sleek bob. Then, we went out to a fancy dinner, and Grandma Betty gave me sips of her wine. She promised it would make me calm, and she was right. My belly felt warm and tingly, and the hiccups I had been plagued with for most of the night vanished after three small drinks.

Grandma Betty explained that middle school and high school were probably the hardest years anybody goes through and that what happens during those years we spend our whole life trying to get over. "Mikayla and you may not be able to be as great of friends as you were before. She's being pulled in one direction and you in another."

Nobody's pulling me, I thought to myself. "Well she's not my friend anymore."

"I know what she did is awful, but I'm not sure you want to throw away a friendship based on one mistake. To err is human, to forgive, divine."

I stuck my jaw forward and rolled my eyes. "And to ignore, practical," I added stubbornly.

"It's your choice," said Grandma Betty.

I found that my resolve wasn't as strong as I thought, because I missed Mikayla horribly. I decided that I would forgo the practical and give the divine a shot, and I went over to her house on Friday evening, three days after she had trimmed my dignity. I was greeted at the door by Annette who told me how sorry she was and that Mikayla was being punished. Then, she smoothed her hands over my hair and told me that my haircut looked spectacular and that I was even more beautiful. She gently steered me toward the staircase. "Now you go on upstairs. I'll let you two work this out."

Mikayla was reclining on her bed with her headphones snug over her ears. She quickly removed them and tossed them to the side.

"Hey," she said, her tone bordering on rude and apathetic.

She didn't look particularly happy to see me. I, on the other hand, could feel a smile starting from the inside and working its way up to my cheeks. I had missed her so much, but I kept my expression neutral.

"Hi."

"Thanks for ratting me out and getting me grounded for two months."

"I didn't rat you out."

Mikayla sneered. "No, technically you didn't, but Grandma Betty did. Because of that old bitch I'm confined to my house like a prisoner. The only things missing are the shackles."

I sputtered in disbelief. "What did you just say?" Mikayla had called people plenty of names, so had I. But we had never insulted each other's family. It was an unspoken rule.

"Oh, nothing. Get over yourself."

This wasn't a denial or an apology. What the hell was wrong with her?

Folding her hands, she laid them on her stomach and stared at the ceiling. "I'm sorry, you know. It's not that big of a deal. I only took a few inches."

"A few inches, three quarters of a foot, yeah, they're like so close you can't even tell." My anger, a persuasive magnet, drew the blood to the surface of my pale skin.

"My dad said he did much worse when he was a kid. He didn't even want to punish me."

"Probably because he's making up for being a crappy dad and husband!" I stopped short of mentioning his affair, which we had found out about last year after overhearing a conversation between Annette and Mikayla's grandmother.

At this insult, Mikayla leapt off the bed. We were standing face-to-face, only hers was five inches above mine. "At least I have a family. I have a mom and a dad and a brother. They're here with me and not in some graveyard, and you've always been jealous of that." Taking a step forward she stuck her finger into my chest and held it there, pushing until I could feel the tip of her nail. With calm malice, she said, "At least my family and my brother didn't die because of me, like yours did."

Beneath my feet, I swore I could feel the spin of the earth on its axis, and it threw me off balance. I stumbled backward, and the rage that had been staining my skin turned to ice.

"You're not my friend anymore."

Like I said, when I say something out loud, it's as good as gold. My follow through is impeccable.

Beating a Dead Horse

From the tenth floor of Mercy General Hospital in Clinton I stand with my feet spread, my hands pushed up against the tinted windows, and watch the bloody sunrise. The air has a crimped quality, and it distorts my view and gives the impression that I'm having a hallucination.

I only wish that were true.

Life has come to a screeching halt in Savage, but rush hour is beginning in Clinton. Traffic congeals in intersections. Horns blare. Pedestrians race across the streets, dodging cars like bullets. Doctors and nurses wipe the sleep out of their eyes and clutch their cups of coffee as they enter the revolving doors into the hospital. Everyone is starting their day, and I haven't yet finished mine.

In the waiting area, a row of televisions lines the wall, and I can hear both national and local reporters rehashing the gory and fascinating details of the tornado that has officially been labeled by weather experts as an F3. Everyone is struck by the irony of the town name, and the play on words is constant. "Savage, Illinois didn't stand a chance against the wild tornado that rolled through last night." "Savage, Illinois was tamed by a beastly, F3 tornado, with winds as high as 202 miles per hour."

Cameras pan the destruction, but it isn't necessary. The adjectives the reporters use are enough to paint the picture. When they announce the death toll, twenty, and the injured, one hundred, I wonder if Grandma Betty is included in these statistics.

Several reports feature testimonials from Savage residents, and I recognize each of the voices. Mayor Richard Stroymeyer speaks in his robotic voice. "Storms can destroy buildings, but they can't wreck the spirit of the community. Our losses have been significant. We will mourn, but those we lost will live on forever in our hearts. As we grieve, we will rise above this and rebuild," he says confidently. He isn't an eloquent man, and I wonder where he stole these words from.

When channel twenty-seven announces that they're speaking with Mitch Atwood, a pilot for American Airlines and Savage resident who survived the storm, I turn around and stare at the screen.

"Mr. Atwood, you are being hailed as a hero for your rescue of your neighbor Betty Kallevik. Can you tell us what happened last night?" The reporter, wearing a concerned expression, sticks the microphone in Mitch's face.

"I'm not sure I can describe it. We heard the sirens, and my family and I took refuge in the basement. When it hit, it was like being in the middle of an explosion. Even that doesn't do it justice. I can't even describe what the storm was like."

"I understand your house virtually collapsed. How were you able to escape?"

"Through the cellar doors."

"What happened next?"

"We were concerned about our neighbors who are good friends of ours. I went across the street to check on them. I heard faint cries coming from near their front door, or where their front door used to be. It sounded like Betty."

"What was she saying?"

"She was calling for her granddaughter, Cane."

"How did you get to Betty?"

"I'm not sure. I somehow managed to pull her out."

"What was her condition at the time?"

"Not good," Mitch wipes at his dirty face with both hands. "Shortly after I pulled her out she lost consciousness. They transported her to Mercy General by helicopter."

"How is her condition?"

"I haven't heard."

"Was her granddaughter found?"

"Yes."

"Where was she during the storm?"

"I'm not sure, but she's fine."

Covering my ears with both hands, I turn and walk away. I don't want to hear one more thing Mitch has to say. It all comes down to the fact that I should have never left the house. If I had been there, this wouldn't be happening.

After being at the hospital for six hours, I've done nothing but analyze my stupidity. Earlier this morning in the washroom, I opened my backpack and took out the bikini that I never had a chance to wear. I wadded it into a ball and threw it in the garbage then covered it with those cheap cardboard-like squares that they claim are paper towels. I didn't want to be reminded of where I had been and why I had gone there. Did I actually think that Justice would have any interest in me?

As I think more about what I should have done last night, I start to pace. Because of the way the chairs are arranged in the waiting area, the path that I take resembles a figure eight. I don't even care that people are looking at me like I'm a mental patient. I walk faster and faster until I'm speed walking, a skill I possess despite my short legs. I've considered entering this event in the Olympics.

It's getting more difficult to maintain my pace now that the waiting room is filling up and a group of people congregate in the corner. All of them claim to have some connection to the tornado. I listen to their aimless conversation.

"You know, my friend Janice lives downtown. I'm so worried about her."

"Some streets weren't even affected."

"I don't know about that, they're saying everything was leveled."

"They'll say anything to get a story."

"Did you hear if the dairy farm was hit? Those cows better be okay, because I need my ice cream!"

Everyone laughs at this, and I want to go over there and slap them all in the face, tell them to shut up, that none of this is a joke. I can't settle down; I wish I had some trivia cards, something to memorize and keep my mind occupied.

Sitting down reluctantly, I close my eyes and think about some of the questions that I memorized yesterday while cutting the grass.

What island is Honolulu on?
Hawaii.
Who was The Sweater Girl?
Lana Turner
What deceased Russian leader said: "We will in my lifetime rule the world by invitation"?
 Nikita Khrushchev
What Peanuts character clings to a security blanket?
Linus.
Isn't that what I've always been, a female version of Linus, dragging around useless things? I have always held fast to my possessions; I've

stored them under my bed, in my dresser, even buried them in the backyard. Now that I may have lost all those things, I no longer see their value and no longer care. The only thing I want is Grandma Betty. If I lose her, I lose my security.

A nurse with a bad perm and a cluster of acne on her chin looks up from the station. "Cane Kallevik," she says my name with a whine.

I go and stand in front of her. After Nurse Frizz makes eye contact with me, she holds out a phone. "You have another call."

Despite the fact that Frank's been working tirelessly throughout the night, aiding the police in every way possible, he's been calling every thirty minutes to check on Grandma Betty's condition and to make sure that I'm okay.

Taking the phone from her I press it hard against my ear. "Hi again."

"How are you holding up?"

"I'm fine."

"And our girl," his voice becomes pliable, "how's she?"

"I still haven't talked to the doctor or been able to see her."

"They're not very forthright with information, are they? Those nurses don't seem to want to share specifics."

"Tell me about it."

"They did tell me that the doctor will be coming to talk to you soon. She has to be holding up. She made it through surgery. I know she can do it! She can overcome anything! She's one strong lady."

Frank has been a cheerleader through all of this; I picture him shaking a set of pom-poms.

"I'm coming to the hospital sometime today," he sighs wearily, "but I'm not sure when I can make it, and I certainly don't want you waiting around. I stopped by the Schaeffer farm this morning. Samson is coming to get you. He should be there shortly."

"I'm not leaving."

"I know your Grandma. She would want you to go home, get some rest, get something to eat. You've got to take care of yourself."

I grind my teeth together. "I'm not leaving until she wakes up." Unless Grandma Betty tells me to leave herself, I'm staying put. "I'm fine," I tell him.

"You listen to what Samson tells you when he shows up."

"Okay," I say to appease him. Not likely; Samson will have to throw me over his shoulder before I go anywhere.

After I hand Nurse Frizz the phone back, I return to the waiting area and sit. Thanks to the conversation with Frank, I'm now consciously aware of my physical state, whereas before I had only been focused on the emotional. Running my tongue across my teeth, I discover that they're coated with a gritty film. And either I'm smelling things, or my armpits reek like swamp muck. My stomach growls loudly, and I press my hands over it and stare at the television to try and forget that I haven't eaten anything since the casserole.

Turns out watching television isn't a distraction but a reminder of everything that went wrong. I stare at the reporters who are stationed in downtown Savage with the carnage behind them; they pan the cameras back and forth. The thing about tornadoes, or any disaster for that matter, natural or manmade, is that they are finite. Over and done, end of story. The media's coverage of that disaster, however, is infinite. The press knows how to beat a dead horse.

I hear my name again and look up anxiously.

"Cane Kallevik." This time it is coming from a gruff, male doctor who I vaguely recognize from the melee last night.

"I'm Dr. Fairchild."

Expecting him to at least come over to me or shake my hand, I'm surprised when he turns on his heels and tells me to follow him. Bedside manner, ever heard of it, jerk?

I follow him through a maze of white hallways to a room that sits diagonally across from the ICU.

"Have a seat." He closes the door with his foot.

The room, nothing more than a cubicle, causes my heart to shrink, and the sudden onset of claustrophobia makes my mouth go dry. I sit, think better of it, stand, and then because Dr. Fairchild is looking at me strangely, I sit again, pressing my arms close to my body. I wonder if he can smell my armpits.

The walls are lined with padded fabric. If I scream, will anyone outside hear me? They must have put the padding here on purpose. Why not wallpaper? Why not paint? Grandma Betty could pick out a spectacular color. My foot starts to bounce and pretty soon my knee and then my whole leg join in the motion party.

The doctor clears his throat, and I begin to braid my hair again. I can't stop myself.

"Your grandmother had a rough night. Her body has gone through a lot."

When they performed CPR, I heard her ribs cracking under the doctor's hands. Is that normal? I want to know, but I still haven't asked anyone.

"Her internal injuries were severe. She had broken ribs, a collapsed lung, a lacerated liver and spleen. We removed her spleen. Surgery was touch and go, but she pulled through. What concerns me most is the head trauma she suffered, and it's causing swelling. She's on a ventilator that's helping her breathe."

"Is she awake?"

"No. She's in a coma."

Coma. Even the sound of that word is ominous. "When will she wake up?"

Dr. Fairchild crosses his arms. "I'm not sure. Even if she does wake up, I can't guarantee what her functionality will be. The next forty-eight hours are critical. I'll know more then."

"Can I see her?"

"Yes. Room 911."

Now isn't that room number ironic? When Dr. Fairchild leaves the room, I take my time walking to the glass doors that block the entrance to the ICU. I can't make myself go inside. I stand there and hold on to the ends of my long braids.

The inside of the unit is a collection of small, windowed rooms with all the doors cracked open; the scant privacy comes in the form of patterned curtains on tracks. Although most of the patients aren't visible, I know by the whir, beeps, and hum of machines that they are there. The sounds remind me of an arcade. Only, in this environment **GAME OVER** has a whole new meaning.

A nurse pushes open the doors and smiles.

"Are you coming in?"

I nod and cautiously step inside. The air smells of urine, bleached sheets, rubbing alcohol, and chicken noodle soup. Room 911 is visible, but I can't see Grandma Betty.

I bravely approach the doorway, step inside, and pull back the curtain.

Grandma Betty looks lost on the bed. Her gray curls are matted against her head; a bandage covers the deep cut on her forehead that they must have sutured because I can see a black stitch. Her skin, ghostly and thin, blends in with the white sheets and blankets; she looks really close to being dead. A wide tube is fitted inside her mouth, and the rhythmic motion of the ventilator is doing what her lungs are supposed to do.

There's a high probability that Grandma Betty isn't going to make it. This is a moment that calls for cinematic emotion. It's the part where a movie director would have me cry, wail, and sob like a baby, *only I can't.* It's an inhuman, inexplicable character flaw that took root sometime after preschool. There have been moments when I was convinced I would cry, like when Mikayla hacked off my hair and said aloud the greatest fear that I had always kept private, but I didn't. The only clue I have that my tear ducts haven't petrified is that on some mornings when I wake up from a dream, I'll find my cheeks wet and eyes completely pasted shut.

Even though I can't cry, I should tell you about the one, mortifying thing that does happen. *Snot.* Instead of normal tears coming out of my eyes when I'm upset, my nose runs like a broken spigot.

So now, as I pull back the covers and take her weightless hand in mine, the inside of my eyelids and sinuses sting, producing the requisite amount of mucus, but the fat alligator tears that press against my tear ducts like pebbles never push their way to the surface.

"Wake up, please, please, please wake up." No response. "I'm sorry," I lean down and rest my head next to hers.

"It's my fault," I admit, choking on the words.

Taking a shaky breath, I carefully tuck her hand back in the warmth of the blankets. After dragging an armchair up to the hospital bed, I sit down heavily, the weight of my irresponsible actions pressing on the center of my chest. I try to keep myself awake by pinching my arms and thighs and biting the inside of my cheeks, but after more than twenty four hours of sleeplessness my eyelids have a mind of their own. They sink downward, and I can do nothing to stop them. Scooting the chair forward so that it's pressed up against the bed, I rest my upper body on the mattress, placing my head next to Grandma Betty's hand. When I close my eyes I have the sensation of tumbling head over heels into darkness.

Minutes or hours later, I can't be sure, I hear rapping. I don't want to wake, so I ignore it, but it's insistent. Reluctantly waking, I rub my eyes and look up.

Since I was expecting Samson to come, I'm not prepared to see Justice with his dimples and shockingly blue eyes.

"Sorry to wake you." He stands in the doorway, fidgeting with the keys he holds in his hand.

He's wearing a dark navy shirt and worn khaki shorts with stray strings on the bottom. Sticking out of his back pocket is a rolled up issue of Sports Illustrated. On anyone else, this outfit would look messy, but on Justice, it looks preppy perfect.

I briefly cover my face with my hands and inhale deeply. Why has God sent him here to torture me? Isn't it enough that I almost killed Grandma Betty just for a chance to see him last night? Shouldn't that have cured me of this ridiculous love-at-first-sight crap?

Hate him, hate him, hate him, I command myself, but I can't find the switch inside my stomach or my brain that turns off attraction. I turn away from him and look at Grandma Betty's face, noticing that under her ear there's a smudge of dirt.

"What do you want?" I ask in a borderline rude way. I take a tissue from the tray next to the bed and wipe away the dirt, hoping Grandma will move when I do this.

"Frank stopped by and told us what happened. We think it would be best if you came to live at the farm until everything can be straightened out, so I'm here to pick you up."

"Live with Jelly Roll? I would rather be homeless." I shake my head and meet his eyes. "I'm not going anywhere."

Justice carries the other chair in the room and places it on the opposite side of Grandma Betty so we are facing each other.

"How is she?"

"Not good." I refuse to meet his gaze, because for one, my nose has started running again. Here I am worried about the snot running from my nostrils and how awful I look, when Grandma Betty is fighting for her life. I'm an evil, vain person. I lower my head and press it into the sheets.

Justice reaches over and puts his hand on top of my head. "I'm sorry, Cane. This is horrible."

His display of affection pleases and embarrasses me. With the weight of his hand on the back of my head, I feel lighter.

"Not as sorry as I am." With my nose and mouth smashed flat against the sheets, my voice is nasally.

He slowly takes his hand away.

"Was she in the basement when it happened?"

I sigh tremulously. Justice hands me a tissue. I take it and press it against my nose; I refuse to blow it in front of him. "No. She was looking for me."

"Where were you?"

Sliding my hand under the covers, I put my fingers on top of Grandma Betty's, but what I really want to do is reach up and cover her ears with my palms. Even though she's unconscious, I've heard that sometimes people in a coma can hear everything. "I was swimming at the gravel pit," I admit to the person whom I wished had been with me.

"You could have been killed. Didn't you know about the tornado warning?"

"Yes," I say defiantly. Wadding up the tissue, I toss it across the room, and it lands shy of the garbage.

"Then why did you go?"

"Because I wanted to see you!" The skin on my face and neck floods with blood. Horrified, I can't meet Justice's eyes. At times, I hate myself for my inability to keep my mouth shut. The truth always pops out, a quick one-two punch. My bluntness leaves everyone down for the count, even me.

In my peripheral vision I see him lean back into his chair and form his hands into a makeshift blindfold. "You could have been killed," he acknowledges with awestruck regret.

"No, actually, I couldn't have. I'm protected."

His hands fall away from his face. "What do you mean? What are you talking about?"

"Because I've been marked by God."

"What?" he asks. "I don't get it."

I shrug and glance down at the floor. "No one does."

We sit in silence and watch the machines that are hooked up to Grandma Betty. They put forth so much effort and noise, and I'm terrified that if someone accidentally turns them off, if the power goes out for even a second, Grandma Betty will die. If I had duct tape, I would tape it to the cords that are stuck into the outlets just to be sure they weren't going anywhere.

"Have you talked to her doctor?"

"Yeah, but it's not like he told me anything I wanted to hear. He isn't sure she's going to wake up, and even if she does, he's not sure what she'll be like. Reassuring, isn't it?"

"I'm sorry."

"Yeah, so am I." I steer the conversation in a different direction. "How's the farm?"

"Only two of the barns have minor damage. The livestock are fine. In fact, I helped hook the sows up this morning. The gardens and the yard are a mess, so I'm sure I'll be busy helping put everything back in order. And there's still the sprinkler system."

"That's Jelly Roll's pet project, she should finish it."

"Most of the projects are hers," concedes Justice.

"Don't say that out loud. I don't like her getting credit for anything."

"You know, you're not going to be a hostage at the farm," Justice says tactfully. "I'll bring you back to visit your grandmother as often as you want."

"I'll be Jelly Roll's charity case, and I don't see how that's any better than being a prisoner."

"You won't be her charity case." His smile is winsome. "You'll be mine," he clarifies.

Even though he probably doesn't mean anything by this, isn't claiming ownership of me, my palms start to sweat, and I can feel the capillaries in my face flooding again.

"Oh, that makes me feel so much better," I respond sarcastically. "And, honestly, I'm having a hard time believing that Jelly Roll offered to take in a stray. She doesn't strike me as that kind of person."

He pushes his hair away from his forehead with his fingers and lets it fall. He puts his hands in the shape of a steeple. "Actually, it was Samson's idea that you stay with us."

I give him a wide-eyed, appalled glare. "Does she know I'm coming?"

"No, well…by now she probably does. Samson wanted to come get you himself, but he got sidetracked with some things and sent me. He said he would talk to Aunt Jenny about everything."

"Spec-tac-u-lar."

"She'll be fine with it, I promise."

"Don't make promises you can't keep," I warn.

Justice pulls his keys out of his pocket and waves them in front of him. "So, have I convinced you to come with me?"

Before I change my mind, I kiss Grandma Betty's cheek, grab the keys from Justice, and walk out the door. We leave the Shaeffer's number at the nurse's station, and Justice tells them to call if there's any change in her condition. I'm thankful that he's here; I wouldn't have thought of this on my own.

When we reach his pickup truck, I catch a glimpse of my reflection in the side mirror. I'm *roadkill Pippy-Longstocking*. Suppressing a cry of revulsion, I open the door and slide into the scorching cab of the truck. Justice's things are spread across the front seat making it difficult for me to find room, so I hover like an idiot.

There's a worn basketball, a pile of textbooks, ranging from early American history to business economics, several pairs of tennis shoes, a duffel bag, and two Walkmans.

"Sorry about this," he apologizes. "Haven't quite got the knack for organization."

"Yeah, me neither." I pick up the economics book. "You can't possibly find this interesting."

"No, just necessary."

He sweeps his belongings in to a condensed pile to make room for me.

Before we're out of the parking lot, I have second thoughts about leaving. I turn and look back at the hospital. *Please don't let her die. Please don't let her die.* I plead with God, but who the hell knows if He's listening. What if she wakes up, and I'm not there? I can't leave her alone; I did that once already and look at where that's gotten me. Then I realize that I hadn't said the one thing that was most important, not last night when we were in the helicopter together and not this morning. I need to tell her. I undo my seatbelt and open the door.

Justice's reflexes are quick, and just as I'm about to leap out of the moving truck, he grabs the corner of my shirt.

I turn and want to say something to him, but my voice box feels squashed.

"She would want you to go home and get some rest. I'll bring you back, as often as you want."

After taking a shaky, deep breath, I sit back into my seat and slam the door.

I expect that we're going to go directly to Savage, into the center of the apocalypse, but Justice goes in the opposite direction. Either he's psychic, or he can hear my stomach, because we pull into the drive-through line at McDonald's.

"What do you want?" he asks.

"I don't have any money."

"No kidding," he acts surprised and laughs. "I kind of assumed that would be the case." He pulls some dollar bills out, spreads them like a fan, and waves them. "I'm on strict orders from Samson to spoil you rotten. "Burger and fries okay?"

"Make it two cheeseburgers, with everything on them, a large fry, and a chocolate shake. Lots of ketchup. Don't forget to ask for ketchup."

He smiles and those small delectable dimples appear. "I take it you haven't lost your appetite."

I wonder what it would feel like to put my lips in those small craters. "Guess not," I say shyly.

After Justice eats and I inhale my meal like a Hoover vacuum, I dare to ask him the one thing I need to know.

"Did you want to see me last night?"

Justice fixes his eyes on me. "Cane, don't," he says.

"It's just a simple question."

He sighs and turns away from me, concentrating too intensely on the traffic. "No, it's not. You're only fifteen."

"Almost sixteen, practically sixteen, days away from it," I remind him casually.

"I'm twenty-one." He says this like he's saying, 'end of story.'

Crossing my arms, I glare at him. "Answer my question."

"That's six years," he says. "Six," he repeats and taps his fingers six times to emphasize his point.

"Congratulations. You know how to subtract," I declare wryly. "But, it's more like five years when you think about it, and I still want an answer."

He doesn't give me one, and I'm gutsy, but not gutsy enough to dig my own grave. The vibration of the engine lulls me into a trance-like state. With a stomach full of fat and starch, I'm unable to resist sleep. Taking my backpack, I arrange it against the window and use it as a pillow.

I'm nearly asleep, possibly drooling, when I hear Justice's voice, reluctant and hoarse, "The answer is yes."

War of the Worlds

As any history textbook will reveal, war is messy. I've been in the thick of it for years now and have learned that messy is an inaccurate description. War is agonizing. It's hell. It's every cliché they say it is. My blood, sweat, and tears (or in my case, snot) have proved that time and again.

The hair incident was something like the shot heard around the world, and it started a nasty conflict between me and my former best friend. During my four year combat with Mikayla, I've employed meticulous tactics, making sure to ambush her when she's most vulnerable and choosing acts with considerable impact. I have to be evasive, crafty, and clever all at once. If that isn't bad enough, my enjoyment never lasts, because immediately after I commit the crime, there's the constant mental strain of bracing myself for her reprisal.

Even though it's true combat, my life isn't at risk. Weapons of mass destruction are nowhere to be found, but it has gotten physical. Last summer, just after school let out, Nate almost ran me off the road when I was on Smurfette; this because two weeks before on prom night I had let all the air out of his tires. If I would have known Mikayla would stoop that low and condone a hit and run, I would have gone one step further and slashed his tires.

The battles have never been documented. Realistically, I don't have time for that, and besides, documentation would be incriminating. However, I do have every last bit of our war filed away in my head. My memorization skills are impeccable, and because I love trivia, I've created the "Cane and Mikayla" game.

Question: What was the first act of war against Mikayla?
Answer: Breaking into her bedroom and stealing her prized

possessions that included: an autographed poster of Kirk Cameron, both of her diaries that were hidden under her mattress, two pairs of Guess Jeans, a Benetton sweater, and every last one of her cassette tapes.

Yes, this was lame, but it holds a special place in my heart because it sent a message loud and clear. We both knew that I had thrown down the gauntlet and was out to get her. She accepted the challenge, and from the start she proved that she had wiles as well.

Question: What was the first thing Mikayla did in return?

Answer: She removed my coveted magazine collection from under my bed and painstakingly went through each, gluing pages together and scribbling graffiti. Imagine my horror when I took my Teen Beat magazines out from under my bed and discovered that they had been defiled.

Question: What prank was the most extensive and took the most amount of preparation?

Answer: The aluminum can prank.

This is the one in which I take the most pride, because it required dedication. I spent a better part of the year collecting cans from the school and the dumpsters around Savage. The best place to score was Savage Suds, where I could easily get twenty to fifty cans at a crack. At around seven hundred cans, my collection was complete. I'm impatient, but I made myself wait until the opportune time.

When the Atwoods left for their summer vacation, I snuck over and let myself in with the key that Annette had given Grandma Betty who was in charge of taking in the mail and watering plants. It took me over an hour to strategically fill Mikayla's walk-in closet, which contained her expensive, name-brand wardrobe that she loved more than anything, with the empty cans. I stuffed them in every nook and cranny, and when I started to run out of room, I filled the clothes, stuffing pant legs, pockets, and sleeves with empty beer and pop cans. By the time I was finished I could barely close the door. The expression on her face would have been the best reward, but I had no way of capturing it.

My only satisfaction came the day they returned from their vacation. That evening, after Mikayla's parents and Grandma Betty had left for a church meeting, I saw Mikayla sneaking out of the house, carrying several large garbage bags of squashed cans. I can only imagine how long it took to flatten them. Anticipating the moment, I happened to be perched comfortably near my window sill at the time, reading a Babysitter's Club book that wasn't nearly as entertaining as what was unfolding across the street. After Mikayla loudly and dramatically deposited the cans in the garbage, she came over and stood directly under my window.

"You think you're so funny, don't you?"

I cackled my answer. "Uh, yes, I guess I do."

"Hilarious, Cane," she said in an angry hiss and stalked away.

Question: What was the worst prank she ever pulled off?

Answer: She went through my closet, confiscated every single thing that was white, took it home, tie-dyed it, and then returned it to my closet.

I arrived home from summer camp and discovered that all of my beautiful white clothes had been sabotaged. If I had appreciated color, it wouldn't have been that big of a deal. Tie-dye was actually cool. However, I was convinced that blue, white, and black were really the only colors that didn't clash with my hair. In order to keep it from Grandma Betty, I bagged up all the clothes and dropped them in a dumpster behind the middle school. It took months to replace what Mikayla had ruined, because unlike her, I didn't have a rich daddy to bankroll my wardrobe.

As far as I know, Grandma Betty and Annette are in the dark about our random acts of hostility toward each other. Because we don't want the adults to put an end to our fun, we cover our tracks. Unfortunately, even the most conscientious perpetrators leave evidence behind. I'm sure Grandma Betty suspects something is going on. You can't pull the wool over that woman's eyes; she's constantly on the lookout for anything out of the ordinary.

Her suspicions were first roused during the aluminum can prank; I could never quite convince her that I was saving those cans for a sculpture. Then, there was the time Mikayla covered my sheets and pillowcase in shaving cream. Even after I cleaned it up, destroyed the evidence, and hitched a ride with a friend to the Kmart in Clinton and bought new linens, Grandma Betty came into my room with that bloodhound nose of hers and demanded to know why my bedroom reeked of Gillette shaving gel. I told her that I had done a science experiment that required shaving cream. She didn't buy it.

The war has gotten old, but I can't seem to make myself stop. I'm just not one to say, "uncle." If anyone is going to wave the white flag, it has to be her.

Here's a confession: sometimes, in moments of weakness, I think I never should have started it. Sometimes, I even wonder what it would be like to still have Mikayla as my best friend. What she did to me, chopping off my hair, that was forgivable, but what she said to me, I don't know if I can ever let that go.

A Moment of Silence

I stir to the sound of Justice turning off the ignition and the massive shadow of Samson standing next to the passenger door. Despite the heat, Samson wears a sleeveless flannel and long pants. He could be a stand in for Paul Bunyan. He opens the door for me. "Good to see you, Cane."

My response is a bungled smile. Groggy from my short nap and the lump of McDonald's that's still digesting in my gut, I stumble out of the car and sling my backpack over my shoulder. I glance over at Justice; he's deliberately avoiding eye contact with me. Maybe he did say what I thought he said; I was sure it had only been a dream.

Samson puts his hand on my shoulder. "How's your Grandma?"

"Not so good. She made it through surgery, but right now she's in a coma." As soon as I say these words, I stare hard at the pale concrete below me because I can feel the snot parade gearing up. I wish I could just cry and be done with it.

"She's going to be fine. She's a fighter. You don't have to worry about anything, Cane. You're going to stay here with us. We'll take care of everything you need. I mean that. Don't hesitate to ask for anything."

Jelly Roll waddles arrogantly toward us. Wearing a pair of crimson jean shorts that have sequins around the pockets, a silver shirt, and a pair of white athletic shoes, she could be a circus director.

"We're so glad you are okay," she says loudly.

This actually sounds genuine.

She shakes her head. "It's just horrible what's happened. The community is in shambles. The reporters have invaded our town, and that certainly doesn't make anyone's life easier, now does it? At least the Red Cross and the National Guard are helping out, but you would think more progress could be made if people weren't tripping over the cameras. And those people that died! I just can't get over what this storm has done. How's your grandmother?"

Jelly Roll's conversational transitions can steamroll you if you aren't careful. Thankfully, I'm spared from having to respond, because Samson answers for me.

"Not so well."

Jelly Roll regards Samson's face, and then her eyes dart back to me. "I'm sure she'll be back to normal in no time at all."

Would she be saying this if she had seen Grandma Betty? I'm leery of her sympathy that's coming off like a glaze. Jelly Roll sugars everything to hide the ugliness below the surface.

There's hardly a pause in conversation, and then when she looks at me, I know it's going to be all business from here on out.

"You'll be staying on the third floor in one of the guest bedrooms. I put some clothes on the bed in there and also some toiletries. I'm sure you want to get cleaned up. I know you need sleep, so feel free to nap the rest of the day away. If you need anything I'm afraid you'll have to fend for yourself. We're all heading to the downtown to help out.

"Speaking of that, Samson, you start loading some of that equipment. You can help him Justice." Jelly roll watches with satisfaction as they both head to the barn.

Some of the kids have gathered around. The oldest, Jeremy, who's only a year younger than me, glances in my direction. "Sorry about your grandma," he mumbles.

"Thanks."

He shuffles off with the other boys to help his father.

Jocelyn bounds out of the house like a kangaroo and stands next to her mother. She stares at me with vibrant blue eyes that are half-hidden in pockets of fat. What must it feel like to be a child and be trapped in the body of an elephant? It disgusts me and makes me sad at the same time.

"Hi, Jocelyn," I say sweetly.

Jocelyn says nothing in return and sidles up to her mother. Jelly Roll slips an arm around her daughter's shoulders.

"If you're hungry, there's plenty of food in the fridge."

"Thank you. I really appreciate all of this."

My politeness slides off of her like butter; she keeps on going.

"Justice will bring you into town tonight. Grace Lutheran is having a short prayer service."

"It wasn't damaged?"

"Not at all."

"Oh." I want to see it for myself. I have to make sure my family's graves are where they're supposed to be.

"If you don't feel like going tonight, I understand, but I know that there are many people who would like to see you. Your neighbor, Annette Atwood, heard that you were staying with us and called here today. She's very concerned about you and your grandmother. She said her family would be at the service tonight, so it would be nice if you could go."

Jelly Roll tugs at her waistband, turns, and shouts. "Get in the car, boys!"

Turning back around, she dismisses me. "Go inside, now. Get some rest. We have to get going."

By the time I'm inside, they're already pulling out of the driveway. From the front window, I watch them leave, wondering where Justice has disappeared to and wondering if he'll avoid me for however many days I'll be stuck here.

Realizing that my body odor is taking up more space than I am, I know I should go upstairs and take a shower. I might need a map to get there, however, because the house is enormous. I'm only familiar with the first floor that includes, from front to back: a formal living room that's adjacent to an office, an elegant dining room, an enormous modern, eat-in kitchen, a bathroom, a master suite wing, and in the very rear a family room. The place is pristine and outfitted with gleaming wood floors, wide baseboards, generous crown molding, and slick wood furniture. Unfortunately, there's a noticeable, obtrusive lack of color. All the walls are dull beige. Grandma Betty would come in with her paint brush swinging.

I climb the stairs and find more of the same: drab walls and glossy wood. There are two bathrooms and six bedrooms. *You've got to be kidding me.* All six bedrooms have plush, country-blue carpeting, and they're exemplary specimens of disorder. I find the mess refreshing. At least Jelly Roll doesn't have control of everything.

The attic stairs, narrow and carpeted in mauve pile, squeak under my weight. Once upstairs, I discover that the recently remodeled space is larger than I thought. It has been divided into three small bedrooms with a decent size bathroom located in the middle. Peeking into one of the rooms, I realize that Justice lives up here, right down the hall. I try to decide whether this is a blessing or a curse and arrive at the conclusion that it's both.

His room is messy; clothes are strewn across the floor. A dozen cassette tapes and CDs are scattered across his unmade bed. I shouldn't snoop, but how can I not? I walk into his room for closer inspection. His varied music selection meshes with mine. He has everything from R.E.M, classic Bon Jovi, Led Zeppelin, U2, Culture Club, the Violent Femmes, and a band I had never heard of, Nirvana. Glancing over at the dresser, I see a framed photo of Justice with his arms around a girl. They're facing each other with their foreheads touching and their eyes closed. The girl, of course, is beautiful. No, correction, she is *disgustingly gorgeous*. She looks like one of the models from Seventeen Magazine; she's the kind of girl that's in the pictures next to articles like, "What to Wear on a First Date," or "How to Flirt with Your Man." Hell, it wouldn't surprise me if she is a model. This must be the girl that he broke up with, and since he still displays her picture, the one he's apparently still in love with. Great.

My room is pleasant, but sparse, with only a bed, dresser, nightstand, and alarm clock. On the dresser are all the essentials: soap, shampoo, conditioner, hair products, deodorant, razors, shaving cream, and embarrassingly, even tampons. The best part is that they're all expensive brands that are advertised in my teen magazines, the stuff that Grandma Betty refuses to let me buy. Jelly Roll's generosity surprises and pleases me, and I'm almost beginning to feel something like affection for the woman, until I spot the stack of clothes on my bed.

I'm horrified to discover that they're Jocelyn's clothes! I pick up a pair of shorts and hold them in front of me. I could probably fit both of my legs into one hole. The shirts are worse; they're wide and have no shape. If I don't drown in them, it will be a miracle of God. Worse than the size, are the colors. Pink, lime green, and neon orange are among the most popular shades. This palette is incomprehensible! Beneath the pile of clothes, I find underwear that belongs to Jocelyn. Disgusting! Flinging them across the room, I shout, "Spec-tac-u-lar!"

I'm being ungrateful. I realize that. In Jelly Roll's defense, I know that she didn't have time to go shopping for me, but couldn't she have at least borrowed clothes from someone my own size? I sit down heavily on the bed and then fall back dramatically. This is what my life has become. Thanks to a tornado, I'm Jelly Roll's doll.

There's a throbbing ache in my temples, and I'm pretty sure that the food I ate has solidified into a mound of gravel in my stomach. I know these sensations aren't from sleep deprivation or junk food, but from excessive worry. What am I going to do if Grandma Betty dies? I can't survive without her. I can't, *I won't*, live here forever, not that Jelly Roll would even keep me.

There's a phone on the bedside table. I pick it up and dial the hospital number, which I took great care to memorize this morning. After holding for five minutes, I'm transferred to the ICU. Emily, the head nurse, informs me that there hasn't been a change in her condition and that the doctor will be by around four this afternoon to examine her.

"Did you take the tube out of her mouth?" I ask.

"No. She's still on the ventilator."

"When will she be able to breathe on her own?"

"I'm sure the doctor will make a decision about that soon."

"Oh." I sit in silence and stare at the wall in front of me. I wish I had a picture of Grandma Betty with me, one where she's awake and smiling.

"Ms. Kallevik." There's a pause, and then Emily repeats, "Ms. Kallevik?"

I finally realize that she's speaking to me. "Call me Cane."

"Cane, we will call the number that you left if her condition changes. I promise."

I work my fingers through my hair, sorting out the knots. "Can you do something for me?"

"Sure."

"Can you please tell my grandma that I love her?"

"Of course I can do that for you."

"Thank you."

After I hang up the phone, I try not to think about anything. I shower and shave all the fuzz off my legs and from under my arms. I use every one of the fancy products that Jelly Roll left me and even put some gel in my hair and blow dry it. This is something I never do, but I'm attempting to look more like that blonde girl in Justice's picture. When I'm finished, my hair is glossy and straight, but that only makes the rich, auburn hue more apparent and for some reason, makes my freckles stand out more. Why can't I have porcelain skin? Why can't I have a less noticeable hair color? Something typical, like blonde or brown.

Although it's torture, I pull on a pair of bright pink underwear that are more like boxer shorts on me. I have to roll them to get them to stay up. There are no bras. But who am I kidding? It's not like I need one. I select the least offensive outfit, a pair of athletic electric blue shorts and a gray Nike t-shirt. My luck runs out when I pull on the shorts and they fall right back down. After searching through the drawers in the bathroom, I discover a safety pin and have to use this to take in the waistband of the shorts.

Once I'm dressed, I take my clothes and swimsuit and go downstairs to locate the washer and dryer. I refuse to wear Jocelyn's clothes again. If I can get to the bank, I can take out some of my money and go shopping.

Back upstairs in the attic, I have the urge to call the hospital again, but I don't want to establish a reputation as a nuisance or an obsessive, compulsive freak.

I debate about what I should do with my free time, but the options are limited and I'm finding it hard to keep my eyes open. My head hits the pillow, and my last thoughts before I fall asleep are of Grandma Betty and Justice.

If you took attendance at Grace Lutheran Church on Easter and Christmas and combined those numbers, there still wouldn't be as many people as there are tonight. The service begins with a long prayer and is followed by a short sermon about trials and tribulations and how tragedy can be an impetus for bringing people together.

Blah, blah, blah. What a bunch of crap.

It's easy for Pastor Fry to say all this when his house was spared, and no one in his family is lying in some hospital bed inches away from death's door. Let's just hope Grandma Betty doesn't knock, because I don't want that door to be opened unto her.

After the sermon, Pastor Fry announces that he will read the list of those who died. There is silent, preemptive crying. As he begins reading the list of twenty names, I sink my fingernails into my palms and brace myself. I recognize several of the names and know two of the people quite well since they were both friends of Grandma Betty. Connie Corbel who works at the drugstore with Grandma Betty and Deborah Fischer, the elderly bank teller, were both killed. Grandma Betty, who knows and loves both of them, will be crushed when she finds this out. I'll keep it from her as long as I can.

The moment of silence that follows the reading lasts more than five minutes, and it's anything but silent. With all the weeping and gnashing of teeth, this could be hell's green room.

An impromptu town meeting occurs after the service with Mayor Stroymeyer and Chief Fitzgerald giving community updates and talking about resources, phone centers, food deliveries, etc.

While I should be listening to all of this, I'm having a hard time concentrating, because I'm sitting next to Justice. Since more people are squeezing into the pew, my thigh is pressed up tight against his.

It's all I can think about. Since we're both wearing shorts, our skin occasionally makes contact. I've never felt this sensation before, and the first thing that comes to mind is chemistry. It's one of the first times I can practically apply one of my trivia questions.

What are the two parts of an atom that carry opposite charges and are attracted to each other?

Protons and electrons.

Or, an alternative answer would be, Justice and Cane.

Our skin touches mostly by accident, but I like to test my theory of attraction and sometimes I force it to happen. I do this now, push my thigh against his, and this time Justice looks at me and smiles. He doesn't move it away, and I'm certain that I can't, that it's impossible. We're bonded together. My heart flutters, and I have to catch my breath. I'm not sure what he's thinking. I'm not even sure what I'm thinking.

So what if he said he wanted to see me last night? It doesn't have to mean anything. He was probably throwing me a bone seeing as how I was almost killed in a tornado. The statistical probability that he'll ever feel anything for me other than friendship (the most dreaded word in the lexicon of a teenage girl) is less than one percent. Although, he isn't moving away from me right now. Does that mean anything?

The meeting draws to a close, and, apparently, our bond has unpredictable evaporative properties. Justice disappears into the crowd.

Annette seeks me out and immediately wraps me in her arms. Yesterday a tornado wrecked this woman's home and here she is, flawlessly made up, wearing a fashionable outfit while everyone else is wearing the bag lady special of the day, including me. Is she ever not perfect?

When she releases me, leaving behind the scent of Liz Claiborne perfume and Clinique cosmetics, I feel the first real smile in more than a day settling itself on my face. Despite what happened between Mikayla and me, I still love Annette and Mitch.

"Where's Mitch?"

"He's at home, attempting to clean up. He sends his best."

"I saw him on the news this morning."

"You and everyone else. He hates being pegged as a hero since he feels like he was doing what anyone else would have done. I'm just so glad that he was able to get her out of there. I wanted to go to the hospital last night with you." She places her right hand over her heart. "How is she?" she whispers.

I tell her the little I know, leaving out the grim details that are making me pessimistic.

"I'll go see her as soon as I have the opportunity."

When I ask about the neighborhood, she doesn't candy coat the situation, which I appreciate. She lets me know that the damage is so bad that most of the neighbors are already gone, staying with family or friends.

"We're living in our RV until the house can be rebuilt. I wish we could have taken you in Cane, but there's hardly any room in that thing! We have just enough beds for the four of us."

Can you imagine Mikayla and I confined to a space like that? In this case, although it's hard to believe, I would pick Jelly Roll as a bunk mate (probably because I know that I have a cushion of five thousand square feet).

"It's okay. I'm fine at the Schaeffers' house."

"I'm so glad to hear that."

Annette grabs hold of my forearm and squeezes. "I'm just so thankful that you're okay."

"You, too," I admit quietly.

The warm moment is abbreviated when Annette turns and waves at Mikayla who's in the back standing next to the BOMMB squad and Nate. I'm horrified when Mikayla starts walking in my direction. She's the last person I want to see.

"I should get going." Annette grabs my arm again. Her grip is a vice. Even if I wanted to escape, I couldn't.

"You take care, okay? You call me if you need anything."

Giraffe legs arrives.

"Hey," Mikayla says casually.

"Hi," I respond begrudgingly.

"I'll let you two talk." Annette backs away and mingles with the church members.

"I'm sorry about Grandma Betty. Is she okay?"

I shrug, partially because I don't want to give her the story and partially because every time someone asks about her, my emotions go into hyper-drive.

"Have you thought anymore about what I said, like, you know, before the tornado?"

"What do you mean?"

"About the war being over between us. That we should, like, move on. We could be friends again. I mean, doesn't the tornado prove that life's too short?"

I look away from her. She might be right, but I don't need

reconciliation-or peace for that matter. I don't need her.

"I knew you weren't home last night. I knew where you were," she adds loftily. "You were swimming at the gravel pit when the tornado hit. I saw it in my head."

How easily I forget that my secrets are shared. The connection that we share, the root of our relationship, is still thriving. I still have moments when I'm connected to Mikayla at a level that I can't explain, when I've known that something is wrong or that she's been hurt.

Two months ago, when I was in the middle of a race at a track meet, I saw a car collision in my head and immediately knew it was Mikayla and Brittany O (the first member of the BOMMB squad to get a driver's license). Thanks to the vision, I lost my focus and the race. I knew she wasn't seriously hurt, so I never sprinted into the stands to tell Grandma Betty about it. If she would have been hurt, I mean really hurt, I would have told someone, at least, I'm pretty sure I would have. I hate second guessing my character, so I try not to think about this.

I discredit her because believing her is too much of a risk. "I could have been anywhere."

"Why were you there?"

"I wasn't there." I'm not sure why I continue to lie.

She shakes her head. "Sure, right. Whatever. If and when you decide to stop being such a stubborn bitch, let me know. For what it's worth, I'm sorry about Grandma Betty and your house."

"Are you willing to take it back?"

"Take what back?"

"What you said that night."

"What are you talking about?"

The fact that she doesn't remember what started this whole thing in the first place is enough to make me write her off for good.

"Nothing, Mikayla, absolutely, positively, no-thing."

She looks to the side, and it's a reflective, memory-lane kind of look, where the eyes go out of focus. I wonder if she does remember. When she meets my eyes again, they're frosty. She leaves without saying a thing.

The conversation with Mikayla has put me in a foul mood. The hoards of sweaty bodies that surround me aren't helping my disposition. With the determination of a prisoner making a run for it, I slice my way through the crowd and exit through the back of the church. I want to make sure my family is right where I left them last.

The cemetery that begins just behind the church spans more

than five acres. Truthfully, I've always been afraid of this place. With the overgrown willow trees, rolling hills, and a grassy landscape punctuated with both modern and ancient gravestones (some date back to the early 1800's), it could be a model for one of those creepy graveyards in children's fairy tale books. Whenever I'm here, I half expect a corpse to tap me on the shoulder.

My parents, brother, grandfather, and uncle are located in a more modern section of the cemetery, somewhat hidden from the church. I walk at a fast pace until I arrive at their gravestones, and I'm instantly relieved. Everything is intact, even the tree above them. Beneath an established oak, they are covered with shade at all times, and I've thought about coming here to trim back the branches. Just once, I would have liked my brother Craig to feel the sun on his face.

Someone touches my shoulder, and I jump a good six inches into the air, thinking that my nightmare is actually occurring. I half expect to see a skeleton when I turn to the side. Instead, I see Justice and look into his tantalizing Caribbean blue eyes.

"I didn't mean to scare you," Justice apologizes.

I take my hand and press it over my heart that is jumping around less from fear and more from being near Justice again. I think back to his leg against mine and my cheeks start to incinerate.

"What do you want?" I ask sharply. "You gave me a heart attack," I add, this time softer.

"Sorry. I was looking for you inside and couldn't find you."

"So how did you know I would be here?"

"Lucky guess. Since half the town is ruined there aren't too many places left to hide."

"Yeah," I say somberly. "But, back here, you can't even tell there was a storm."

Justice is nervous. He fidgets with the keys in his pocket and keeps looking back toward the church. He pulls a pack of Wrigley's spearmint out of his back pocket. That's what his breath always smells like. The floor of his truck is littered with tiny aluminum balls. He opens a piece and pops it into his mouth.

"Want one?"

"No, I can't stand gum."

"I never chewed it before either, but now it's my crutch."

"Why?"

He sighs heavily. "Because after the breakup, I started smoking like a chimney. I don't know why I did it, I just couldn't think of anything better to do. Hated it at first, but then I actually started craving the things. I became a borderline addict, and then it started to affect my running. Not to mention the fact that I was disgusted with myself. Basically, I needed something to get me off cigarettes. Gum was the cheapest thing."

"What's her name?"

"Whose name?" he asks, but I can tell he's asking just to ask, which annoys me.

"*Her* name?" I need a name to go with the face in the picture so that I can personify my hatred and jealousy.

"Nikki."

He says this with detachment, but his eyes go all pliable and hurt. I jump to a less personal subject. "You run? I thought basketball was your sport."

"Not just basketball."

"Oh."

"We'll have to go running sometime," he suggests.

"I would love that!" I put little kid enthusiasm into my reply. Pa-the-tic.

Justice offers a brittle smile, but it breaks suddenly. He furrows his brow so that his dark eyebrows nearly touch. He lowers his head. I wonder what he's thinking about; my guess is that it's probably Nikki. She probably ran with him all the time.

I stare at the modest gravestones in front of us, and I notice a detail that until now has never really meant anything. Grandma Betty's name is next to Grandpa Henry's. Her date of birth, July 29th, 1931 is followed by a hyphen. A hyphen, like she's expecting her death date. My stomach and heart cave in at the same moment. "If she dies I have no one left," I whisper.

Justice crosses his arms. "That's not true."

I point to the graves spread out in front of us. "My entire family is right here. All of them. Grandma Betty is all I have."

He doesn't say anything because he knows I'm right.

"Do you know what happened to all of them, to my parents and my twin brother?" I ask. "I never have to tell the story because everyone in town already knows it. I'm not sure what it's like to meet someone who doesn't know."

"Cane, I-"

"It's legendary."

"No," Justice hesitates, chews hard on his gum and then looks back at me. "It's personal. I wasn't really sure until today, and then when Samson told me Granmda Betty's last name and I saw it on the sheet at the hospital…and now being back here. I was hoping it wasn't the case, but I guess I couldn't be that lucky. Fate has its fair share of irony."

He gets quiet and stops chewing his gum.

My curiosity piqued, I ask, "What is it?"

He's about to answer, when I hear a shout from behind.

"HELLO, you two!"

It's Jelly Roll's big mouth. We both turn at the same time.

What the hell does she want? She's moving toward us with the gait of a determined penguin. For a large woman, she moves fast. It must be the momentum. Although, it's obvious from her pinched expression that it takes effort.

"What are you two doing back here?" She puckers her lips. "We've been looking all over for you." When she sees the graves, she looks at me and doesn't say anything more.

"Did you need something?" Justice's tone hedges on annoyance, but Jelly Roll doesn't notice because she's armed with an agenda.

"Frank wants Cane to meet him at her house in the morning. He wants to start going through things and taking things out of the house. Can you take her, Justice? Maybe you can help?"

Justice pulls his pack of gum back out of his back pocket and rotates it in his fingers. "Sure."

"Good. I'm leaving town for the night. I'm going to drive some friends of mine downstate. They're going to be staying with some relatives. I'll be back late tomorrow."

As soon as she leaves I look at Justice expectantly. "You were saying?"

"We'll talk about this later," he assures me.

He pulls out a new piece of gum and holds it like a cigarette.

"How about now," I insist.

He makes a sound that falls short of an actual laugh. "How about not?"

"I want to know!"

Like an addict, he shakes slightly as he opens another stick of gum. After he puts it in his mouth, he wads up the foil and forms it into a tiny silver ball. His eyes are guileless.

"No, honestly, you probably don't."

Needle in a Haystack

Justice turns into Mr. Mute on the way back to the Schaeffer farm, which pisses me off to no end. It's not like me to back off, so I continue to prod.
"Just tell me already. What's the big mystery?"
"We'll talk about it later. Now's not a good time."
It irritates me when someone has something to say and they keep it to themselves. What is the point of that?
Since so many roads are barricaded to keep out the nosy freaks who get off on tragedy and mayhem, we embark on several detours to make it back to the Schaeffer Farm. I don't like seeing what the tornado left behind. It's beyond discouraging. As we drive through town I see people bent over the rubble rummaging through their ruins in the pitch black June night. I'm not even sure they know what they're looking for. Most stand up straight after a short time, pressing their hands to their lower backs wearing expressions that are haggard and confused.
Witnessing their despondency makes me think about what I will see tomorrow at my own house and what little may be left. There are specific things I want to find. Picture albums, trivia cards, clothes, and the newspaper article about the car crash are my top priorities, but I wonder if finding them will be like looking for a needle in a haystack.
There comes a point when the views are too depressing; I just can't take the visuals anymore so I squeeze my lids tightly over my eyes.
When we finally arrive at the Schaeffers', I get out of Justice's truck and slam the door on purpose. My sour and uncooperative expression is for his benefit, but either he doesn't notice or doesn't care. After retrieving my swimsuit and clothes from the dryer in the basement, I make my way upstairs.
Most of the kids are already in their beds. When Jeremy opens

his door, we mumble "Hi," to each other but avoid eye contact. I wish I were back in my own house, alone. Sharing a house with more than one person is a foreign concept, and now I'm living with eleven. I sprint up the attic stairs and begin to walk down the hall when Justice steps out of his room and blocks my path.

"Move it," I reach up, push him in the chest, and try to walk around him. He sidesteps and blocks me like a defensive lineman. I sigh and look up at him.

"What?" I demand.

We're so close that it's hard to look straight at each other without feeling like our eyes are crossed. I can feel the heat coming off his skin.

"I'm sorry. I've been a jerk tonight."

His breath smells of bitter spearmint. I want to stand on my tiptoes and kiss him. It's nearly impossible to stay angry at him.

"And?" I prompt him.

He takes a deliberate step back.

"I *will* tell you, just not tonight."

I see him reach for his pack of gum, but then he stops. He turns and leaves.

"Tomorrow then?" I ask.

"You're relentless." He closes his bedroom door.

"Didn't I tell you? *Relentless* is my middle name," I shout at him.

I go into the bathroom and lock the door, refusing to look at my own reflection because I'm blushing again. I can't be near him without this happening. I wouldn't be surprised if my skin stayed permanently red. Before going to bed, I call to check on Grandma Betty. A nurse who isn't anywhere near as friendly as Emily tells me that her condition hasn't changed. Although I have no reason not to believe her, I think she's lying and contemplate stealing a car so that I can drive to Clinton to check on Grandma Betty myself. Even though I don't act on my impulse, this thought stays with me through the night and I don't fall asleep until well after two in the morning. What if she wakes up and I'm not there?

Worse yet, what if she dies?

Breakfast is an absolute, chaotic nightmare. Joshua and Jordon, who have inherited their father's unnaturally large physique, toss the Cocoa Puff box back and forth between them, keeping it out of Jonas' reach. Jonas proceeds to throw himself on the floor and cry. Jeremy slaps Jordon in the back of the head and grabs the box midair and hands it to Jonas. Jordon, hell-bent on revenge, chases Jeremy out the front door. I watch them run around in the front yard. Jeremy, obviously quicker and more agile, taunts his slightly younger brother with an evil smile. I expect Jordon to be angry, but when I see his face, he's a smiling fiend.

Meanwhile, three of the other boys are having an impromptu pillow fight in the living room. Jade, who sits contently in the middle of the floor watching television and picking his nose, isn't distracted by the roughhousing.

I sit next to Jocelyn who still doesn't look at me but makes an effort at conversation. "Aren't you going to wear my clothes today?"

"No, I washed my own."

She glances my way. "Are those clothes all you have left?" She shoves a donut gem into her mouth. There's a ring of chocolate around her lips.

"As far as I know. Guess I'll find out this morning when I go to my house."

"Can I come with and help you?"

I nearly choke on my toast. "Um, probably not."

When she shoves two donuts into her mouth, I realize my answer probably hurt her feelings. "It's just that Justice is taking me, and there's not really much room in his truck. Plus, it's probably going to be boring," I explain patiently.

"Oh," she says, spraying some crumbs onto her plate.

"Maybe we can do something later," I offer.

"Okay!" she says eagerly. "Like when?"

"Um, soon I guess."

When I'm finished with breakfast, I wander outside to find Justice. He and Samson are helping the hired summer crew; they're in the process of hooking up the hoses to fill the milk trucks. I'm impatient to go to my house but don't want to bug Justice. I'll go myself. I'm tired of being carted around everywhere. I miss Smurfette. Despite the mockery I received because of her, she did offer legitimate transportation and independence. I take off in a run and am almost to the end of the driveway when I hear Justice shouting.

"Hey, where you going?"

I stop and turn around. "*To my house!*"

"Not so fast. I'm going to drive you. Just wait a minute."

I sit down under the oak tree out front and pick at the grass while I wait for Justice to pull around in his truck. *God*, I miss all my stuff. My trivia cards, magazines, and my romance novels (have I mentioned those?). I love mainstream fiction and the occasional classic, but I'm a sucker for romance novels, particularly historical romances. Sure, these books are brain candy, but everybody needs a sugar fix every now and then. The cheesier the story, the more I love it. My all time favorite: *The Flame and the Flower*. It's not as innocent as it sounds; Grandma Betty would pass out if she knew what was in that book. Talk about graphic sex education.

Jocelyn peeks out the window at me; she has a can of Coke in her hand. When I wave at her, she disappears behind the curtain.

During the ride to my house I attempt conversation with open-ended questions. "So, when do you graduate?"

"In two years."

"Where do you want to work?"

"I'm not sure."

"Have you thought about where you want to live?"

Justice drags his hand along the top of his stained blue jeans. "Not really."

The return of Mr. Mute. What the hell is his problem anyway? I give up. "Are you in a bad mood?"

He looks at me with an amused smirk. "You're direct, do you know that?"

"And you are a *pain in my ass.*"

He briefly rubs the spot just over his left eyebrow and then half shrugs. He flips off the air-conditioning and rolls down his window. The unbalanced pressure causes my ears to pop, and I roll down my window to compensate. Now my hair is being whipped in all sorts of crazy directions. I gather it and hold it at the side.

When we reach my street, most of the branches have been cleared so Justice is able to maneuver his truck easily. The Atwoods' RV is parked on their lot, but they don't appear to be home. Thank God for that, because after last night, I don't have any desire to see Mikayla. I'm confused about how to handle our relationship now that she's so intent on making nice.

When we pull into my driveway, Frank is already there, equipped with boxes, a camera around his neck, and a notebook. As Justice and I exit the car, I take a cautious look at my house. I'm relieved that the damage isn't as horrible as I thought it would be. Even though there isn't much of a roof left, three quarters of the house is intact. Only the living room and entry way have been slaughtered by the storm. This does nothing for my guilt. If Grandma Betty had just been in the basement or in any other room, she would have been fine.

"Hi! Good to see you Cane." Frank comes over and gives me a hug.

It's awkward since this is the first time we've ever officially touched. My head barely reaches the top of his barrel chest; he's a block man, very square and hard, all straight edges. Being hugged by him would be painful if he squeezed hard, but he's gentle. He smells like those tiny film canisters; I guess that makes sense since he loves photography.

Frank extends his hand to Justice. "Good to see you again. You folks getting along okay up at the farm?"

Justice nods solemnly. "We're counting our blessings. We lucked out."

"That you did, that you did." After briefly surveying our street, Frank turns back and faces me. He claps his hands once and then rubs them vigorously. "Let's get started. Cane, do you know where your grandma kept her office?"

"In the back, just off the kitchen."

"Great. We should be able to navigate that part of the house relatively easy. I thought Justice and I could look for some insurance papers, bank statements, things like that. We're going to need to contact the insurance company soon so that we can get the ball rolling on getting a check for you and Grandma Betty. There's plenty to rebuild."

"Oh, okay." I nod knowingly but haven't even considered these details. This is way out of my league.

"I'm also going to take pictures of each room, the foundation, the roof, and the surrounding property so that we have something tangible to offer. Do you know who your grandma's insurance provider is?"

"No." I glance over at the house and bite my lip. I realize how ill-equipped I am to handle this. What happens if Grandma Betty doesn't wake up? I stare at the ground because my chest tightens and my nostrils snot up.

"Do you know what medical insurance your grandmother has?" Frank asks hopefully.

I shake my head slowly. "No."

"How about where she keeps her social security card and important documents?"

"I, I-" I scan our yard and notice that the oak tree that stands outside my bedroom window has split right down the center. Turning back to Frank, I say, "I don't know where anything is."

"Don't worry. We'll find the documents," reassures Justice. "We'll take care of everything."

"No doubt about that," adds Frank cheerfully, bouncing on his toes. "Everything will be okay."

I've never felt more like a kid in my life. Here I was, convinced that I was almost an adult, and this tornado zooms in, picks me up, and drops me back on square one. Everyone keeps telling me that it's going to be okay, that it's going to be fine, but *when*? Life should come with an emergency fast forward button.

"See those boxes over there?" Frank asks. "Fill them with anything you think is important. Whatever you want to take, you can."

"We can put them in the back of my truck," offers Justice. "Samson will let you store things in the house and even in the barns if you have to."

"When Justice and I are done finding the documents, we'll start filling the garbage cans I brought. As we throw things away, we'll take a detailed inventory."

"Okay," I agree helplessly. At least he has a plan, because I wouldn't know where to begin.

Once the work is divided up, I separate from Frank and Justice and begin to truly assess the damage. When I arrived I had been under the assumption that it wasn't that bad, but when I enter through the back of what used to be my house, my optimism goes to pieces. While the layout is the same, and the house is relatively square, the windows are gone. Everything we own is spread haphazardly throughout the space. The television is smashed to pieces in the kitchen. The cupboards are open, and the dishes are missing. I think I saw bits of them smashed outside. The appliances are tipped over, and I don't even see the dining table and chairs. While I have free range of the back of the house that includes our large country kitchen, a full bathroom, back hall, and two small bedrooms, I can't access the living room at all since that part of the house is impassable. Thankfully, we have a front and back staircase, and so despite the destruction in the front of the house, I still have access to the upstairs.

Frank, who has come into the house with Justice, sees me at the base of the stairs. "Cane, I'm not sure it's a good idea for you to go up there."

"It's probably not structurally sound," adds Justice.

"It's fine."

Frank examines the stairs, puts his foot on the bottom step, and presses.

"See?" I move past him. "It's fine."

Frank rubs his jaw. "I'm not sure."

I throw my shoulders back and push past him. "Everything I want is up there."

"I'm coming up with you," says Justice.

For once I don't want him anywhere near me. I want to be alone. "No. I'll be fine."

"Just be careful. I don't want you falling through the floor and getting hurt," says Frank. "You call for help if you need anything."

I climb the stairs carefully, gingerly stepping over paper, silverware, mittens, and skeins of yarn. Seeing the disarray, the irrational way that things have been rearranged by the twister, is like being in the middle of a Dr. Seuss book. Too bad that Thing One and Thing Two aren't going to come in and do a quick cleanup.

Rafters are all that remain of the roof; dappled sunlight floods the space. Pieces of plaster and lath are missing, and I can see clearly into the bathroom and then directly into Grandma Betty's room.

When a sparrow darts in front me, I duck and suppress a screech. I'm sure they already have a nest somewhere in here. It doesn't take long for nature to come in and make itself at home.

The hallway is littered with clothes, pictures that have fallen off the wall, and oddly, a can of paint that has somehow opened and spilled, the result being a soupy, purple mess. Picking up the can, I look at the name of the color. *Lively Lavender*, from Grandma Betty's purple phase.

Tossing the can back down, I press the box against my chest and bravely enter Grandma Betty's room. In a mess this big it's hard to know where to begin. I'm knee deep in sweaters, underwear, yarn, books, and linens. Her bed is stripped bare. How does a tornado have enough finesse to leave the mattress and headboard but take the sheets?

It takes me more than an hour to organize and pack up what should be saved and another hour to separate the garbage and haul it outside where Justice and Frank are taking inventory. I have the urge to ask them how their search went, but I'm too afraid of what they'll tell me. Defeat is on their faces.

After three more trips outside to load the boxes into Frank's car and Justice's truck, I go upstairs. It's time to face my room. The door is closed, and that alone makes me nervous since all the other doors upstairs are flung wide open. Expecting obstacles, I turn the knob and push hard. The dense pine door swings open and smacks the door stop. For a moment, I wonder if it's a mirage, if my mind is playing tricks on me. But, my gift and curse is that I always see things for what they are.

There isn't one thing out of place. It's how I left it. God shut my door and waited for me to come home.

By early evening Justice and I have made it to the hospital and are sitting on either side of Grandma Betty like we did yesterday morning, but yesterday seems like an eternity ago. Was it really only yesterday? Time is all bent out of shape lately, and I've invested so many emotions into the last forty-eight hours that I feel years older.

Neither of us is particularly comfortable with speaking in a normal voice, especially after the grim report Dr. Fairchild gave when we arrived. As soon as he said it wasn't looking promising, that she wouldn't be coming off the ventilator and that when she did, he wasn't sure she would wake up, I tuned out. After Dr. Death (my nickname for him) left the room, every time Justice or I spoke, we whispered, like we were afraid speaking loudly would have catastrophic consequences. Even the nurses used hushed tones when they came in the room to check her vitals.

I tried to wake her up as soon as we got here tonight. I brought Great Grandma Lily's Bible from home, the one Grandma Betty reads from every night. I stuck it under her nose, hoping that it would work like smelling salts. It didn't, so I carefully placed it under her hand, hoping she could sense the shape and texture of it and remember that she needed to get up because she hadn't gone to Bible study yet this week.

"You don't have to stay here, you know." I fidget in my seat, but I don't look at Justice. "You can leave."

"I want to be here."

"Why?" I start massaging Grandma Betty's forearm and moving it around like the physical therapist showed me. "It's boring. You don't even know Grandma Betty."

Justice starts to do the same to her other arm. "I feel like I do."

I roll my eyes. "You honestly want to be here?"

"Are you trying to get rid of me?"

This, of course, is the last thing I want to do. "Not really."

"Okay then."

I move to her leg next, and, again, Justice does the same. We're supporting her knees and moving her lower legs up and down. "Does this really help?"

"I'm sure it does. They don't want the muscles to atrophy."

"I guess. I just wish she would wake up."

"She will. The doctor said that she was doing better today than yesterday."

"That's what you got out of it? That isn't what I heard." Guess I should have listened instead of just nodding my head. "Besides, what yardstick do they use to measure progress?"

"I don't know."

Defeated and sullen, I sit back down. Justice continues to massage Grandma Betty, taking great care. When he's finished, he sits down across from me again.

"Aren't you going to quiz me?" He sits up taller and looks in my pocket. "You must have fifty cards in there."

"History major? Right?"

He nods.

"Let's see how smart you are."

"Fire away."

I pull out the cards, shuffle them, and try to find a challenging one. "Okay, who was the star witness at the Senate Watergate hearings?"

Justice crosses his arms and leans back until the two front legs of the chair hover above the floor. "John Dean the third."

"That was too easy," I remark.

"Did you know it?"

"No, but I haven't memorized these yet, and I'm not the history aficionado, remember?"

He concedes by holding out his hands.

"What was Uncle Sam's biggest real estate deal?"

He scoffs. "The Louisiana Purchase. Something harder please." He makes a show of yawning. "You're losing my interest."

"Fine." I move on to the next. "What plan to rebuild Europe was unveiled on June 5th, 1947?"

Justice doesn't hesitate. "The Marshall Plan."

"The last ruler in the Egyptian dynasty of the Ptolemies?" This should stump him, I think smugly.

"CLE-O-PATRA," he smiles confidently. "Next."

I groan. "Who were 'overpaid, oversexed, and over here'?" I never would have read this had I known that the word, *sex*, was coming.

I start to turn a lamentable shade of fuchsia, and my armpits get the slightest bit slimy. Saying *sex* around Justice isn't an easy thing to do, since I think about what sex would be like with him. I don't have much experience to draw on, more like *no experience* at all.

"You got me on this one."

I flip the card over. "American GIs." I almost expected to find my name on the back, although, then it would have read, 'overpaid, *under*sexed, and over here.'

Game Over. After dropping several cards on the floor due to nervousness, I put them safely back in my pocket.

Justice leans across Grandma Betty toward me and gently pushes the hair off my forehead. Instantly, a tingle starts at the base of my spine and shoots all the way up my back to my neck. His fingertips against my forehead are by far the most erotic sensation I've ever felt.

"What's that?" he asks softly.

Confused I reach up to the spot he has touched. It's my birthmark that stands out in relief when I blush.

"Beautiful, isn't it?" I ask sarcastically. "It's a birthmark. My mark from God," I say jokingly, but it's not at all a joke.

"It's shaped like a cross."

"It was intentional."

"What do you mean?"

"It means I'm safe. God leaves me alone. My name is Cane, get it?"

He looks at me thoughtfully and sits back in his chair.

Since Justice is being so quiet, I compensate by talking. Not the normal kind of chatting, but the uncontrollable, verbal diarrhea where it's sometimes hard to catch my breath.

I tell him everything I can about our family, from my Grandpa Henry to my Great Grandma Lily. Hoping she can hear me, I occasionally glance at Grandma Betty, but she hasn't stirred at all. She's lying so still it scares me.

I'm not sure why, but I can't seem to get off the topic of death. I tell Justice again about the accident involving my parents and all the details of that night, but he really doesn't seem to want to hear it. He sits there with his head down and hands folded in prayer form, pushed up under his chin. I wonder if he's going to jump in and tell me that thing that he still hasn't told me, something about it being personal, but he doesn't say a thing, so I keep on going.

Maybe I do this next thing hoping Grandma Betty will hear me and that she'll be shocked to learn what her little Cane is capable of, wake up, and throttle me. I tell Justice everything about Mikayla, every single thing I have done. I use him like a priest, confessing all my sins to him.

He's clearly amused. "Don't you get sick of it, tormenting her like that?"

"It's old now, but how do I stop?"

"It sounds like she's the one who's making the effort to stop it. She's asking for it to be over."

"Sure, but you don't know what she said to me."

"Is that what started it, something she said?"

I don't answer. I lean back in the chair and study Grandma Betty's face for a moment. Her white skin blends in with the pillow. Her hair is matted flat against her head. This is a woman who coordinates her makeup, outfits, and handbags, and always has her hair perfectly curled.

"So I just give in and do what she wants?" I ask, jumping right back into our conversation.

"Are you afraid of losing?"

"I don't know."

"She's the one waving the white flag." Justice reaches in his pocket and pulls out a piece of gum.

"I guess."

By the time we leave the hospital that night, Justice not only knows all my family secrets but also my dreams and ambitions. When I tell him I want to be an archeologist, he says that he doesn't see me being able to sit still for that long. I tell him I don't want to be the kind that sits, but the kind that goes on adventures and treasure hunts. The female version of Indiana Jones. He laughs, and my feelings are hurt until he confides that his love for Indiana Jones movies is what actually led him to study history.

We walk through the Schaeffer's door a little after ten that night, and Justice and I have our arms loaded with boxes of my things.

"It's about time you got home!" Jelly Roll directs this verbal reprimand at me.

"We were at the hospital."

"I know that. That's not the point," she whines. "You just shouldn't make promises you can't keep."

Knowing that this conversation is going to take more than a second, I set my boxes down on the floor.

"I don't know what you're talking about."

Jelly Roll's face looks odd, even though she wears no makeup, she still has on lipstick. Maybe she's had her lips tattooed.

"You promised Jocelyn that you would do something with her. She told me all about it."

"But," I shake my head thinking back to our conversation this morning, "I didn't promise her anything."

"She said you did, and she cried herself to sleep waiting for you."

Around Jelly Roll, I've always had a governor on my tongue, but the events of the past few days have shorted a few circuits in my brain. "Obviously she misinterpreted or maybe she was imagining things because she was on a sugar and caffeine high from the Coke that she inhales every day. *I didn't promise her anything.*"

"We've taken you into our house, and that's how you speak to me?"

Justice plays referee. "Aunt Jenny, she didn't mean anything by it."

I glare at Jelly Roll with as much hatred as I can muster. "I'm not a part of this family, and I am one hundred percent sure that my being here doesn't make you happy."

Jelly Roll narrows her eyes. "That's one thing that can't be misinterpreted."

I want to say something back, but she leaves the room muttering loudly under her breath.

I'm not going to stay in a house where I'm not welcome. I'm already carrying the boxes back out the door when Justice comes out after me.

"Not so fast," he says.

"What?" I throw the box of clothes into the back of his truck. "You think I'm actually going to stay here after that? News flash, I'm finding somewhere else to live."

"You're being a little sensitive."

"Give me a break, Justice! She's your aunt and all, but she's a vindictive cow! I don't know why she hates me."

"Yeah, about that-"

"What about it? She hates me based on my genetics or something. It's common knowledge, isn't it? Don't you see the way she looks at me? You wouldn't believe some of the stuff she's said to me over the years. It's so obvious! I'm tired of it. Drive me back to my house. I can stay there."

"There isn't even a roof, Cane. You can't stay there."

"My room is fine." I pull back my hair and expose my birthmark. "See this, I told you that it protects me. God marked me just like he marked Cain in the Bible. It all started the night I killed my whole family, and-"

"You don't honestly believe-"

"I do believe that! You don't know how many times I've been spared. God's always looking out for me, but when it comes to everyone else in my life, he picks them off one by one. It's like he keeps on punishing me. If Grandma Betty dies-"

"She's not going to. She's going to be fine."

"*Oh, please.* Enough with the platitudes. I'm sick of everyone saying that; it's like that's all they can think to say. I would much rather have someone say, 'Sorry Cane, don't think she's going to make it, better start planning the funeral,' because then I would have permission to get mad as hell, which is much better than feeling helpless and waiting for something awful to happen."

Merely speaking of the possibility that I may lose Grandma Betty deflates me; emotionally drained, I stagger backwards and lean against the cab of Justice's truck.

He stands there with his hands deep in the pockets of his jeans, watching me.

"If I lose her, I have no one left."

He takes a small step toward me. "You have me," he says with certainty.

I laugh and look away. "I don't have you."

He reaches out and holds his palm against my cheek. "Yes, you do."

On account of my heart beating so fast I can feel it vibrating inside my mouth, I'm unable to say anything in return.

Justice takes his hand away from my face, and I can tell that he feels like he crossed a line. It shows in his face; his eyebrows are knitted together and he stares off to the side.

"You need to stay here."

"She doesn't want me here."

"No, probably not," he concedes, "but I do."

I'm not an expert at flirting or any of those other games that kids my age play, but I know how to read people. When he finally looks straight at me, I can tell that he likes me and not just in a friend kind of way, but *really* likes me. At least I think so.

"Are you tired?" he whispers.

"No," my mouth moves, but I barely make a sound.

"Let's go for a run."

He takes his aviator sunglasses off the top of his head where they've been perched for most the day and tosses them through the window of his truck. He grips the lip of the window sill and takes a deep breath before looking back at me. "There are some things I want to tell you."

Throwing Caution to the Wind

I'm an avid collector of stories about my parents, but my material isn't as substantial as I would like it to be. No matter how much I hear, I want more.

Naturally, I know more about my father because his mother is raising me. I'm more familiar with his childhood than anything else. When Grandma Betty reminisces it's usually about a time that took place before all the tragedy, a time when her husband and sons were still alive, when she had more of a reason to live than just me.

My favorite stories are about my father and his best friend, Samson Schaeffer, and how they were always getting into trouble.

"You know that Samson was your father's best friend. Those two were inseparable, just like you and Mikayla." Grandma Betty winked at me. "Oh, and I was so thankful for Samson. He was the level-headed one, the cautious one. Your father," she sighed heavily. "Well, he wasn't afraid of anything. He was my little adventurer. I used to take Samson and your father to the park, and Samson would start crying if the swing went too high, and that made me laugh, because that boy was so sturdy and big even at three-years-old. Your father on the other hand, just a skinny runt, cried if it didn't go high enough. When he was able to swing by himself, I was sure that at some point he would eventually go all the way up and around the bar. At times, I would cover my eyes with my hands because I was sure it was going to happen.

"He scared me half to death with the things he would do." Grandma Betty covers her heart and catches her breath. "He would leap off furniture, climb up doorframes, and do tricks on the monkey bars that I don't even think monkeys know how to do! I had to watch him constantly, and by the time he started kindergarten, I was amazed that he had only broken a wrist, thanks to a trapeze mishap. When he started school and got older, I wasn't always around to tell him to stop or to be careful, but I knew I could count on Samson for that.

"But your father rarely listened to Samson's warnings. It wasn't only that he didn't listen, but somehow he managed to persuade Samson to join in the fun. Your father could talk anyone into anything.

"When both of them got to that age where they were just enthralled with fire, I knew that eventually there would be trouble. They were always asking your Grandpa Henry to let them build a fire out back. Most of the time Grandpa would help the boys and allow them to have their fun, but he wasn't so keen on going through the fuss during the summer months when it was hot; he said there was no need for a fire when it was eighty degrees out.

"Well, your father must have been about ten, or maybe eleven, when he got the bright idea to experiment with fire and see what would happen to various objects after they were thrown into the flames. He and Samson built a small fire back behind the garage. They collected so many things to put in that fire! They also managed to get a hold of some aerosol cans, a dozen or more of them. You know what happens to those when they are put under heat and pressure, don't you?

"Thank God Samson had half a brain, because sometimes I wonder whether your father really understood the consequences of his actions. When those cans started to hiss and spit, Samson took off in a dead run and threw open the screen door on the back porch so hard and fast, one of the hinges broke! He didn't have to say a word. I knew right away that something was wrong. I told him to stay put, and I sprinted out back and dragged your father away from that fire, giving him an earful of words that I can't even repeat.

"As soon as we made it back to the house, we heard an explosion. My heart just about stopped beating. Either from fear, anger, or both, I started crying like a mad woman! I think your dad was more scared from that than from anything I had said to him. It was years before he built a fire again."

The fire story only scratches the surface. My father did everything from tractor surfing, where he had Samson tie a sled to a tractor and drag him through fields, to cow-tipping at Samson's farm. An adrenaline junkie, he thought nothing of rock climbing without ropes (which rendered a broken leg), parachuting out of an airplane when he was only seventeen (Grandma Betty didn't know about it until afterwards), or white-water rafting on the Colorado River (a trip he took with Samson and several other friends the summer after high school graduation).

The stories about my father are nail-biters, but I know that he comes out victorious and alive in every one of them, thanks to Samson, his faithful, more level-headed sidekick. If it weren't for Samson, I might not have been born.

Grandma Betty claims that raising my father gave her every single one of her gray hairs. "The day he was born I got my first one, and by the time he left for college, I didn't have a single brown strand left on my head."

When I study pictures of my parents, it's obvious that I'm a miniature version of my mother, but the comparisons stop there since I don't know what she was like as a little girl. Because of what I know about my father, I see more of myself in him.

I'm like my father, but in a more stealthy way. When no one is looking, I'm the daredevil. Every now and then, I throw caution to the wind, and I like to imagine that my dad is my sidekick, that he's watching over my shoulder.

On Your Mark, Get Set, Go

As soon as we come to the end of the Schaeffer driveway, Justice starts running at a breakneck speed. I'm one or two strides behind him, and he keeps slowing down, waiting for me to catch up to him. I'm quick, but his legs are twice as long as mine.

"Am I going too fast?" he asks. "I took off too fast, didn't I?"

My heart is punching a hole through my rib cage. "No."

My answer, nothing more than a gasp, gives me away. He immediately slows down. The muscles in my quadriceps burn from anaerobic strain. It takes awhile before I'm able to get control of my breathing, because even before we started running my heart rate was maxed out from excitement.

"What's so important that you had to bring me out here?" I try to sound casual when I ask this.

Justice reaches up and swats at a bug that has landed on his square jaw. He has the kind of profile that would make a superhero jealous. I try not to think of my own profile, my disappointing cheekbones and pointy chin. Grandma Betty has told me I have the face of a Tinker Bell; I don't see how that's a compliment.

"It's just that I can't stand being in that house sometimes," he says.

I laugh disbelievingly. "You can't stand it! Give me a break. At least Jelly Roll doesn't hate you."

He turns his face and spits. "That's why I don't like being there, because of how she treats you."

This is as close to chivalry as it gets, and I'm not sure it's possible to be more in love. I keep silent, because who the hell knows what might come out of my mouth? It would probably be something like, "You are my knight in shining armor. I love you." Sometimes I make myself barf. I swear those romance novels have rotted my brain.

"She doesn't really hate you."

I scoff. "Don't patronize me. Of course she hates me. It's obvious."

Justice shakes his head. "There's some history you don't know about."

"Oh, I know it all. I know that Jelly Roll was in love with my father, and he didn't pick her, he picked my mom. Really, it was like the love triangle that really wasn't a triangle at all since my father never wanted anything to do with Jelly Roll."

We've entered the forest preserve, and the path that winds its way around the perimeter is four and a half miles. Justice turns right, and I follow him. The moonlight, neon in intensity, makes me look like an athletic Casper. I wish I could upgrade my freckles for a tan.

"Your father and Samson were best friends, you know that?"

"Of course." Because I'm looking at Justice, the way his shorts sit on his thighs and the way his t-shirt every now and then exposes a sliver of his ridged abdomen, I stumble on a tree root and almost fall face first into the dirt. I brace my fall with my hands.

"You okay?"

Shaken, I stand and brush myself off. "I'm fine." Thank God for the cover of night. My whole body is turning red from embarrassment.

"Anyway, I doubt you've heard the whole story." Justice says forcefully. "You know that Samson, your dad, and Jenny Ryanne grew up together and all went to the University of Illinois. You know that Jenny was always in love with your dad."

"I know all of that, and do you think you could refer to her as Jelly Roll, instead of Jenny?"

Justice looks sideways at me and offers a crooked smile. "Sure. Anyway, your dad, Samson, and Jelly Roll remained good friends in college, until Mary came along. When Mary and Alex fell in love, Jelly Roll was heartbroken about it and kind of broke off from the group. She couldn't get over the fact that Alex would never love her; she even dropped out of school mid-semester and returned home."

"Hence, the cosmetology school stint where she learned the fine art of applying makeup like Tammy Faye-Baker," I add.

"Right, but the story doesn't end there. Jelly Roll wasn't the only one who had her heart broken. The part of the story that's usually left out is that Samson also fell in love with Mary, which I'm sure you can imagine caused trouble. He eventually told her how he felt and kissed her, and unfortunately that also happened to be the same moment your dad walked in the room. Long story short, the friendship between your dad and Samson was never quite the same again. Your dad felt betrayed by Samson, and Samson felt guilty for loving his best friend's girl." Justice lets this information sink in, and I'm trying to figure out why Grandma Betty neglected to tell me this part of the story that has all the makings of a classic country song.

"Samson left school before senior year was over and stepped right into the family dairy business. I'm not sure he ever stopped loving Mary. Your dad and he were eventually friends again, but not like they were before Mary came along. Samson couldn't be around the two of them for long; it got to him because the feelings for Mary were still there.

"Fast forward a year. Jelly Roll and Samson announced their engagement. Jelly Roll has never gotten over the fact that both men in her life loved Mary more than her. I still think Samson loves your mom, even after all this time. He was devastated when your parents died. He lost the two people he loved most. I'm not really sure that my uncle was ever head-over-heels in love with Jelly Roll. I mean he loves her, but it doesn't run deep. I'm sure she's well aware of that. I think they ended up together more out of circumstance and heartbreak than out of genuine affection or love."

"How do you know all of this?"

"My mom, Sharon, isn't just Samson's younger sister but Jelly Roll's best friend from high school. I've overheard many conversations between them. I wanted to give you the background so that you could better understand how dysfunctional it is."

"The sins of our fathers," I laugh bitterly.

Justice gets a dark look on his face. "Something like that," he says reluctantly.

"If Samson and Jelly Roll's relationship is so dysfunctional, why did they have eight kids?"

He shrugs, and as his shirt moves, I notice his skin peeks through; I try not to look for too long.

"I have my theories," he says thoughtfully.

"And, those would be?" I ask leadingly.

As we run around the curve, I spot a car a mile or so in the distance; it's parked in a grassy clearing. Probably some teenagers making out, and that makes me think about Justice and me making out, like that will happen.

"Maybe it's a distraction. I know Samson loves kids."

"What are Jelly Roll's reasons?"

"I'm not sure, but I think she's trying to prove that she's happy. She has what your mother and father never had the chance to have."

His insight, harmless and plausible, stirs up the silt of grief that

I feel, not for myself, but for my parents who never had the chance to finish what they started.

We're nearing the back of the forest preserve, and the car I had seen earlier is now in clear view. Despite that the night has leeched its color I recognize that it's the Atwood's car. I'm sure Mikayla and Nate are busy going at it in the backseat. I can't confirm this because the trail turns away from them, and the early summer growth is jungle thick.

"What's Nikki like?" I ask, taking myself by surprise at the daring subject change.

Justice laughs a bit awkwardly. "Why do you want to know that?"

"I know she's beautiful."

He glances curiously in my direction. "I only know that because I saw the picture in your room," I confess to him. "I wasn't snooping or anything."

He laughs again. "Sure."

"Fine, whatever," I state dismissively and then add, "I just want to know."

It's awhile before he begins talking, but when he does, I can tell by the way he runs, slightly faster, and the mechanical way he speaks that he still has feelings for her.

"We met freshman year. I had to take this poetry class to fill a requirement, and she sat next to me all semester. It just happened. Everything was fine until this last year. I don't know." He shrugs. "We just kind of grew into different people. She really wasn't the same person I fell in love with. She became manipulative and demanding. I still couldn't bring myself to end it. I kept hanging on. She broke up with me, handed me back the ring and that was the end of it."

"Ring? You were engaged?"

"Yes."

"For how long?"

"Two years."

"Weren't you kind of young to be engaged?" All the guys I hear about or read about in Cosmopolitan are commitment-phobes.

"I hate it when people ask that."

"Sorry." Of all people, I should know that being young shouldn't be a disqualifier.

"No, I see your point. It's just age is a yardstick for too many things. It really shouldn't be."

I agree one hundred percent. "And so why do you torture yourself by keeping the picture?"

"The girl in the picture is not the same girl who broke up with me. That was taken in the beginning. I'm not really sure why I hang on to it. I threw everything else away."

"Even the ring?"

"Not that," he gives an abbreviated laugh. "I'm not that stupid."

"Hey," he grabs my hand, and I'm so unprepared and thrilled I almost snatch it away. "Let's walk for a minute," he suggests tentatively.

He's still holding my hand, and I love the way his fingers mesh with mine and how I feel more feminine when he's near, not like the scrawny tomboy Jelly Roll thinks I am. The contact doesn't last long.

We walk together in silence, but I can tell from the way the air sits heavily between us that Justice wants to say something else.

Our run has taken us more than halfway around the forest preserve, and I want to venture off the path and visit my favorite place. I want to share it with Justice.

"Can I take you somewhere?"

"Sure."

With me leading, we hike off the path through the thick of trees to an open field. In front of us is the daunting hill where the lone maple that is half alive grows. We hike to the top. When I reach the tree, I drag my hands along the bark expecting to feel a pulse on the half of the tree that's alive, but there's nothing. I put my back against the trunk so that it supports me, close my eyes, and listen to the sound of my heartbeat as it slows. When the rush of my blood becomes inaudible, the sounds around me, the crickets' consistent song, the gurgle of the stream that borders the forest preserve, and Justice exhaling and shifting his weight, are heightened.

When I open my eyes and turn my head I notice that Justice is standing with his back against the opposite side of the tree. His hands hang to his side, as do mine, and I know that if I reached back we could clasp hands.

"Why do you think Grandma Betty didn't tell me the whole story, you know, about Samson being in love with my mom?"

"Maybe she thought it was ancient history."

"Nothing's ancient history. Do you think she left those details out on purpose?"

"Why would she do that?" he asks.

The more I think about it, the more it makes sense that she didn't tell me. Why would she need to? The outcome was that her son had married Mary, and then I had been born.

"I need to tell you something else that I'm not sure you're going to want to hear," Justice says regretfully.

I wait for him to continue.

"I told you last night that what happened to your parents was personal, and I want to explain. When Frank stopped by the house the other day, he mentioned your last name, but I guess it didn't click until I went to the hospital and saw Kallevik in black and white outside Grandma Betty's door. Then I started connecting the dots. I realized who you were, that you were the baby who survived.

"Cane, do you know everything that happened the night you were born?"

His voice is thin and strained, and I fear that there must be something I don't know. I've always feared this.

"I know about the accident, that they were struck by another car and that their car flipped. I know enough."

"Do you know who caused it to happen?"

"Yes."

He sighs unevenly. "So you already know?" he asks in resigned relief.

"Kevin Price," I say out loud for the first time to someone other than myself. He's always been the other villain in my story, besides me, and as soon as I say his full name, I understand what Justice is telling me.

"My father."

I take the information and swallow it whole, and it doesn't get lodged in my throat. It slides down to the same spot in my gut where all the other bits of tragedy are. Knowing that it was Justice's father doesn't make it any easier or any worse. I'm still the one who set things into motion, who was trying to kick my way out of my mother.

"I wouldn't blame you if you hate me," he states evenly.

I don't hate Justice for what he has told me. In fact, I believe tragedy has brought us together and holds us together. Slowly, I reach back with my hand and my fingertips find his.

A piece of the past has been put in place with new associations. I love a man whose father killed my parents. My mind plays leap frog, going from past disaster to current, and I'm not thinking about my parents or Kevin Price, but I'm grappling with the reality that Grandma Betty lies unconscious in a hospital bed.

"If she dies..." I can't even finish the sentence.

Looking out over the forest preserve, I can see the sinister and cruel damage the tornado left behind. *Who will love me*, I ask myself.

Justice works his fingertips up the length of my palm and then laces his fingers through mine so that they are tightly joined. My entire body vibrates from the inside out.

After a moment, he releases my hand and leaves his side of the tree to come stand in front of me. He inches closer so that my back is pressed up against the trunk; the bark presses into my skin making ridges and patterns that would read like Braille against fingertips. What would it be like to have his hands run the length of my bare back?

"Cane," he whispers and squeezes my hand tightly.

He's so close that I lose the natural rhythm of breathing. I can't make myself look him in the eye, and so I watch the motion of his chest as he breathes. He smells fiercely sweet, a combination of spearmint, sweat, and pheromones. He takes his free hand, raises it to my face, and delicately traces my cheekbone. My body loosens up and contracts at the same time, and I don't know what this sensation is, what it means, all I know is that when he touches me, the pleasure is wild.

I close my eyes and wait for him to kiss me; I can feel him contemplating it. If I had any courage at all, I would make this happen. I would wrap my free hand around the back of his neck and pull him to me.

Then, all I feel is wide open air. Had I imagined it?

He clears his throat and turns away from me, and I don't know what to make of what just happened or if anything did happen.

"We should get back," he states with detachment.

I peel myself away from the tree. The blood rushes back and fills all those tender pleats the bark has made in my skin.

Justice runs too fast again. I swear, it's like he's starting a race, and he skips the, "On your mark, get set," part and just goes. This time I notice he doesn't make much of an effort to slow down for me. I don't bother to try and keep up. I need some time alone to process what's happened and to accept that Justice is probably repulsed by me. It's discouraging. No matter how much I love him and how many articles I read in Cosmo and Seventeen, I doubt I will ever get him to love me back.

I also wonder how much longer I can live at the Schaeffer house. It's only a matter of time before I open my mouth and say something to Jelly Roll that will lead to a fist fight. Grandma Betty always tells me that I know too much for my own good, and now I can finally see how this is true. I know so much now that I have a definite advantage over Jelly Roll.

Justice is ahead of me, and I'm just about finished with the trail and catching up when I see the Atwood's car about to pull out onto County N. Due to the thick flora, my view is slightly obscured, but I can see Nate sitting in the passenger seat. I slow my pace and walk so that I am still camouflaged by the trail. I don't want to chance them seeing me, especially Mikayla. The trees and weeds thin out, and I can clearly see both of their profiles. Only, it isn't Mikayla driving the fogged vehicle. My stomach turns into a marble as I realize that no one is as perfect as I want them to be.

Realizing that I have stopped, Justice turns and comes back to me. Out of breath, he bends over slightly and rests his hands on his knees. He wipes his forehead with the bottom half of his shirt and stands.

"You okay? What's wrong?" he asks with concern. "You look like you've seen a ghost or something."

I stare after the Atwood's car as it speeds down N. Instinctively, I reach up to braid my hair, forgetting that it's pulled up in a high pony tail.

"No, nothing like that." Shaking my head miserably, I look at Justice, who disappoints me when he won't look me in the eye. "I just know too much for my own good."

Part Two
July 1992

The Daily Grind

Last Friday Grandma Betty was moved to a long-term care facility that's attached to the hospital. She looks more human, more alive, now that most of those machines are gone and that tube is out of her throat. She's breathing on her own, which is progress, but it isn't enough to give the doctors confidence and the freedom to pat themselves on the back, because she's still in a coma. Dr. Fairchild, who was born without a heart and I believe has no desire to sign up for a transplant, says there isn't much more that we can do but wait.

I've used every tactic to rouse her out of her preternatural slumber. During my visits, I've said things hoping to shock her awake.

"Hey, I just had sex for the first time last night, Grandma Betty!" I exclaimed excitedly.

I've also tried, "I was at a party with Mikayla and got arrested for underage drinking."

"I'm experimenting with drugs."

"I've decided to drop out of school and backpack across the country."

None of these things have worked. Truth is stranger than fiction, and I should be telling her: *Connie and Deborah are dead. The tornado destroyed our town. I've fallen in love with the son of the man who killed my parents. Annette isn't perfect after all; she's screwing her daughter's boyfriend.*

Why can't I bring myself to say these things?

At times I'm tempted to be candid, but since Justice is usually in the room with me, I keep my mouth shut.

Justice has become my unofficial bodyguard. Don't get me wrong; I love having him as my shadow. There isn't anything better, but I can't figure out what's going on between us. He's the king of mixed signals; I've thought about making him a crown that says this. Some days he hardly speaks, and during these vexing moments of silence, I repeatedly ask him what the hell his problem is. Instead of giving me a verbal break, he looks at me with those soulful, beautiful eyes of his and shakes his head like he's sorry. It's impossible to hold a grudge against dimple man; I can't even get enough momentum going to get truly pissed off.

The predictability of my life wears on me at times, but at least I know what to expect. At least I know that Justice is going to be by my side for most of the hours that I'm awake. My routine is something like this: wake up, work on the farm, work some more, visit Grandma Betty with Justice, eat dinner at the hospital with Justice, return to the Schaeffer farm, go running with Justice, talk to Frank when he calls (and he calls daily to give me updates on what's going on with the house, the insurance company, and to talk about Grandma Betty), and go to bed with a fair amount of exhaustion and sexual frustration. I'm getting a crash course in sexual frustration. Before Justice came along, I never really understood, but the lesson has been learned.

I often walk around feeling stuck in a straightjacket. It has nothing to do with my routine or with Justice, but everything to do with my warden, Jelly Roll. Even though there haven't been any knock-down, drag-out fights, or even a volley of heated words, there have been plenty of dirty looks exchanged, the kind that say *I would like to pound you to a bloody pulp.* Because I'm living in a fantastic house and spending all my time with the love of my life, I don't want to jeopardize my situation by saying something stupid. For now, I'm trying to be civil to Jelly Roll.

Being civil typically means avoiding her. Currently, I'm sitting in bed, because I'm dreading going downstairs for breakfast where Jelly Roll always comments about my food selections.

"Oh, eating healthy again. Cereal and fruit."

"Pop tarts aren't good enough for you, are they?"

"For a little thing, you sure eat a lot."

If it hadn't been morning when she said these things, I might have retaliated, but my brain has the consistency of oatmeal until ten or eleven. Hours later I think of the perfect comebacks. "Sausage and pancakes again? Don't you have enough pigs in your blanket?" Sadly, I never get the opportunity to say things like this out loud.

Today is Saturday, my one and only day to sleep in, and I should be taking advantage of it. But the sun and I have struck up quite a friendship. Any sign of light on the horizon, and I'm instantly awake. Grandma Betty would be proud of my progress, because weeks ago it took mild electrocution to get me going. However, early rising isn't a cure for laziness. I have a fondness for lingering in bed. I love the feel of the sheets against my bare, freshly shaved legs (I've taken great care lately to keep them that way, one guess as to why).

I'm growing tired of lying here and thinking, and so I reach for the romance novel that I bought at the hospital gift shop called *Write Me a Love Song* and attempt to finish a chapter that I started days ago. I can't focus; stories such as these are starting to bore me. I have my own romance brewing, and it's much more interesting than anything I've ever read in a book.

Casting the book aside, I tackle some trivia cards; I'm trying to memorize history questions so that I can impress the history major down the hall with my knowledge. To my horror, I can't remember a thing! My short term memory has taken a hit. Is it possible to get Alzheimer's when you're only fifteen?

I rummage around on the nightstand and pick up a pen. The new freckles on my forearm make some interesting patterns, and oddly enough, it doesn't take too much effort to connect them in such a way so that they form the name *Justice*. I take the pen and push into the belly of my forearm, traveling over the letters carefully again and again, filling up my pores with Justice's name. After admiring my new tattoo, I decide I can't prolong the inevitable, so I get dressed and go downstairs to face the wrath of Jelly Roll, hoping by some miracle of God she won't be in the kitchen.

No such luck.

"You're finally up!" she exclaims.

Never mind that all her kids are still snoring upstairs. Her face looks odd this morning. Her lips are naked; they're a waxy, pale pink and they disappear against her tan skin.

"Justice is gone for the day," Jelly Roll slides a cereal bowl down the kitchen island toward me. "He went with Samson to a business meeting in downtown Chicago."

"Oh," I say, knowing that I sound disappointed.

Jelly Roll raises her eyebrows at me like she's trying to read between the lines. I suddenly remember the ink tattoo and try not to let her catch a glimpse of my forearm.

"Since it's Saturday, I hadn't really planned any farm work for you. But, I would like you to spend the day playing with Jocelyn. She wants you to take her swimming and show her how to do her hair," Jelly Roll stops and pushes her pale lips together, then looks down at me over the tip of her nose. "But, I'm not really sure you would be adept at playing hairdresser. That doesn't really matter, though. As long as you keep her busy, it will be fine. I need to take the boys to a basketball tournament, so I'll be gone most of the day. I should be home by four in the afternoon."

She thrusts a white envelope filled with cash at me. "Do you think you can manage?"

I've earned this money, but the way she's giving it to me makes it seem like I don't deserve it. And, if I refuse to watch Jocelyn, I can guarantee she'll snatch it out of my hands.

"Um, sure."

At this moment, Jocelyn appears in the doorway.

"Are we spending the day together?" she asks and claps her chubby hands together.

Jelly Roll rolls her lips into a messy smile and looks at me.

I paste a smile on my face and turn to Jocelyn. "Yeah, we are."

After breakfast my day consists of making Jocelyn happy, and it isn't hard to amuse her. The girl is excited to be around me, and she hasn't stopped talking since Jelly Roll left, something I find both endearing and annoying. Clearly, in her eyes I'm a rock star. I've never had anyone worship me in this way, and I have to admit, it's flattering. Is this what it's like to have a younger sister?

As we swim together in the pool, she asks me every question imaginable.

"Why don't you paint your fingernails?"

I shrug. "I don't know. I just don't see the point. It's not my thing."

"Oh, my mom likes makeup. She went to beauty school after college. She always has her fingernails and toenails painted."

Jocelyn fans her fingers wide and regards her naked nails. "No, it's not my thing either. Do you color your hair?"

I laugh and grab a strand. It looks almost brown when it's wet. "No! Why would I need to? It has enough color in it."

"Oh. My mom says your hair isn't a normal color, but I think it's pretty."

"It *is* normal. It's *hers* that isn't." For fear this will be repeated verbatim, tone and all, I amend my last comment. "It's just that your mom likes her blonde hair, so she has to have it colored so it looks just right."

"Oh. Why are all your clothes the same color?"

I glance down at my navy suit with white trim around the edges. "I like them blue and white. They're classic colors and it's almost impossible to wear anything that clashes."

"Oh," Jocelyn takes a sip of her Coke and pushes the inner-tube she's floating in away from the side of the pool. Her thighs are twice the size of mine. I wonder how big she'll get if someone doesn't do a diet intervention. "I love classic," she adds seriously.

"Hey, Jocelyn."

"Yeah?"

"I don't like Coke. Actually, I like just plain water. Drinking Coke just makes me hungrier and thirstier."

"Oh." Jocelyn paddles over to the side of the pool and deposits her Coke can by the ladder. "Me, too. I'm tired of drinking Coke."

Lying on my back, I float around the pool and let bright sun burn my eyelids. Relaxing my arms, I flip them so that my white forearms are exposed; I can feel them getting pink. I should get out and put more sunscreen on, but I like it when my flesh sizzles.

"Why do you have Justice's name on your arm?" asks Jocelyn as she grabs onto my arm and inspects it.

I open one of my eyes and squint at her. "I don't know. He's my friend," I say defensively and pull my arm into the water.

"Oh." She flutters her feet and paddles away. "His mom is my daddy's sister, so he's my cousin."

"I know."

"My mom used to be best friends with Aunt Sharon, but they had a big fight. Mom's still mad about it and won't talk to her."

"What did they fight about?"

Jocelyn bobs up and down in the water making gigantic ripples. "I don't know."

"Fights are no fun."

"Fights are no fun," she repeats.

For the remainder of the morning and the better part of the afternoon, Jocelyn plays parrot, and it damages my ego. The things that come out of my mouth aren't nearly as profound as I had believed. I wonder what Justice must think of me.

By three in the afternoon, the intensity of the early July heat and Jocelyn's incessant chattering has given me an enormous headache that sticks to the inside of my eye sockets. After I put in a movie for her, I call Grandma Betty's nurse at the care facility since I obviously won't be able to make it in today. Her condition is the same, but it doesn't feel right that I'm breaking routine and not going. I've become superstitious about my daily visits, and this schedule change makes me jumpy.

I glance in the living room; Jocelyn is asleep. Her mouth hangs open, and her arm dangles over the side of the sofa. She has carefully drawn my name in large, block letters with a purple pen. Sighing, I look at my own arm and see that my graffiti has faded from the swim.

Outside, I hear a car door slam. Samson and Justice have returned. Justice laughs; his laugh has such a rich timbre that it sends shivers to places I didn't even know could get shivers. Part of me wants to bound out the door and jump right back into our everyday routine, but the other part of me is so fed up that our relationship hasn't gone in the direction I want it to go that I want to get far, far away from him.

With this thought in mind, I head upstairs, change into running clothes, and pull my hair up into a high ponytail. Being careful not to wake Jocelyn, I emerge soundlessly from the front door. I catch Samson's eye and wave, and then I start running. The humidity pastes itself to my body. I'm completely saturated, dripping wet, and I should turn around and go back, but I can't make myself change direction. Besides, I've wanted to return to my house for days so that I could do what I had planned.

Now, whenever I arrive in my neighborhood, it's always a bit of a shock. In addition to wreaking havoc on the houses, the tornado tried its hand at some impromptu landscaping. Many of the mature trees are gone, and it's unsettling to see so much blue sky when this street used to be a shaded and verdant cocoon.

Thankfully, everything is accessible now; most of the garbage has been hauled away. A few of our neighbors have even started to rebuild. Three construction trucks are parked in front of the Atwood's house, and I can hear hammers and power tools in their backyard. The door to their RV opens, and Annette emerges holding a phone against her ear. I duck behind the shell of our garage. She's the last person I want to see.

From an awkward squatting position, I survey our property. It's exceptionally tidy. Frank has taken care to plastic over all the windows; even the roof is covered with tarps that are tied securely to the framing. The two large dumpsters on the side of the house overflow with miscellaneous possessions. Even though I've pitched in a few times over the last four weeks, it's been a weak effort. I can't give myself credit for this transformation. Frank has been more committed to helping us than I've been. From the beginning he told me not to worry about a thing, that he would handle it all, but it's become so out of balance that I'm embarrassed and ashamed. Every time we talk all I can say is *thank you*, but it doesn't feel like it's enough.

Sometimes I wonder why Frank is so involved. I know he's a friend of Grandma Betty's, but he's gone above and beyond the call of duty. If Grandma Betty knew how much Frank had done and how little I had helped, she would be spitting mad. I make a mental note to tell her this during my next visit; maybe that will get her attention.

I peer around the garage and see that Annette has disappeared. Standing, I make my way to the rear of our property in search of a shovel. The one that Frank has been using leans against the garage. I take it and go to the base of the willow tree in the far back of our property. The scraggly and ancient willow escaped the wrath of the storm with the exception of its leaves. The tree is completely bald, and I wonder if it was the wind that blew them off or if the poor tree had such a fright that the leaves simply fell off from sheer terror.

I find the soft, mossy low spot and get to work. After three minutes of serious digging, I reach the small wooden crate. I lift it out of the ground and carefully pry open the nailed down lid with the shovel. All of Mikayla's things that I had taken are there, and because I had taken care to seal them in plastic bags, they're as good as new. I'm not really sure she'll have much use for an autographed poster of Kirk Cameron, her old diaries, cassette tapes, and clothes, but it's not about the things. It's about ending the war.

I've been thinking about it for days now, and I wish I could say that my motivations were pure and that I finally decided to forget the past and rekindle a friendship with Mikayla. I even wish I could say that I had outgrown it. In reality, I'm ending it because of what I found out about Annette and Nate; Mikayla has enough problems without me tormenting her.

Reluctantly, I walk across the street and knock on the Atwood's trailer door. Of all people, Nate, Mr. Pretty Boy himself, answers the door. His Mustang is nowhere to be seen.

"What do you want freckle freak?" He regards me with disdain.

I could destroy his world with what I know. This gives me a confidence I typically don't have around him. I put my hand on my hip. "Is Mikayla around?"

"Maybe she is, maybe she isn't."

"Who is it?" Mikayla asks in the background.

He steps away from the door. "See for yourself."

Mikayla comes to the door, looking tan and every bit the cover girl I'll never be. "What do you want?" she asks wearily and leans her head against the doorframe.

"I came to give you this." I hand over the bounty that I had stolen from her over four years ago. "It's over. I want it to be anyway, and I should have never started it."

Once the look of disbelief leaves Mikayla's pretty face, her lips grow thin and hard.

Nate returns to the door and slides his arm around Mikayla's shoulders. "What the fuck are you doing here anyway?"

"I see you've been taking a vocabulary course this summer. Good for you," I say sarcastically. I look at Mikayla. "I just wanted to give that stuff back to you."

She runs one of her hands over the small poster. "Is this a truce?"

"Guess you could say that," I respond awkwardly.

She smiles hesitantly. "It's a start."

"I guess," I concede.

By this time, Annette has made her way from the backyard into the front, and I want to get the hell out of there. "See you later."

"Sure." Mikayla steps back, and Nate slams the door in my face.

I'm in a mad rush to leave, but Annette stops me.

"Cane!" she shouts. "How are you?"

Reluctantly, I turn around to face her. There's an invisible magnet pulling my eyeballs to the ground. For the life of me, I can't look her in the face. I keep picturing her in the car with Nate.

"You okay?" She reaches out and touches my arm.

"Yeah." Far from it, I think.

"Frank has been over at your house quite a bit." She glances across the street. "He's done a fantastic job cleaning up your place."

"Yeah."

"How's Grandma Betty? I haven't been to see her in over a week; we've just been so busy."

"She's the same," I answer softly.

"She'll get better."

"Yeah," I say noncommittally.

Annette turns and regards her house with pleasure. "It's coming along, isn't it? It was just a miracle that Mitch had some connections and we were able to get a contractor. We should be back in our house by August first. Maybe then you could come and stay with us?"

"I'm happy at the Schaeffers' farm," I reply stubbornly.

"Sure you are. I'm glad." Her smile is unsteady. "So many horrible things have happened because of this storm, but it has brought people together, don't you think?"

I make a sound that comes out like a grunt. "In more ways than one," I say suggestively. She misses the innuendo.

The trailer door opens, and Mr. IQ himself emerges with a large duffel bag in one hand and a football helmet in the other.

Annette smiles tensely. "Hi, Nate."

"Hi, Mrs. Atwood," he responds in a respectful tone that I've heard him use with authority figures. "I was wondering if you could give me a ride to football practice?" His tone is neutral and detached, but he angles his body toward her. His posture, sloppy and familiar, is enough to expose their relationship.

"Of course. Let me go get the keys." Annette's breathing is so shallow she sounds out of breath. "Honey, it was so nice seeing you. Stop back anytime."

I'm so disgusted I can't say anything. When she disappears inside the trailer, I turn to leave, but Nate stops me by grabbing my arm.

"What are you doing here?"

"None of your business." I shake his hand off my arm.

"I guess not, but this shit with Mikayla has to stop."

"I think I made it clear that it was going to."

"What? Was that your idea of a little peace offering or something? I don't trust you."

"No, Nate," I pause and glance at the trailer and then back to him, so that he can get the full gist of what I'm saying. "It's *you* I don't trust."

"What's that supposed to mean?" he asks arrogantly.

"A private midnight rendezvous is never as private as you would like to think."

He narrows his alligator green eyes at me. "What is that supposed to-"

The trailer door opens abruptly ending our conversation. Nate is going to have to figure it out on his own, because I'm not sticking around to watch Annette and him drive off into the sunset. I sprint across the street to my house.

Since I can't contemplate returning to the farm, at least not now, I spend the rest of the afternoon and early evening picking through some remaining items inside the core of my house and trying to figure out if I should tell Mikayla. But, seriously, how do you tell someone that's her mom is sleeping with her boyfriend? It's an impossible situation, and I've never stumbled across an advice column on that one. I've done many things to Mikayla, but the one thing I don't want to do is break her heart.

After I forage the house for treasures and emerge with a five dollar bill that I found in an old handbag in the basement, I walk outside and turn my attention to the garage. It didn't sustain as much damage, but what I'm looking for happens to be in a section that was hit. Once I make it past Grandma Betty's car and the pile of boxes that Frank has been storing in here, I squat down and survey the spot where I stored Smurfette. Unfortunately, part of the roof has caved in, and I have to crawl into the tight space to retrieve her. It takes some effort and a profuse amount of sweating, but I finally manage to bring her out of the rubble. I unwind the tarp from her frame.

My low blood sugar warns me that dinner time has come and gone, and my thirst is enormous. Feeling woozy, I get on Smurfette, and now that my allegiance to this old bike has waned, I'm thoroughly embarrassed to be riding it. I pedal furiously toward downtown, trying to look straight ahead the whole way there so I don't see what a mess everything still is.

At the drugstore, one of the few places that survived, I buy Gatorade, a king size Snickers bar, and chips. I would love a meal, but there isn't much to choose from in a town that has been hit by a tornado. Hell, even before the tornado there wasn't much to choose from. After my nutritionally deficient dinner, I begin the journey back to the Schaeffer farm and arrive just as the sun is setting. I park Smurfette against the oak tree and head toward the back of the house, thinking I should just jump in the pool since my skin is a crust of salt from all the sweating I've been doing. I'm just about to leap in, clothes and all, when I hear arguing inside. When I hear my name, I carefully make my way to the screen door and listen. Jelly Roll and Samson are sparring in the kitchen. The boys and Jocelyn are nowhere to be seen.

"Your daughter was crying when I got home. She was just devastated! It's Cane's fault! This is the second time it's happened, and I'm tired of it."

"It's not Cane's fault," explains Samson calmly. "Jocelyn's overly sensitive, Jenny, you know that. All she does is cry when something doesn't go her way."

"How can you speak about your daughter like that? The bottom line is that Cane left Jocelyn alone! Just up and left without telling anyone!"

"No she didn't. I keep telling you that. Justice and I got home, and then Cane left."

"But she didn't tell you."

"No, but she didn't have to. She's old enough to go for a run by herself. Justice and I both saw her leave."

"Is that all you're going to do? You're just going to stand there and defend her?" Jelly Roll slams the dishwasher shut and spins the knob to turn it on. "Typical."

"Jenny, I'm sick of you treating her like you do."

"Treating her like what? I've never been anything but nice to her."

Samson laughs softly. "I don't know about that."

"*I agreed to hire her! I have taken her into my house, given her everything she needs and-*"

"Your heart has never been in it. You have never gotten over what happened in the past, and now it's affecting how you treat Cane."

"How dare you accuse me of that! This has *nothing* to do with that."

"It has *everything* to do with it, and you know it."

Jelly Roll scoffs and points her finger at Samson. "She's been your charity case. She always has been. She's trying to win this family over."

Samson laughs disbelievingly. Justice enters the kitchen, and Jelly Roll looks at him, stops herself for a moment, but then continues.

"She can't stay here anymore. I refuse to have her in this house any longer. She can stay with one of her friends."

Jelly Roll tries to push her way past Samson, and he blocks her path.

"She's staying here," Samson says decisively. "You're not kicking her out."

Justice crosses his arms and regards his aunt and uncle. "What's this about?"

Samson looks at Justice and shakes his head firmly, as if to say *now is not the time.*

"Like hell I can't. She's your charity case, not mine. And for the record, you're the one who has never gotten over the past. I see the way you look at her. She's the spitting image of her mother, and it's you who can't get over it."

My body has succumbed to a fight or flight response. I experience a primal instinct to defend myself, and I burst in through the screen door and stomp all the way into the kitchen. They all turn toward me. "I didn't leave Jocelyn alone."

"Of course you didn't," Jelly Roll responds condescendingly. "You never do anything wrong."

Justice pulls the sunglasses from off the top of his head and tosses them on the counter. When he speaks his voice is impatient and laced with anger. "Aunt Jenny, you're making a fool of yourself. Don't-"

Jelly Roll interrupts. "*Don't what*, Justice? I see she's won you over, too."

"I'm not trying to win anyone over!" I yell at her.

Samson steps forward, blocking my view of Jelly Roll, not an easy task considering her circumference. "Cane, don't worry-"

"Yes, Cane. No need to worry," Jelly Roll says with mock compassion. "Everyone is on your side."

Samson spins around to face his wife. "You're embarrassing yourself. You're acting like a child."

"No, Samson. I'm merely being honest."

"*This has gone on long enough,*" he warns.

Samson and Jelly Roll exchange a glance that seems to communicate vast amounts of grievances and old arguments.

"There's something we can agree on after all," Jelly Roll says quietly and leaves the room.

Samson approaches me and puts his large mitt of a hand on top of my head. It's a kind, fatherly gesture.

"Don't pay any attention to her. You're welcome to stay here. I mean that. I'm sorry you had to hear that argument." He glances over his shoulder. "Justice, could you take Cane somewhere fun for a little while? Maybe to go get ice cream?"

Samson looks back at me. "Would you like that?"

Spec-tac-u-lar. I've been reduced to a child who needs an ice cream cone. I smile and respond with a weak, "Sure."

"Great. Well, then I'll see you two later." Samson walks down the hall toward the master bedroom with his head lowered and hands deep in the pockets of his jeans.

Justice and I are left alone in the kitchen. He's already dressed in his running clothes. I wonder if he missed me today, if he planned on running with me tonight.

"How about a run?" he asks.

Thank God he's not going to take me for ice cream. I nod. As we walk outside, he reaches over with his hand and grabs my pinky finger with his. Touch is the best substitute for words; this is all the reassurance I need. He releases my finger and starts running, and I follow.

Our run is silent, furious, and determined. My body moves like an ocean wave, gathering speed and strength, and I have no trouble keeping pace with Justice. We run in tandem, and although we are silent, we seem to be having a conversation with the movement of our limbs and with the way we breathe. During a sprint, I trip over a pothole in the road. When I fall, my knee slams into the ground. I'm an expert at ruining the moment.

After unsuccessfully trying to resume our pace, Justice suggests that we return home. Reluctantly, I agree. By the time we reach the farm, the cut has become Niagara Falls. Blood rolls down my shin and stains my sock.

"I'm not going in the house," I say defiantly.

"You have to clean that up."

"I'm not going back in yet."

Justice looks around. "Come on. We'll go into the office. I'm sure there's a first aid kit or something like that in there."

Samson's office is in the back of the milking barn. All leather and wood, it's a warm, comfortable place. It has a full bathroom attached to it. Maybe I could spend the night in here. Justice walks ahead of me and flips on the bathroom lights.

He turns. "Let me see the cut."

I limp past him, taking care to keep my leg extended. I open the vanity and look for the first aid kit. "It's fine. I'll take care of it."

Justice shakes his head. "It's not fine. I want to look at it. Sit on the counter."

Unable to find anything useful under the sink, I shut the doors and sigh in frustration. Bending over awkwardly, I try to examine the gash, but it's under my knee cap and so covered in dried and fresh blood, that I can't see it clearly.

Justice steps toward me. "Just let me look at it."

"Fine," I say tersely. I hop up onto the counter and sit on the edge.

The run distracted me from the pain and from the emotion of the fight, but now the cut stings like hell, and I'm shaking with anger. While Justice searches in the cabinets for the first aid kit, I unload all the things I've been stewing about.

"Can you believe her? How can she say those things about me! I'm not a charity case! I'm not trying to win this family over. And if that's what I've been all these years, if that's why Samson hired me, then-"

"No, that's not what you've been. You're a hard worker, and you know how much you help out here. So does she, even though she won't admit it."

Justice finds what he needs. He unzips the first aid kit and removes some gauze. He wets a couple of pieces under cold tap water.

"So what! Initially, I probably was a charity case. I know that Grandma Betty was asking around for jobs for me! Who is to say that she didn't come and ask Samson? Samson probably thought to himself, well, sure, s*he's my best friend's kid. I still feel guilty for everything that happened. My brother-in-law is the one who slammed into Alex and Mary's car. I owe her big. She needs a job. Why not? We're rich. Let's give* *her some easy money.*

"Now it makes sense why they pay me ten dollars an hour! No one else my age can make that! But I know Jelly Roll has never liked it. And, now that I'm beginning to look more and more like my mother, she hates me all the more. By living here, I'm giving her more ammunition against me. She turns and twists everything I do. And then to have the nerve to say that I left Jocelyn alone, that I was the one who caused her to bawl like a baby, I mean where does that woman get off? Seriously!"

When he pushes the gauze against my leg to stop the bleeding and carefully cleans the cut, I lose the ability to talk. *Poof,* it's gone just like that.

After he's finished cleaning it, he holds a dry piece of gauze against the cut with his right hand and his left hand is on the countertop, just outside my right thigh. Either my abrupt silence has tipped him off that something isn't right or we do have chemistry after all, because he raises his head and looks straight at me with those eyes of his, so like pieces of sky that I feel myself freefall every time he looks at me.

My eyes are level with his throat, and he swallows hard, as if he's trying desperately to keep something inside. Then, I look back up at him. I think he's going to leave, but instead he angles his body and reaches up across me with his free hand to get something else out of the cabinet.

Without thinking, I reach up and grab onto his wrist when it's just over my head. He nervously glances at the wrist that I've captured and then back at me. I hold on tightly, and I slowly take control, moving his arm back down and placing his hand firmly on top of my thigh. I angle his fingers so that they wrap around the inside of my leg, against my bare flesh. The pressure of his hand against this tender spot makes my insides hum with anticipation.

"Cane." My name is said like a protest and a reprimand, and I suspect he's going to put an end to what I've started. But, he moves closer to me instead. Does he want me to make the first move?

I've never been one to back down, and so I reach up with my other hand and grab the back of his neck and pull him down to my level. His fast breathing warms the base of my neck. He adjusts his position and moves himself closer. I return the favor and scoot closer to the edge of the counter.

When our lips touch, I don't think about the fact that this is my first real kiss and that I don't know what to do, because it turns out, I do know. I've never been so sure of anything. When our lips move against each other and our tongues meet, I can feel gravity disappearing and then reappearing in increments. He tastes so good, like wind, spearmint, and salt.

The pressure he's applying on my cut is harder, and it hurts and feels good at the same time. He releases his hand from my leg, wraps both his arms around me, and pulls me to the edge of the counter. Instinctively, I hold onto his shoulders as he lifts me. It takes no effort for him to pick me up, and when I'm settled against him I can feel how solid and strong he is and how small and light I am in comparison. I feel hollow and full at the same time.

With his hands around me, I actually feel like a woman, not some scrawny girl. I know he's excited, that he likes this, because I can feel something I know about but have never seen or experienced.

Then, without warning, he turns his face away from me, disrupting our kiss. He squeezes his eyes shut and his hold on me relaxes. I slide to the ground. "What?"

He staggers away from me. "I…I can't."

He pulls his shirt back into place, hunches over, and puts his hands on his knees like he has sprinted and needs to catch his breath.

He has streaks of my blood on his hands. "*Why not?*" I demand, more angry and hurt than I've ever been.

"*Why not?*" I ask again, this time with such desperation it makes the hair on the back of my neck tingle.

He roughly grabs my forearm and turns it over, running his fingers across his name, the one I have tattooed on myself. I didn't know he had seen it.

"You're," he pauses and looks at me with eyes that have turned to cobalt ice, "just a kid."

It's the worst thing anyone has ever said to me.

"I'm sorry." His hand is on the doorknob. "This shouldn't have happened. It's my fault."

He opens the door and leaves. The only thing I can think to do is erase what happened, to scrub it off of me. I turn the faucet on and rub my skin raw, until all the ink disappears down the drain. I find, however, that sunscreen and blue ink make for good protection against ultraviolet rays. Even though the blue is gone, his name remains. I've been branded.

The Weight of Hope

She's told me that I'm her reason.

"When I saw you for the first time, I knew that God had given me a reason to go on living. You were the most precious thing in the world. After all that had been taken away from me, God gave me the perfect gift."

Grandma Betty had a right to think that I was the only good thing, because starting in 1973, three years before I was born, God decided that he was going to take everything near and dear to her and flush it down the toilet. During the time when the Grim Reaper made himself comfortable in Grandma Betty's life, I envision a colorless world. I imagine black and white photographs of the family I never knew. Uncle William, a Navy pilot, is waving to me from his helicopter, his helmet riding so low I can barely make out his eyes. Grandpa Henry, an avid fisherman, is riding along a country road with his fishing pole sticking out the window. Even though I can't see his face, I have a clear view of his crooked fishing hat and the back of his thick neck, burned from the sun and covered with fine gray hairs. My great-grandma Lily sits on a bed in William's bedroom, staring out the window, her bones as weightless as the birds that she watches every morning. Then, I see my mother and father, standing together at the altar, eyes closed and lips almost, but not quite, touching. Lastly, in the center of all the other pictures I store in my head, is my infant brother, Craig, whose eyes are wide open and seem to ask, "Why?"

I've taken liberty in creating this imaginary picture collage, but doing so has made the stories more real, as if I had lived through the events and felt the blunt force of grief just as Grandma Betty had.

The descent down sorrow road began on a warm October evening when two high ranking naval officers showed up at Grandma Betty's front door. They wouldn't tell her what happened until Grandpa Henry was standing next to her. When he came out onto the porch and stood beside her, they were told that their eldest son, Pilot William Kallevik, had died by enemy fire in Vietnam. Not one for tears in front of strangers, Grandma Betty let go of her husband's hand and walked primly down the front steps of her house, past the two naval officers, and kept walking until Grandpa Henry had to go looking for her in his pickup truck. When he pulled up next to her, she refused to get in or talk to him, and so for the entire night Grandpa Henry drove at a snail's pace down country roads with his wife walking next to him, her hand clutching the side mirror of his truck while she wept so fiercely she was half blind for days afterward.

Shortly after William's funeral, when Grandma Betty was squatting in front of the open refrigerator attempting to make room for all the casseroles and pies that had been delivered by friends and family, she yelled at Grandpa Henry to come into the kitchen and take the garbage out. She handed him a bag overflowing with garbage. When he took it from her, he made a funny sound.

"What did you say?" she asked. When there wasn't an answer, she grabbed hold of the bottom shelf and shook her head.

"Why don't you answer me, Henry? I'm trying to get some work done, and I can't hear what you said!"

Frustrated, she slammed the refrigerator shut and stood with creaking knees. That's when she saw his body buckling out from under him and his hands grabbing at the center of his chest. After she called the ambulance, she sat with his head in her lap.

"It's alright now. They're coming. Now, don't you do this to me! William left, but you can't go. You can't leave me and Alex behind. That boy still needs his father. Henry, don't do this!" she begged.

The doctors told her it had been a massive heart attack, but Grandma Betty knew better; Henry had slid out of bed every night since their son had died, went into his old bedroom, and cried like a baby. Grief clots stop more hearts than blood clots, and Grandma Betty told everyone this at his funeral that followed William's service by a scant ten days.

The next year was dormant, but Grandma Betty said that even though no one died, her sorrow had put her into emotional hibernation. The only time she woke up is when her younger son Alex would come home from college to visit. When she saw Alex and hugged him, her cheeks felt like they were cracking. Reaching up and touching them, she realized how much effort it took to smile.

When Grandma Betty had gotten to the point where her lips could curve into a smile without strenuous effort, her mother, my great-grandma Lily, fell ill with cancer. Grandma Lily moved into William's old bedroom, and Grandma Betty nursed her until the day she died six months later. Grandma Betty told me that although she had six months to prepare for what would happen, she wasn't prepared when the time came.

"Death doesn't take its time, even when it seems to. You've got to remember that, Cane. One minute the heart is beating, the next it isn't. No matter how much you think you can cope with it, you can't, not when it comes to people you love."

After so many endings, there was finally a beginning. On June 15th, 1975, Alex and Mary were married at Grace Lutheran Church, the same church where Grandma Betty married Grandpa Henry and also where Great-Grandma Lily pledged her life to Great-Grandpa Samuel. Alex and his new wife settled into an apartment just off the square of downtown Savage, an upper flat that was an oven in the summer and a freezer in the winter thanks to its exposed brick walls and old pine floors.

On New Year's Day, 1976 Alex and Mary came over to Grandma Betty's house with a small gift. Smiling, she led them inside and told them she didn't need anymore Christmas presents. "I've got enough things in here to open up a resale shop. Besides, you're saving for a house, so shame on you both for buying me something!"

"It's just something little we picked up. It's not much, really." Mary shrugged off her coat and gingerly sat down on the edge of the sofa, gripping the armrest.

"You okay, sweetie? You're pale."

Gritting her teeth, Mary smiled reassuringly. "I'm fine."

Grandma Betty placed the back of her hand against Mary's cheek. "I don't think so, honey. You don't look so good." She shot a disparaging look at her son, "Alex, if she wasn't feeling good why did you drag her over here for dinner?"

"I'm fine," insisted Mary.

"I don't buy it."

Alex thrust the gift in his mother's direction. "Open it, Mom!" he commanded enthusiastically.

"You're wife isn't feeling well and all you're worried about is me opening a present."

Sitting in the recliner across from Mary, Grandma Betty opened the gift. On the inside of a small shoe box there were two skeins of yarn, one pink, one blue, and two knitting needles. Frowning, Grandma Betty picked them up and looked them over, the meaning slowly turning every cell in her body inside out with happiness.

Alex reached out and took his mother's hand. "We're not sure... it's too early to know if it's a girl or a boy, so we got both."

This story about my parents is one of my favorites, and I've recorded every word to memory.

"It was only seven weeks before your mother's due date that we found out there were two of you! They didn't do ultrasounds back then, not like they do now, but Mary insisted she felt two sets of feet, and since she was measuring big, they did an ultrasound and discovered you and Craig. Your mom told me that you were the kicker, always moving around and never sitting still. She said you were so impatient that you were the one who was going to put her into labor! Well, we were scrambling to get ready for the two of you! We needed double of everything, and I had already thrown a baby shower so we had to go it alone.

"Your mom was so excited, and she had the nursery all ready for the two of you. I had a bad feeling the night of the storm, and I knew that she would go into labor. Every time it goes from being sunny to rainy, you can count on lots of babies being born.

"I don't even remember driving to the hospital in Clinton. I knew it was bad when Frank wouldn't look me in the eye when I asked him if anyone had survived. I turned to the others around him, the other police, the paramedics, and no one would tell me what I already knew had happened. My son, his wife, and their two unborn children were killed. I knew that it was the end of things for me. I was ready to turn around, walk out, and throw in the towel.

"But before I could, a doctor stormed through the doors with this joyous look on his face. 'She made it! The little girl made it!' Oh, Cane, you don't understand what you being born did for me. I was Job from the Bible. I had lost everything, and then you arrived kicking, arching your back, and pounding your fists in the air. You were so feisty I could barely cuddle you. At first I thought that somehow even as an infant you knew what had happened, but then I realized that you weren't angry, just ready to fight the world, for yourself and for me. You rescued me. You gave me hope. I wouldn't have made it through without you."

Sometimes when Grandma Betty looks at me, I see how she casts her hope, and it gets tangled around my waist. I have learned that for me, hope is fickle; it can drag me down just as easily as it can pull me up by my bootstraps, so high that my feet don't even touch the ground.

A Friendly Game

 This summer I've come to love the quiet ritual of Sunday mornings, and it isn't for the reason I'm *supposed* to love it. It isn't because I enjoy having my butt go numb while I sit in a wooden pew at Grace Lutheran and recite creeds that I'm sure God could give a damn about.
 It's because the whole day begins and ends with Justice. While the Schaeffer crew piles into their extended van to go to church, Justice and I get to ride alone in his truck with the windows rolled down and the redolent, delicious breeze lifting our hair by the roots. When we arrive, we always sit next to each other, so close that our thighs touch and our hands occasionally brush. We listen to Pastor Fry say prayers for everyone whose lives have been ruined by the tornado and then get on our knees to confess our shortcomings. Yet, when I kneel next to Justice, I'm not thinking about my past sins but about my future sins, all of which involve Justice.
 This morning, however, I've broken ritual. After last night, I can't imagine seeing Justice. The thought is too mortifying. I don't want to have to face Jelly Roll either. So, I've slept in, and when I finally get out of bed, I'm dizzy and groggy because it's late, nearly eleven. A long, hot shower and a marathon shaving session, where I manage to nick my other knee with the razor, don't refresh me at all. In an attempt to comfort myself, I dress in my favorite pair of cut off shorts and vintage, white t-shirt that over the past year has gotten dingy. The soft cotton against my skin makes me feel a little better, but not as much as Justice's hands had felt on my body.
 After breakfast, where I eat three bowls of Froot Loops cereal and stare at the white tattoo on my forearm, I wander outside and sit by the pool, occasionally testing the temperature of the water with my

toes. The July heat is a meaty leech, and I'm considering leaping into the water despite the fact that it took me fifteen minutes to blow dry my hair.

The gate opens behind me. Squinting, I turn around and see Justice, who happens to be wearing athletic shorts instead of the typical blue jeans. I consider ignoring him completely, but he's not someone you can ignore. "What are you doing here?" I snap and then turn back around to commence staring at the water.

He's nervously rolling a Sports Illustrated magazine in his hands. "Didn't feel like going to church this morning."

Sunlight skitters across the bottom of the pool. "That makes two of us."

"Thought I might run, but it's too hot." He bangs his magazine against his leg and looks out over the landscape. "Want to go see Grandma Betty?"

Is this his attempt at reconciliation? My affirmation is a slow, steady exhale and a shrug.

"Let me grab some shoes."

He pulls his aviator sunglasses down over his eyes. "I'll be waiting out front in the truck."

I rush upstairs to get my shoes and some other things to take to the hospital. In the truck, there's an uneasy silence between us. If I've learned one thing, it's that once you kiss the man you love, it's *all you can think about*. Apparently those romance novels are right about some things after all. He's thinking about it too, I just know it, but I'm also realistic. While I'm thinking about how great it was, he probably hasn't stopped asking himself how he could have been so stupid.

Justice pulls up to a red light. He drums his thumb against the steering wheel, reaches up, and adjusts his glasses.

I love his sunglasses. He's one of the few people that I know who can wear them without looking like an insect. Tom Cruise in Top Gun doesn't look anywhere near as good as he does.

"Cane, about what happened," Justice says tentatively, "last night."

As if he needs to specify or to clarify.

He clears his throat and looks out the window. When Justice is anxious he has this habit of placing his index finger in the middle of his forehead and drawing small circles. He's been doing it a lot this morning, and if he doesn't stop, there's going to be a permanent ring on his forehead.

"It never should have happened." He stops drawing and looks at me.

I discreetly avoid his stare and carefully observe the traffic light ahead. "Green light," I announce listlessly.

I don't want to be around him anymore, and yet, it's *all* I want. I never knew it was possible to know that something was doomed, and despite that knowledge, invest all my heart.

"I'm sorry," he states quietly.

"Apparently." I can't keep the hurt out of my voice, much less my expression, so I turn my head to the far right and stare out the window.

We pull into the hospital parking lot. Justice shuts off the engine, but neither one of us takes off our seatbelts and opens the doors.

"Cane."

"What?" I look at him. *Big mistake.* It only makes me want to kiss him again. To make matters worse, he takes off his sunglasses. His eyes are high quality sapphires today and so clear I can see right to the bottom of his soul.

He smiles gently. "Still friends?"

His question smothers me. I reach down and release my seatbelt.

"That's all." My tone indicates that it isn't a statement but a question.

Our visit with Grandma Betty is brief. I'm past the sad stage; it's full steam ahead to anger. Grandma Betty is never one to yell, but she can throw you a look that could kill and give a silent treatment that can make you beg for mercy. Is that what this is, the longest silent treatment ever? Is she doing this on purpose? After an hour of stewing about this possibility, I tell Justice that I need to leave.

As we enter Savage, Justice enthusiastically suggests we go to the high school and play some basketball. He's working hard at being my buddy, and although this infuriates me, I'm so desperate to spend time with him that I'll play along with this little charade. I'm determined to make him see that I'm more than someone to hang out with.

"Sure, whatever," I agree apathetically.

Even though I've never been on a basketball team, I'm not a terrible player. Unfortunately, I'm not good enough to impress Justice, nor do I have enough skill to make it possible to play one-on-one. We play a few games of horse, but the scorching sun makes it impossible for us to be too energetic. I'm the first to give up. Sitting on the grassy area in the shade, I watch Justice practice his three-point shot.

Eventually, he gives up as well and comes over next to me. He plants the basketball on the ground and uses it like a stool.

His profile is magnificent and strong, like one of those mythical Greek gods, yet his nose is regal and straight, not the typical aquiline Roman nose.

Is he an exact replica of his father, just as I'm a replica of my mother? His father has always been my enemy. If I saw him and Justice side-by-side and the resemblance was uncanny, would I hate only his father, or would I hate Justice as well? "What's your father like?"

He wipes his mouth. "Do you make it a habit of always saying what's on your mind?"

"There's no filter from my brain to my mouth."

"You really want to know about him? I'm surprised you have any interest at all."

I lean back so that I have a perfect view of Justice's butt, and for the record, he has the world's best ass. *Yes*, I am that shallow.

"I'm curious."

"I don't know much about him."

"Was he a jerk?"

Justice shrugs. "I was seven when the accident happened, but by that time my mom had already kicked him out. He had been having an affair."

When someone delivers information like that without showing emotion, I don't know what to say. *Sorry* doesn't seem appropriate.

"Oh," I respond idiotically.

"He moved away when I was eight. We've lost touch." Justice half stands, yanks the basketball out from under himself, and then sits on the ground next to me. He spins the ball on his finger.

This simple trick of motion and balance has always amazed me; Justice does it effortlessly.

"I have a few memories of him, but he was never an award-winning dad. He didn't seem too interested in the role. Samson was more of a father to me. He used to come to my little league games and then my basketball games."

"Really?"

"Yeah. He's been a great uncle."

"I'm sure Jelly Roll didn't come with him."

"Actually, she did."

"Because she was best friends with your mom?"

"Yeah."

"They're not best friends anymore, though, right? They had a fight."

"How did you know?"

"Jocelyn." Reaching over I flick the ball, and it falls out of his hands. We watch it roll over the cement and bounce off the court where it finally lands up against the chain link fence that wraps around the football field. "So what happened between them?"

"Jelly Roll loves a good fight." He points at me. "You should know." He reaches into his back pocket for his gum. "Damn it."

"What?"

"I didn't bring any." He takes his sunglasses off and fidgets with the stems.

"What was the fight about?"

"I wasn't around for it. From what my mom told me after the fact, it was about divorce. I guess Aunt Jenny was fed up with Uncle Samson. Said she had, had enough and wanted to walk out. What was my mom supposed to do, side with her friend or her brother?"

"I'm guessing she chose her brother."

"You guessed right."

"Why did Jelly Roll want a divorce?"

"I never asked."

I half laugh, half grunt. "You would think it would be the other way around. That Samson would want the divorce."

Justice looks at me again, with those marvelous eyes of his. "You'd think," he says again, grinning. "But, I have my theories about it. I've inferred some things. I think she wanted a divorce because she didn't really love him. She resented him for not being your father."

"And she stayed and had eight children?" I scoff. "Brilliant."

"The kids aren't to blame, but I do wonder why she didn't stop after two or three."

"I have my theories about it." I elevate my brows and lower my voice, trying to mimic Justice. "I've inferred some things."

"You have, have you?" He smiles. "Such as?"

"Excess. Jelly Roll doesn't do small. Jelly Roll isn't small. Look at her house, her wardrobe, the Schaeffer business. Nothing about it is small. Two or three kids would have never been enough. She had to set herself apart; eight kids and all J names." I pause and roll my eyes. "If that doesn't make their family unique, I don't know what does."

"You're too insightful for your own good, you know that, don't you?"

"I've been accused of that before."

Justice draws circles on his forehead again, and I bust him. "What's wrong?"

He pulls his hand away from his forehead and exhales slowly. "Nothing."

"You've practically got a target on your forehead. Something's bothering you."

He shrugs. "I'm just thinking about how different things would have been for me if my father had been in my life."

"Do you want him in your life now?"

"Not as much as I did as a kid. I would have liked him in the bleachers during basketball games. Having Samson was awesome, but…" he falters.

"It wasn't the same," I finish for him.

"Not really, no."

He slides his sunglasses back on.

"I know what it's like."

"I'm sorry that you don't have your father, that you never had a chance to have him."

I shrug. "I don't know. I have people in my life that care. Frank is turning out to be something like a father, and I feel like Samson has always watched out for me. Anyway, you can't really miss something you never had."

Justice makes two fists and pushes them together, so that his knuckles are lined up. "I thought about contacting my dad at the beginning of the summer, but I never did. Then, I met you, and I don't know. It got me thinking about everything that happened, what he did that night. He took so much away from you, and now, I really don't have any interest in seeing him again."

"Forgive and forget, isn't that what they say?" I don't want him avoiding his father or punishing him because of what happened sixteen years ago.

"It's never that easy." Justice lightly pounds his fists together. "How do you love someone who leaves?"

"I don't know. I love my father, as much as I can anyway, and he left me."

"It wasn't his choice."

I can't argue with that, but I don't want Justice to banish his father from his life. Any shot at having both a mother and father shouldn't be wasted, no matter what happened in the past. "If it was the other way around, if my father had done something like that, I don't think I could just spend the rest of my life not talking to him or pretending he didn't exist. And, the harder you try to pretend you *don't* need someone, the harder you pretend you don't love someone, it ends up eating away at your soul. Lying to yourself never works out."

Justice gives a soft, amazed laugh. "I think you have more figured out about life than I do."

"Actually," I smile with complacent assurance, "I do."

There's a commotion coming from the parking lot. Three or four cars arrive at once, and one of them is Nate's Mustang. Mikayla is with him. Great. His own little cheerleader.

This interruption is so typical of my luck. My meaningful discussion with Justice is brought to a premature conclusion.

"They practice on Sunday?" Justice asks.

"The football team practices day and night, seven days a week. Football is their life."

"It's only July."

"They start in June." I stand. "Which is probably why they suck come September."

"Want to get out of here?"

"Absolutely."

"I'll go get the ball." Justice leaves and walks across the court. I have no choice but to come out from under the shelter of the trees.

As soon as I'm out in the open, Mikayla sees me and waves. I wave back. It's awkward, considering a week ago we would have been greeting each other with our middle fingers.

Justice is taking *for-ev-er*, and by the time he saunters back over to me, there's no way to avoid Mikayla and Nate who are headed in my direction.

"Hi, Cane." Mikayla smiles at me as she approaches. Nate holds his helmet at his side and says nothing.

"Hi." I half shrug with my shoulder.

"This is Justice, Justice, *Mikayla*," I say with emphasis, hoping Justice will make the connection.

Justice gets the reference, and when he looks at me peripherally, he smiles knowingly.

When Mikayla sizes Justice up, I begin to reconsider our peace treaty. Yet, it's worse when I see the reverse happening. Justice is appraising her as well. Can I blame him, though? Mikayla has power over every male.

"What are you guys doing out here?" asks Mikayla, who speaks more to Justice than me.

Justice holds the ball up in front of him. "Shooting hoops. What about you guys?"

"Nate has practice. I came along to watch."

"We've got to get going," insists Nate, who glares at me with disdain.

His eyes clearly reveal that he remembers our little conversation yesterday.

"Later," says Mikayla and follows Nate who's walking so fast he's halfway to the field.

"*That was her?*" Justice asks incredulously.

"Yeah."

"Not what I expected."

Of course he didn't expect her to be Miss Teen USA. My jealousy has curdled my mood and left a sour taste in my mouth. I slam the truck door. Justice doesn't comment. The air grows denser between us, and I wish I had a knife to cut it or a match to burn it. He turns off the air-conditioning and rolls down the windows. This is a tactic I've come to know well.

"What's wrong?"

"Nothing," he says casually and doesn't look my way for the rest of the trip.

Nervous and annoyed, I spend the rest of the drive separating my hair and braiding it. When it's finished, I start all over again, repeating the process so many times my hair will be a kinky, knotty mess if I don't knock it off. When we get back to the Schaeffer homestead, Justice gets out of the truck without so much as a goodbye and heads toward the barn. I go into the house through the back door, slamming it for good measure.

"Hi." Samson nods at me. He's at the sink refilling a thermos.

"Oh. Sorry about that."

"Sorry for what?"

"Slamming the door."

"It wasn't that loud," he says kindly. "You have every right to still be mad about last night, but Jenny Ryanne isn't here."

"She isn't?"

"No. She took the kids to Chicago for a day or two."

"Really?" My relief is audible.

Samson reacts by making a sound that falls just short of an actual laugh. "Yes." He rubs one hand through his shorn crew cut and follows through until his hand rests on the back of his neck.

"Why don't you sit down for a minute?"

"Sure." I sit at the kitchen table.

He pulls out a chair and lowers himself carefully, steadily, like an old man would. "I should apologize for the way Jenny has always treated you."

"It's okay," I say quickly, feeling embarrassed that he's apologizing for something he can't control.

"It's not okay," he sighs and grabs a hold of his thermos. There is a thin layer of dirt under every one of his fingernails.

"Cane, there's a lot of history between your family and mine and a lot of old feelings that I don't think have ever gone away."

"I know."

"You know?" There's no surprise in how he says it. Samson has a habit of speaking with his head dropped forward and his eyes raised. Justice does the same thing.

"I just want you to know that you are welcome here. That you're like part of our family."

"For better or for worse?" I joke.

Samson sits back and gives a satisfied laugh that reminds me of an engine purring because it's so deep. "Guess that's about right." He stands, preparing to leave.

"What was my dad like?" I didn't mean to sabotage him with a question about my father, but now that I have, I'm not sure why I've never asked him before.

"Daring, adventurous, brilliant, and sometimes," Samson shifts his weight to one leg, "arrogant, but rightly so. He was the best at everything. He was extraordinary."

"Am I anything like him?"

"You're exactly like him," he responds instantly.

"Am I anything like my mother?" I ask quietly.

Samson looks me in the eye and then moves his gaze out the window in one fluid motion.

"Yes."

His reply is coated with an assurance that masks other emotions. "Do you think that sometime we could talk about my parents?"

"I think that would be a good idea." He twists the lid tight on his thermos. "I'll see you later."

After he leaves, I rush up to my room and find the Ziploc bag that holds the article about my parents' accident. Even though I know the words by heart, I read through it several times. When I'm finished, I slowly and deliberately rip it into long strips, and then take those long strips and shred them into smaller and smaller pieces until it's confetti. I gather it in my palms, every last piece, and marvel at how light it is, how inconsequential. I place it back in the bag and seal it shut.

Because I woke up so late this morning, the day is over before I feel it really had a chance to begin. With the exception of visiting the hospital and playing basketball with Justice, I've spent the majority of it in my room, sitting on top of the floor vent to absorb some cool air.

After a dismal dinner of macaroni and cheese and peas, I read a few more chapters of *Write Me a Love Song*. The characters are sex-crazed imbeciles with no morals. But, who am I to judge? Still, I can't read this crap anymore. I need to take a trip to the library and pick a different genre.

Casting the book aside, I decide that I need to escape and go for a run, preferably without Justice. I dress and grab the plastic bag that has the remains of the article.

Don't get me wrong, I love running with Justice, but I've missed being alone. When I'm by myself, I'm not thinking about what I look like, whether my armpits reek, wondering if I will have embarrassing gas (farting definitely wouldn't help my chances of attracting Justice), or obsessing about whether Justice likes me or not. When I'm running alone, I can be anything I want to be. I can think anything I want to think. The road doesn't pay any attention to me and that suits me just fine.

Dusk has set in, and even though it's hot, the atmosphere has layers to it. By my face, it's unbearably warm, the peel and stick kind of heat that refuses to budge. However, my shins and ankles are cool and slippery thanks to a heavy mist that skates gracefully across the landscape. The mist gets heavier as I run down County N toward the forest preserve.

Picking up speed, I tuck the Ziploc bag in the waistband of my shorts and run faster. As my heart beats faster to offset my intense exertion, I find, as always, what a miracle cure it is for worries. I'm not thinking about Grandma Betty, Mikayla, Justice, or Annette and Nate. I'm not thinking about my parents and their history with the Schaeffers. I'm not thinking about the one hundred and one ways that I would like to torture Jelly Roll. All I'm thinking about is myself, of how it's possible, if only for a minute, to feel invincible when I'm running this fast and hard.

I follow the narrow path out of the thick of trees and see the intimidating hill in the distance, the very spot where Justice and I had held hands, where he almost kissed me. I'm pissing myself off by thinking about him again. In a fit of anger, I sprint to the top. When I finally reach the tree I remove the bag from my waistband, open it, and sprinkle the shredded newspaper on the ground at the base of the tree, but only by the side that has died.

Upon turning to leave, I have a superior vantage point, and in the distance, snaking its way along the small road, I see a familiar vehicle making its way toward the exit.

Without thinking, I take off and run as fast as I can, and my fury makes me agile and quick. It doesn't take as much exertion as I thought it would to reach them, probably because Annette is driving slowly, reluctantly. Even though I want to confront them both, I'm not sure how to go about doing this. Do I jump out in front of the vehicle and risk getting run over? Do I run up to the side of the car and start banging on the windows like a crazy person? Unsure of what I should do, I duck into the row of trees on the right side of the road and keep my pace so that I'm no more than twenty or thirty feet behind them.

When they finally reach the stop sign, I'm even with them. Annette grips the top of the steering wheel with both hands, looking anxious and guilty as she turns her head to the left to yield to oncoming traffic, of which there are three cars. Nate, his jaw slack with satisfaction, sits messily in the passenger seat with one foot propped up on the dashboard. I emerge boldly from my hiding place and stand only a few feet from the passenger window. Nate's peripheral vision obviously works. Our eyes meet. There's no alarm in his stare, no pretense of conscience. Annette pulls out; the tires squeal, and when she casts a hasty look over her shoulder, I wonder if she's seen me.

I return to the Schaeffer house pissed off, sweaty, and confused. After a long shower, I go into my room and wonder just how I should handle this situation. Talking with Nate didn't do a damn thing, not that I'd expected it to. The only way to end this is to approach Annette, and just what the hell am I going to say to her?

I hear Justice in his room, and I'm itching to fight with someone. I go down the hall and storm into his bedroom, pushing open the door until it bangs against the door stop. I started out with a clear sense of purpose, but Justice stands in front of me, shirtless no less, and my anger loses consciousness and falls flat on its face.

"Ever heard of knocking?" he asks irritably.

"No, I was born in a barn," I say plainly, hoping my dry humor will win him over. Crossing my arms I try my hardest not to stare at his ridged abdomen, which of course means my eyes are darting all around the room like some maniac.

"Well, now that would explain a lot," he says with an edge of sarcasm that hurts my feelings.

"What's your problem?" I demand.

Justice turns his back to me and sorts the pile of laundry on his bed. He doesn't fold his clean clothes so much as he wads them into a ball. "I don't have one."

"*Like hell you don't!* I want to talk about what happened between us last night." I do and I don't. I can't believe I just said that.

"We did that already."

"You talked about it, I didn't."

He shakes his head and stops folding clothes. He leans against the mattress, bends slightly, and supports his upper body with his arms. His head hangs as if deep in thought.

"Aren't you going to say anything?" I'm yelling now, and I'm pretty sure I sound like a whiny brat, like Jocelyn does when she's complaining to Jelly Roll, but I'm too mortified and hurt to care.

Justice slowly raises his head and speaks softly. "What do you want me to say?"

"I want you to tell me that you like me, and not just as a *friend!*"

It's official. I've made an ass of myself and broken the cardinal rule of dating. If you force a guy to share his feelings, '*It will scare him off,*' this sage wisdom straight from the mouths of the dating experts at Seventeen magazine.

He stands upright again and wipes at his face with his hands. "Don't do this."

"Why? You know that I like you!" I glare at him and continue. "*If I looked like Mikayla we wouldn't even be having this discussion, you would be all over me. I saw you checking her out today! I saw you-*"

"I wasn't checking-"

"*Don't lie! She's beautiful, that's what you were thinking. If only I were beautiful, if only I were good enough for you.*" By now my emotions are so far out of control that I snatch the picture of Nikki and Justice off his dresser and throw it across the room. As soon as I do this, I know that it is the lamest, most idiotic thing I could have done. My jaw falls open in response to my stupidity.

Justice looks at the closet door that now has a dent in it. The frame is cracked in three spots. I should apologize or offer to replace it, but I'm so mortified at what I've done that I'm incapable of speaking.

"Cane, I know you're upset, but let me explain-"

I cut him off again. "You don't know anything," I say calmly. If I don't leave now, my eyes will turn red and snot will start rolling out of my nose. I spin on my heels.

Justice moves across the room and steps in front of me. Taking hold of my shoulders with a hard grip he backs me up until I'm pinned against the wall. Is he angry at me for destroying his frame? Is he tired of me antagonizing him?

Unable to interpret his intentions, I feel a mixture of fear and excitement, and when twined, they are the most venomous of aphrodisiacs. His hands haven't left my shoulders yet, and he's applying so much pressure my collarbone is going numb. My heart pounds so ferociously, I can feel it in my lips, my fingertips, and in the lowest part of my abdomen.

Unable to read his penetrating, serious expression, I hiss, "Sorry," even though, it's clear to both of us that I'm not sorry for anything.

He puts his hands on either side of my face. "When I was looking at *her*, I was thinking about how she doesn't measure up to you. You are all I can think about. You are always asking me what my problem is, and *that's* my problem. I can't get you out of my head."

He inches closer until the only thing that divides us is the thinnest cord of heat.

This time, he makes the first move. He kisses me, and it's slow, purposeful, deliberate, and I make a small noise of pleasure in the back of my throat. He responds by pulling me away from the wall, and we are sufficiently melded together. He leads me over to the bed until the backs of my legs are up against it. My body responds to him so effortlessly and so violently, I'm faint with pleasure. I want to have him on top of me, to have his weight pushing me down or I may float away from this world, and I can sense this is what he wants. His hands slide up under my t-shirt, and his fingers skate across my skin. I shiver with wild delight and ferociously cling to him, inviting more. One of his knees is already resting on the bed, and his hands move to my upper back so that he can cushion the fall.

Just as we are about to make the transition and fall back on the bed together, there's a noise. Samson appears in Justice's doorway before Justice and I have a chance to properly untangle ourselves. For something that's so right when it's happening, that's so natural, all it takes is one harsh look of disapproval to make it horribly wrong.

Fruit of the Forbidden Tree

It isn't all that hard to figure out why Eve went for the apple. Something becomes overwhelmingly appealing when someone says you can't have it, which is probably why Mikayla and I became obsessed with Ouija boards.

We first learned about them in the Sunday school room at Grace Lutheran Church the summer before the sixth grade, when the BOMMB squad had yet to come into existence and Mikayla and I were still as close as sisters.

Our teacher, Mrs. Steinbach, a curly haired woman of undetermined age who preferred shapeless clothing and had the uncanny ability to talk more with her flaring nostrils than her mouth, made a list of the evil devices that were linked to devil worship. Ouija boards were number one on the list.

Mikayla and I were fascinated by this, probably because the Atwood family had one hanging on the wall in their basement. The antique wooden Ouija board had been given to them by their adventurous Aunt Susan, a true nonconformist who had been everything from a Catholic to a Wiccan. Whenever Annette spoke of her sister, one of the comments was always that Susan changed religions like she changed outfits.

The afternoon of Mrs. Steinbach's lesson, Mikayla and I went straight to her house and pulled the Ouija board off the wall.

Mikayla waved it front of her mother's face. "Can we use the Ouija board, Mom?"

"I don't see why not."

Mikayla and I looked at each other wide-eyed. Apparently, Annette had never been lectured by Mrs. Steinbach and was unaware of its evil power, not that you could tell it was evil. It was so ugly you wouldn't suspect a thing. Warped and splintered along the edges, it wouldn't win any beauty awards. However, it was more than usable. The letters, numbers, and frightening symbols and pictures were faded but clear. It also came with a small device that had a hole in the center.

Clueless as to how to use the board, we went to the library in town and did some research. We discovered that the small rounded triangle was called a planchette and that the board itself was used as a fortune device. It could answer questions and give the players an opportunity to communicate with spirits. We checked the book out of the library and took it home, planning to follow the step-by-step instructions.

We took the board up to my bedroom and created the right mood by drawing the curtains and lighting a tapered candle that we had confiscated from the dining room. Before our eyes had completely adjusted to the darkness, we sat down facing each other with our legs crossed and knees touching, just like the instructions said, and placed the board on our laps.

Mikayla played the medium and began by asking a friendly spirit to join us and help us along on our adventure. For some reason, this struck us as incredibly funny, and we couldn't stop laughing.

After we settled down, it ended up more as a series of complaints and accusations than a game. Mikayla said that I was asking stupid questions, and I blamed her for moving the planchette. I told her there was no way it was moving on its own, but she insisted it was.

"I'm not kidding! I'm not doing anything."

"I don't believe you." I narrowed my eyes. "I watched you moving it. There's no way it's doing it by itself."

"Think what you want." Mikayla took her fingertips off the planchette and tossed her blonde hair over her shoulders. "I'm only helping it along when I need to."

An admission. I smiled. "So, you admit that you're cheating?"

"Maybe if you wouldn't ask such lame questions. Like I really want to know when we are going to start our periods. I could care less! That's so gross. It's hard enough sitting in sex-ed class listening to Mrs. Miller talk about pads and tampons. Dis-gust-ing."

"I just want to be prepared. I want to know when it's going to happen. Don't you?"

"I don't know," Mikayla shrugged dramatically. "I don't see what's so evil about this thing. Mrs. Steinbach doesn't know what she's talking about! It's not even fun."

"Come on!" I was determined to make this thing work. I wanted a way to communicate with my mom, dad, and brother. "Let's just try again."

Mikayla exhaled mostly through her nose and scratched the inside of her wrist. "Fine," she said and delicately placed her fingertips back on the planchette.

"Don't press down too hard. Don't move it," I instructed.

She gave me an irritated stare.

"I've got an idea," I suggested cheerily, "why don't you close your eyes? That way, when it moves, we'll both know that you aren't doing it. And I'll tell you what it says."

"Fine." Mikayla squeezed her eyes shut so hard that her whole face wrinkled.

"Spirit of Good, please be patient with us. I want to know if Mikayla and I will be best friends forever?"

The planchette slowly moved, seemingly without help from Mikayla, and since I expected it to move to the word, yes, I could barely breathe when it moved to the first letter, T. It moved again to the W.

"What's it saying?" Mikayla asked.

Instead of answering, I watched in amazement and fear as it finished spelling out its answer.

"Cane!" Mikayla opened her eyes and blinked at me in expectation. "So?"

"It spelled out 'yes,'" I lied.

"Let's go do something else." Mikayla stood so quickly the board flipped upside down into my lap. "This isn't evil, it's absolutely boring."

That night, after Mikayla had gone home and Grandma Betty had fallen asleep, I tried to play with the Ouija board myself, but nothing happened.

Slipping back into bed, I picked up the pen on my nightstand and set to work on my freckles, connecting them to spell out the word that the Ouija board had given me. TWIN.

A Knight in Shining Armor

Despite the fact that the cleanup is a monumental, ongoing effort that starts before sunrise and ends well past sundown, the downtown is still a holy-hell of a mess. The buildings centrally located, like the post office, Savage Bar and Grill, Dennis' Dental Office, and Paulo's Pizza Parlor, endured an ashes-to-ashes, dust-to-dust, kind of fate. The library, located diagonally across from the post office, however, was pardoned by Natette. (They give hurricanes names, why not tornadoes?) That's what I've christened the tornado, Natette, and I really don't have to explain why, do I? There are four measly shingles missing, a window with a swirl crack, and a few strips of aluminum siding with craters the size of golf balls.

Coincidences must have a statute of limitations. Every place that is important to me, my room, the library, the drugstore, the Schaeffer farm, was barely touched. God spared this place because I love it. If that isn't proof enough that the mark on my forehead means something, I don't know what is. Unfortunately, during the tornado God was so busy looking out for me, he didn't bother to check in on Grandma Betty. I'm not sure if I'm even going to get to see her today, especially after what happened last night. It's not like Justice is going to offer me a ride, and I'm sure as hell not going to ask Samson.

I've taken up residence at the library, and while I should be searching the shelves for books to check out, I'm in one of the aisles, sitting cross-legged on the floor. A book, titled *A Time to Kill* by new author John Grisham, rests in my lap. I'm finally departing from the romance genre and into drama, and given my current situation, it seems appropriate. I have yet to read the summary on the back, but that's because I'm more interested in what is going on back at the

Schaeffer farm and if Samson has killed Justice. This morning when I left I hadn't seen either of them.

When Samson caught us last night, he stared so hard at Justice that I could almost visualize the stream of belligerent vocabulary being communicated to his nephew. Samson barely looked at me, but he did tell me I should get my things and go downstairs and stay in Jocelyn's room. Since I knew in my heart that Justice and I belonged together, that this wasn't wrong in any way, I planned on defending what had happened, but I couldn't think of one measly thing to say. Even though I hadn't done anything wrong, my cheeks were stained with red blotches of anger and shame. I left the room as quickly as possible. Samson closed the door behind me.

I'm not sure what was said between the two, but when I carried a bag of my things downstairs I could hear them whisper-screaming at each other. It lasted for ten minutes, not that I could keep track of time that well, and then I finally heard Samson's heavy footsteps and the creek of the attic stairs. He walked down the hall and stopped in front of his daughter's room. He cracked open the door, and I laid my head on Jocelyn's pillow that smelled of strawberry shampoo and pretended to be fast asleep. He closed the door behind him, pulling extra hard so that the knob clicked securely into place.

After tossing and turning and telling myself that there was no way sneaking back upstairs to Justice's room would be a good thing, I fell asleep. I dreamed that Justice, Grandma Betty, and I were all living together in our house on Scott Road. Jelly Roll and Samson came to visit, and all of us sat around the living room and looked at pictures of my parents, but no one could see anything because the rays of sunlight coming in through the rafters blinded us.

When I woke, it was after seven. Despite my horrible morning breath and creased face, I dashed upstairs to find Justice, but he was already gone. Disappointment filled up my gut, and I couldn't even eat breakfast. At least Jelly Roll wasn't around to torment me. God only knew what was going to happen when she came home and found out about this.

How can I concentrate on finding a new novel, when I'm still obsessing about what happened last night? I regard the book in my hand; maybe *A Time to Kill* isn't the best story given the circumstances. I shelve Grisham and move on, discovering an Irish author, Maeve Binchy. The covers of the books are cheery and have a water-color quality, but none of them seem too heavy on the romance. Perfect. I tuck a few under my arm and check out at the front desk.

When I emerge from the library, I head over to Smurfette. I'm throwing my books into the white basket when I hear the rumble of a familiar car. I don't have to turn around to know who it is. A confrontation with him is the last thing I want. Instead of turning to acknowledge him, I pedal insanely out of the parking lot so that I can avoid eye contact. He's traveling close behind me, too close, and I'm forced to ride in the narrow gutter. My heart rate explodes, and my nervous system pumps adrenaline like crazy. Nate isn't backing down, and I can't go any faster. The rumble of his engine is louder than ever.

Where the hell are the police when you need them? I expected it to happen, even braced myself for the possibility, but when he knocks into the rear wheel of my bike with his car, Smurfette and I crash to the concrete.

Shock and fear make it impossible for me to move much at first, but when I do, there's a searing pain in my knee. My scab has been ripped open and the cut enlarged. Standing upright is a challenge because my hip throbs and I'm shaking like JELL-O that hasn't set all the way. Nate kills the engine and pops effortlessly out of his car, racecar driver style.

Looking around, I check to see if there have been any witnesses, but everyone is too busy working on buildings and going about their business to realize that I've almost been killed. Turning, I finally face my enemy.

"*What are you trying to do, kill me? You're such a prick.*"

"Aw, come on," he says in a way that minimizes what just happened. "I just bumped your tire." He smiles with those thick, rope-like lips of his and walks to the front bumper, checking to make sure his car is unscathed.

"No harm done," he speaks at the car and not to me.

When he's finished inspecting the chrome fender, he regards me with contempt.

"Always the retard, aren't you? *Still* riding that bike?"

"*Still* having sex with Annette *and* Mikayla?"

"About that," he pauses and crosses his arms. "I need to talk to you."

I make a small, sweeping gesture with my hand to indicate what just happened. "Hell of a way to start out a conversation, don't you think?"

He leans into his car.

I grab the handlebars of Smurfette and use them for support. Just to be sure he's paying attention to what I'm about to say, I make eye contact with him.

"I'm not going to keep your secret."

"You don't have a choice. I've got a good thing going, no, actually, a *great* thing going, so you're going to keep your mouth shut. I mean that."

"Or what, Nate?" I cross my arms. "Going to run me over again?"

His laugh, an irritating cackle, is a cruel, raspy sound, and goes perfectly with his vagabond haircut and intimidating, reptilian eyes. "That would be too obvious wouldn't it? Besides, I've got more inventive ways."

"Is that a threat?"

He raises his eyebrows sharply and pops back into his car and starts the engine. The tires squeal as he drives away, once again coming within inches of my bike. I'm beginning to think I've underestimated Nate. A few weeks ago, I was certain all he could do was speak and play football, but he's proven beyond a shadow of a doubt that he's capable of deception and depravity. But, he can't bully me. It's the end of the line for his twisted fun, and I'm going to see to that immediately.

With this goal in mind, I pedal out of the downtown, this time slowly, since my knee is throbbing and bloody. I pass all the buildings and houses whose decaying states are starting to look familiar.

I finally reach my house on Scott and park Smurfette against the side of our garage. Our street is sleepy, the only exception, a rowdy squirrel that chatters noisily while it taunts a stray cat. Across the street the Atwoods' RV is no longer there. They must have moved back into the house. Annette's car is parked in the newly painted and restored garage. It's now or never.

I'm prone to rash actions. Often my passion trumps good judgment, and I'm sure whatever I say or do will be wrong. But, I'm not backing down. Determined and anxious, I cross the street, swinging my arms like a soldier. Slowing down, I take a deep breath and knock on the front door.

Annette answers promptly. "Cane! So good to see you. Oh, have you hurt yourself?"

I've forgotten about the fresh wound, and now that I'm reminded, the ache returns. It looks rather hideous, and my entire shin is streaked in dried blood.

"Let me go get something so we can clean you up."

She walks into her house, leaving me to shut the door and follow her into the kitchen. "The painters just left yesterday, and I've been busy putting things back and figuring out what we need to replace. Mitch is away for a long trip, so we've been fending for ourselves around here and-"

"Is Mikayla home?" I interrupt.

"No, she's at practice, but Nate should drop her off soon." Annette puts her fingers to her lips as she searches for a washcloth and some ointment. "I'm so glad you two have made up. I can't even really remember what started it."

I grab onto my pony tail. *Hair* is what started it, words are what finished it. *Can no one remember that?*

Annette bends over to help me, but I yank the damp washcloth from her hands. How can this woman who has always been so much of a second mother to me be sleeping with *Nate*? The thought is repulsive.

"What happened?"

"Someone ran me over."

She laughs. "It looks like it."

If only she knew this wasn't an attempt at humor and that it was her lovely boy toy who ran me down with his Mustang. Before I can figure out how to phrase what I know about her and Nate without degrading either or us, I blurt it out. "I know about you and Nate. I know that you're sleeping with him."

Nervously, I bunch up the bloody washcloth and squeeze it.

"*What?*" Annette tucks her smooth honey-colored hair behind her ears, not once, but twice, and laughs nervously. Her composure teeters for a second, and then she raises an eyebrow and calmly holds her chin between her thumb and pointer finger, as if posing for a picture. Her nails are perfectly manicured, a lovely shade of fuchsia that reminds me of the bleeding hearts in Grandma Betty's garden.

"Now, Cane," she says admonishingly, "why would you even accuse me of that? It's absolutely ridiculous."

She recovers well and sounds so absolutely convincing that I begin to doubt myself. I didn't actually see them having sex. Is Annette counseling Nate or something? I'll admit, there are times when my imagination spins out of control, and sometimes stories that begin with *Once Upon a Time*, seem incredibly real. But, I know I'm right. I remember the fogged windows and the look of guilt. My skin turns a lovely shade of flaming red.

"I *know* that you are."

Annette gives a throaty, dismissive laugh but won't look me in the eye.

"That's just absurd."

Outside, there's the familiar purr of the Mustang's engine, and Annette and I both look out the large front window just in time to catch its shadow as it slinks into the driveway.

Annette remains absolutely still and poised, but she flinches ever so subtly, the motion mostly in her eyelids and her neck. When she suddenly pales at the sound of Nate's voice, I know that I've imagined nothing.

"I've seen you with him out at the forest preserve. You have to stop."

I toss the white washrag that is now stained with my blood on their new countertop. Just as Mikayla and Nate enter through the back, I'm about to leave through the front door. I know that they've both seen me and sense that something is amiss, because the room succumbs to an unbalanced silence. Annette douses the stillness with a hefty dose of chatter that seems odd. Even after I shut the front door of their home and sprint back across the street, I know that what I've said has left a mark, a bruise larger than the one that's forming on my hip.

When I arrive back at the Schaeffer farm, thankfully avoiding anymore hit-and-run attempts by Nate, the first thing I notice is that Justice's truck is missing. I wonder if Samson kicked him out for good. This frightens me more than anything, almost as much as when I knew that Grandma Betty was hurt, and I'm about to run inside and check when Samson comes out the back door. We nearly crash into each other.

"Hi," I say shyly, finding that it's impossible to look at his face. Have I committed as big a sin as Annette?

His large hands are hidden in the back pockets of his jeans. "I was just looking for you. I have a couple hours. Would you like to go visit Grandma Betty?"

The last thing I want to do is ride in a car with Samson, but I can't refuse. I want to see Grandma Betty more than anything, especially after seeing Annette. I can't believe there have been times when I've favored Annette over her, even thought that I loved Annette more than her.

"Sure."

"Good, let's go."

"I haven't eaten lunch yet." Like Pavlov's dogs, my stomach growls in response to my statement.

"We'll stop and get something on the way." He pulls his baseball hat down a little further and draws his eyebrows together in a way that reminds me of Justice. "It will give us time to talk about some things."

Spec-tac-u-lar, I mutter soundlessly.

As it turns out, Samson doesn't have much to say. I know by the way he keeps sneaking glances at me, tugging at the bill of his hat, and clearing his throat that he wants to initiate conversation. We're sitting in a booth in the back of Subway when he finally says something.

Samson rips the paper off of his straw, "What happened between you and Justice can't happen again."

I didn't expect him to come right out with it. I glance up at him quickly, and then my eyes fall back down again. I don't care what he says, because it's not going to make a difference.

When I don't say anything, he adds, "I made it clear to Justice as well."

"Why?"

Samson sighs and pulls off his cap. He pats at his crew cut like an old lady might pat at her freshly curled hair.

"You're just too young."

"Five years isn't that much of a difference," I say defensively.

He takes a drink of his pop and glances at the front of the restaurant. "The difference between fifteen and twenty-one is a lifetime."

"I'm almost sixteen, and I'm mature for my age." I'm grabbing onto the tip of my straw and bouncing it up and down. It's making a horrible squeaky noise. I stop. "I think I've proven that over the past few years," I declare confidently.

"I'm not saying you aren't."

"Did you kick him out?"

"No, nothing like that." Samson takes a monstrous bite of his sub and chews thoughtfully. After he swallows, he wipes at his mouth with a napkin. "But, I think it's better if you two have a little distance from each other. I'm giving you the next week or so off from work. I know cross-country practice is starting soon, and I'm sure you'll want to hang out with some kids your own age."

"I could probably move back to my house. It's not in that bad of shape."

"I don't want you to leave, that's not what I'm insinuating. I want you to stay. I'm just trying to prevent...well, you know, it's just that what I saw happening last night, you and, um, he...." his voice trails off and he's uncomfortable with the direction he has taken the conversation. He shakes his head apologetically and takes another bite.

While I'm thinking about how to get around all this and how it will be possible to sneak moments in with Justice, I plunge my straw up and down again. The squeak is irritating but oddly satisfying.

Disobeying Samson won't be that hard, but it occurs to me that there's one person who might make this impossible.

"Are you going to tell Jell-I mean, Jenny Ryanne what happened?" I almost slipped; sometimes I actually forget her real name.

"I don't see the need."

Thank God. The last thing I need is Jelly Roll installing hidden cameras and motion detectors; she would go that far.

"No one else needs to be involved," Samson states simply. "It's over and done with. Nothing really happened."

His cavalier declaration infuriates me. *Of course something happened, and it's far from over.* It will never be over. Adults are sometimes so blind I wonder if they can see anything at all. Pouting, I finish my lunch in silence, focusing my eyesight on the brown, plastic tray.

Samson clears everything away after we are finished, and I deliberately decide not to thank him for lunch, forgoing manners as a type of protest.

The hospital is ten minutes from Subway, and Samson and I are trapped together in a hot car, which seems more uncomfortable because of the grudge I carry with me. I'm sure he knows I'm pissed. I'm practically hugging the passenger door, and I've pulled my hair out of my ponytail and taken to separating and braiding it. My fingers don't even need the attention of my brain, and so I let my thoughts wander to Justice. Already I'm thinking of ways to be alone with him. Tonight, after Samson is asleep, I'll sneak into Justice's room.

"I've been thinking a lot about your dad and mom lately."

Samson's announcement derails my train of thought; my fingers stop braiding.

"With you living with us, I can't help but think about them." Samson rests his forearm on the windowsill. "They were both...I don't know." He sighs. "I guess it's hard to put into words."

He's baited me, and I want more. "Tell me a story about them."

He chuckles and pulls at his hat. "Grand gestures. That's what your dad was about. When he couldn't convince your mom to go out with him, he resorted to some pretty ingenious tactics."

"But, I thought they fell in love right away."

"Your dad fell in love with your mother right away, but I'm not sure it was love at first sight for her. Alex had something of a reputation." Samson turns up the air conditioning and holds his palm in front of the vent, testing the temperature.

"He was quite the ladies' man, and your mom knew about his reputation, so she was reluctant to say the least. But, your dad was relentless in everything he did. If he wanted something, there was no stopping him. And with your mom, it was no different. He knew that she was *the one*, kept telling me that over and over again."

"What did he do?"

"What didn't he do is more like it. The first time he asked Mary out and she refused, he somehow found out her favorite flower-"

"Red poppies," I insert into the conversation, proud that I know at least that much about my mother.

"Right. It just so happened to be spring, the season for poppies. Your father always had luck like that. So we spent one Saturday driving around Champaign, Illinois gathering every red poppy we could find. The car was filled with them. We snuck into her dorm room and literally filled the place with flowers." Samson laughs quietly at the memory and turns to look out the passenger window.

"What happened?"

He looks back at me. "She was stubborn, so what do you think happened?"

"She didn't change her mind."

Samson nods succinctly. "After the red poppies, he found out she loved poetry, so he wrote some for her. He had many talents, but, sadly, writing poetry wasn't one of them. But he wasn't concerned with making a fool of himself; he would have done anything to win her over. The last poem he delivered himself, wearing nothing other than a suit of armor that he rented from a Halloween store. He never did live that down. From then on, he was known as Knight Alex.

"He was starting to wear her down, but in the end, the thing that won her over was rather simple. He showed up at her door with a picnic basket and an invitation to join him for lunch at the park. After that," he nods once and presses his lips together, "they were inseparable."

Hidden beneath his blunt statement of the facts is an old sadness and regret that I wouldn't have seen if it hadn't been for Justice telling me the other half of the story.

Samson's face has gone foggy; he's retreated into the past and stays there for the remainder of the drive.

He pulls into the hospital parking lot, and we walk inside together. I glance over at him and have the strangest compulsion to take his hand and hold it.

We reach the care facility where Grandma Betty is located, and Samson slows his pace. He stops just shy of the front desk and looks down at me. He reaches up, pats at his crew cut again, and shifts his weight nervously.

"Why don't you go on ahead? I'll give you a few minutes alone, and then I'll come in and visit."

"Okay."

Samson sits down and handles some of the outdated magazines that litter the coffee table in the visitor's lounge, and I walk down the hall toward Grandma Betty's room.

I've come to a decision, if only in the last few minutes. I'm going to come right out and tell her everything. I'm tired of keeping my life a secret from her even if she is unconscious. Besides, I need to talk to someone about Justice, and with her, at least I'll have a captive, non-judgmental audience.

Since I'm so accustomed to seeing Grandma Betty alone on that slim white hospital bed with the starchy cotton sheets, I'm astonished that someone is beside her and even more so when I realize who it is. Frank sits next to Grandma Betty, bent close over her upper body, and he's whispering something in her ear and holding her hand. With his free hand, he gently strokes her forehead in the way of a devoted lover. His lips brush hers and linger there.

Now it's clear why he's done so much, why he's made grand gestures. When he sees me, he reacts like I did last night. He looks the same way that I looked at Samson, like he had been caught doing something wrong, when in fact, neither Frank nor I are guilty of anything but loving.

Half-Empty

Grandma Betty loves the silver lining. She always wants me to look on the bright side. I make an effort, but, for me, the glass is usually half-empty, and by the time I want something to drink, there's nothing left. Go figure.

This is what I'm thinking when we arrive back from the hospital and discover that Smurfette has been destroyed. The bike, scattered across the driveway, has been systematically dismembered by hand and machine. Seeing my childhood bike that has been a living thing, an extension of myself, mangled like road-kill knocks the wind out of me.

Samson brakes hard. Leaning over the steering wheel, he peers angrily at the remains. "What the…who would do such a thing?"

I hop out of the vehicle and survey all the pieces before me. The frame, bent and disfigured, is still blue, but the paint is laced with deep gouges. Kneeling, I run my fingers over scratched metal and press against the joint as if feeling for a heart beat.

Samson stands over me, his shadow blocking what remains of the sun. "Do you know who did this?"

I take the frame in my hand and stand carefully, favoring my knee and hoping it won't bleed again. "I have a pretty good idea."

"Who?"

"Nate."

"Nate Radcliffe?" Samson asks in disbelief. "The star quarterback?"

I nod and gather more pieces.

Samson sets his large hands on his hips and looks around. "We should report this to the police."

"That would only make it worse." Carrying the frame and the pedals over to the grass, I dump them in a pile. "It wasn't worth anything."

"Why would he do this?"

I shrug forlornly. The fallout has begun.

"Do you want me to talk to him? I know his father, I could call him."

"No," I try not to look too alarmed, "please don't. Really, it's fine."

Samson and I carry all the pieces into the equipment barn. "I'm sure it can be fixed," he assures me with sober optimism.

I nod. There's a garbage can right next to where we lay everything; I can't make myself tell him to just throw it away.

Even though I've asked him not to call Mr. Radcliffe, he seems inclined to do so. If he goes through with this, I can only imagine what Nate might do next. For someone without a frontal lobe, Nate sure knows how to kick where it hurts. First a hit and run that I barely escaped and now murdering Smurfette, what's next?

At dinner Samson tries unsuccessfully to pry information out of me about Nate and why he would do this. Can you imagine what Samson's reaction would be if I said that Nate was having sex with Annette, and since I put an end to it, Nate's determined to make me pay. Samson finally gives up, and we finish eating in silence.

When he heads out to his office to make some calls, I wash the dinner dishes and start picking apart the day. How come my whole summer has become all about forbidden relationships? I'm stuck in Romeo and Juliet purgatory. Shakespeare didn't have half the drama that I do. I could write a series of scandalous plays that would put Savage on the map for good.

I still can't get over Annette and Nate. What would a thirty-eight-year-old married woman want with a seventeen-year-old boy? If she wanted out of her marriage so badly, then why didn't she just get divorced? If she wanted to have an affair, why not pick someone her own age or at least someone that's not dating her daughter? Honestly, the scenario makes me want to vomit, especially when I consider that Mikayla might have had sex with him as well. I hope she isn't as ridiculously stupid as her mother.

While Nate and Annette's relationship is illicit, Grandma Betty and Frank's is perfectly acceptable. Now, all those days when she would come home and talk about him make complete sense and so do the visits on the weekends and evenings when they would garden together. How could I have been so blind? More importantly, why did Grandma Betty keep their relationship hidden? Did she think I would be upset?

I would like nothing more than to ask her why she has kept her mouth shut, but she still won't open her damn eyes. If Frank hadn't been there today, if I hadn't been so shocked to see him there under *those* circumstances, I would have remembered to tell Grandma Betty everything I needed to tell her.

I put the last dish away and squeeze the sponge dry. I'm wondering how I will spend the rest of the evening when I hear someone pull into the driveway. Justice has come back! In my excitement, I rush through the family room, out the back door and sprint past the pool, and then when I see who it is, my heart falls all the way to my ankles. I should have known Smurfette was an omen. My night is turning into a living, breathing nightmare.

She's home already? One measly day of freedom and she's back, looking haggard despite her tan and the careful application of makeup and a thick coat of raspberry lipstick. She regards me like a stray farm cat that she's been dying to accidentally run over.

The boys file out of the van, and Jocelyn squeezes her way past them and bounds toward me. She wraps her arms around my waist. The kid is a linebacker, and I stumble back and scrape my elbow on the wrought iron fence.

"We're back," she announces. "Mom wanted to come home for the fireworks. I missed you!"

Because of the tornado, the fourth of July celebration had taken a backseat to the cleanup. I had almost forgotten that they were scheduled for tonight, two weeks past America's birthday.

Jelly Roll approaches me carrying a suitcase. Her face is all business. "Where's Samson?" she asks.

"In his office making some phone calls."

"Where's Justice?"

Even though Jelly Roll has no idea what has happened, at the mention of his name, I experience a pervasive feeling of guilt.

"I don't know," I respond lamely.

"Did the trucks come this morning? We were supposed to send out a large shipment of milk today."

"I'm not sure."

Jelly Roll sniffs impatiently and pushes open the gate. "Get back here boys! You have to unload the car before you do anything else."

Jocelyn, gripping the bottom of my shirt so hard that the seams strain, smiles up at me. "You can sit next to me at the fireworks tonight. Okay?"

"Oh," I smile down at her and gently remove her hands. "I don't think I'm going."

"Why not?"

"I have to go running." More like, I have to get the hell out of this house.

"I'll come with you."

This girl is completely unaware of her obesity and of the fact that she gets winded walking up the stairs. "Not tonight."

Disappointed, Jocelyn frowns and shuffles away, dragging her feet for effect.

"We can go swimming tomorrow," I offer, knowing this will cheer her. She turns and cocks her head. "Okay! I got a new swimsuit."

"Really?" I try to sound interested. "What does it look like?"

"It's navy blue and white, just like yours." She smiles wide, showing off her front teeth, which are disproportionately large for her tiny mouth.

I follow Jocelyn into the house, noticing that my name is once again scribbled on her arm in lime-green ink.

Jelly Roll lines up the suitcases and takes inventory of the kitchen.

"Who used that sponge to wash dishes?" she asks.

"I did."

"That's the sponge I use for cleaning. The washrags are in the drawer."

"I didn't know."

"Obviously." She sighs and leans against the kitchen island, tapping the butcher block counters with her long fingernails that are painted the gaudy color of Barney the dinosaur. She commences issuing commands.

"Can you please get the dishes out of the cupboards, the ones that you washed with that sponge," she clarifies in a snotty tone, "so that I can put them in the dishwasher? And boys, carry all of those upstairs and go back to the van and unload the rest. Jocelyn, you can go get the blankets and load them in the van."

"What blankets?" asks Jocelyn.

"The old ones, honey, so we can sit on the ground at the fireworks."

"Oh."

Everyone else does precisely as she says, but when I don't make a move, she looks at me expectantly, her painted-on eyebrows raised. "The dishes?" she asks, prompting me to do something.

"No," I say with thoughtful impudence, "I don't think so."

My defiance stuns her. Her fat face falls, and then she draws it back up again into a disbelieving smile.

The fact that I have affected her this way makes me want to do it again. I'm tired of putting up with her crap. It's been a horrendous day anyway, why not make it worse?

Her fingers stop tapping. "It's a simple request, and I prefer my dishes not to be washed with a dirty old sponge."

"Get the dishes yourself." It feels so incredible to stick it to her.

"*Excuse me?*" she asks, drawing out the words so that they take up more time than necessary.

"The dishes are clean. They were soaped up and rinsed in hot water. I don't see any reason to get them out, other than the fact that you are on some power trip and like to boss me around. I'm not your little servant." My exterior is icy smooth; my hands aren't even shaking, but my hammering heart is a dead giveaway. My mouth has the consistency of a cotton ball.

"I'm not home for two minutes, and already you're looking for a fight."

"I'm not the one looking." By this time, the two oldest boys, Jeremy and Joshua, sense a showdown and both stand eagerly awaiting the draw. An audience provides me with more bravado.

I point my finger accusingly at her. "You're the one who's always looking. You hate me, and let's just say the feeling is mutual, Jelly Roll."

The back door opens, and I hear Samson in the family room greeting his youngest children. "What are you guys doing home already? I thought you might stay for another night."

"*What did you just call me?*"

It's only after she asks this that I'm aware that I've called her by her nickname. In anger, she squints, and her eyes all but disappear. It's clear that she's taken the name and run with it. She knows what I called her and why.

"*You are an evil, ungrateful, manipulative, little…*" she stops short, noticing that two of her sons are watching closely.

"Just finish the sentence," I say forcefully and raise my arms up so they form a V. "*Why not say it out loud?*"

"Say what?" asks Samson, who enters the room with Jade and Jocelyn hanging on his biceps. He glances uncertainly at his wife. "What's going on?"

"Cane's moving out," Jenny Ryanne announces with a pop and forges a smile. She overcompensates with the expression and looks demonic. She stares right at me with dagger eyes. "Aren't you?"

"No, that's not what we were talking about. If I remember right, you were just about to call me a name."

"Boys," Samson looks at his sons, "go upstairs."

They reluctantly shuffle out of the room. "You, too, Jocelyn."

"But, Daddy, I want to stay,"

"Jocelyn-"

"Daddy, I want to show Cane my new swimsuit, and then maybe she can go to the fireworks-"

"Later," Samson says firmly.

Looking up at her father's face, Jocelyn lets go of her father's hand and leaves the room. She stomps on the stairs to let everyone know she isn't happy.

When all the kids have left, I'm no longer enthusiastic about this confrontation.

"She's leaving. I'm not having her under my roof, and I don't know why we offered in the first place." By this time Jelly Roll barely has control of her voice, and the cadence of her words is unnatural.

Samson wraps his fingers around the loops in his jeans. "We've agreed on-"

"*Nothing!*" shouts Jenny Ryanne. "We've agreed on nothing."

"You could have stayed another day and taken some more time to cool off."

"This is my house, and I'll decide when I want to come home! I need to be here on the farm. Things get out of control when I am not around, that much is obvious."

"Control freak," I mumble under my breath, but neither Samson nor Jelly Roll notices.

"She isn't leaving."

Jelly Roll ignores her husband. "Go upstairs and pack your things. I'll call the Atwoods and make arrangements. If they can't take you, then I'm sure you can stay at Frank's." Jelly Roll puts her hand on the phone. Samson pulls the plug out of the wall.

"Just what do you think you're doing?"

"I'm stopping you from embarrassing yourself any further, Jenny Ryanne."

Jelly Roll turns the color of her lipstick. She picks up the nearest thing to her, a ceramic rooster complete with tiny metal bells around its neck, and hurls it across the room. It slams against the wall and explodes. Ceramic shards fly unpredictably, and when the miniscule bells make contact with the backs of the chairs and wood floor, they mimic the sound of delicate wind chimes.

The cacophonic noise sets off something inside of me, and I can't help but say what I really think. "Just because I look like my mom doesn't give you the right to hate me. You can call me an evil, ungrateful, manipulative, little bitch, but I think it's the other way around."

Samson steps forward with arms spread, impersonating a referee, "I think it's best-"

"If you leave!" finishes Jelly Roll. "*I'm finished with you. You're no longer welcome here."*

"Jenny," says Samson imploringly. "That's unacceptable."

Jelly Roll turns to her husband and leans forward. With her bright makeup and spiky, short blonde hair, she resembles the rooster she just destroyed. "There's nothing more to say. My decision is final."

Jelly Roll storms out of the room, the fat around her middle jiggling with her anger.

Samson stands helpless, with his arms at his sides and his palms spread open. I'm sure he is begging for deliverance from this. I sprint upstairs, ignoring all the sets of Schaeffer eyes that are looking at me.

"Are you mad?" asks Jocelyn.

I don't stop to answer her but continue up the stairs to the attic and change into my running clothes. When I come back down, Jocelyn's in the hallway holding up her swimsuit and smiling, asking me if I would please go to the fireworks. I shake my head and run down the stairs and out of the house.

Justice's truck is back in the driveway, but I don't stop to look for him. I keep running, my lungs working as hard as my fury. I expect to feel a release, but muggy nights have a knack for keeping things at a stand still. My anger is trapped inside of me, expanding like a balloon, and the endorphins, effective needles that pop anything, don't do their job.

While my feet are moving quickly, I can't enjoy the motion because I'm thinking about how the events of today have grabbed me by the ankles, yanked me upside down, and given me a good shake. Nothing is the way it should be. I love Justice, but clearly he's not about to love me back. Frank and Grandma Betty are lovers. Nate destroyed Smurfette, and I'm sure he wants nothing more than to destroy me. Jelly Roll's hatred for me is out of the closet, and I've made it clear to her that the feeling's mutual. I miss the good old days when everything was status quo. I miss the monotony of my life before that damn tornado.

My pace makes fast work of the forest preserve, and I'm up on top of the hill, standing beneath my ugly tree, struggling for breath and a quiet conscience. Should I have confronted Annette? Should I have said those things to Jelly Roll? Haven't I just made myself as awful as she? The high road is long gone, and I wonder at what point I veered off the main drag and took an unprecedented detour.

A stream of purple and silver rain into the night, and the explosive sound lags a second behind the brilliant colors. Savage celebrates America's independence as well as its own. The tornado is being avenged with hope.

I sit down on the obtrusive roots of the maple tree, and they cradle me. The fireworks shape themselves into magnificent flowers and scepters, wonderful pieces of transitory pop art that use the sky as a canvas.

The landscape in the valley below is fickle; the shadows frolic, making it difficult to get a clear outline of things. One in particular is more alive than others, and as it approaches I realize that it is, in fact, human. Out in the open, I recognize who it is. His form, the broad shoulders that slope just slightly and thin torso, is so familiar to me that I would know it blindfolded.

So, he's come to find me, but to what end? It is a mystery what this man, who would make the statue of David envious, sees in me, a wiry girl with more mouth than brains, more moxie than refined beauty. I watch his steady, determined approach and brace myself for what is to come.

"Thought you might be up here. Samson told me everything that happened, about the bike and the fight with Jenny."

"Par for the course, isn't it?" I ask disgusted.

"I'm sorry." He puts his hands flat against the tree and pushes like he wants to bring it down. After his breathing is steady, he says, "I need to talk to you."

When he takes great care to focus on everything but me, I know that he's not here to proclaim his love but to do the opposite.

"You're just going to end it, aren't you?" I drag my hands across the bumpy surface of the roots and surrounding ground. The grass, which has gone to seed, tickles my palms and forearms. "That's the reason you're here."

"It's gone too far already."

"How can you say that?"

An explosion that casts patriotic colors answers me; he says nothing. I lower my head and draw my knees up to my chest, waiting for him to speak. Resting my cheek on the crest of my knees, I glance up at him. "So, you have no feelings for me?" I ask coldly.

"I have too many feelings for you, and that's the problem."

"We aren't committing a crime," I argue, with my tone nearing a whimper.

"You're not committing a crime," he says pointedly and sits down across from me in the mess of roots that are more plentiful on the dead side. They must be reaching for something.

"I am," he adds regretfully.

"It's not a crime if no one convicts you."

"Samson already did that."

"What did he say to you?"

Justice chuckles miserably and grabs for a bunch of grass. He yanks it out. "Everything I should have been saying to myself."

"That's not fair," I insist. "If I were two years older this wouldn't be an issue. So why does it have to be now? We can just not tell anyone. It wouldn't be so hard. Would it?"

Justice ignores me, and I am fearful that the curtain is closing on whatever we had together. The only silver lining is the one that has been created by a firework. It fades fast against the black night.

In a gesture of sheer and greedy desperation, I grab at his hand, and he finally meets my eyes. His eyes, usually blue, have smoldered to a charcoal gray. He stares at me with adoration and reluctance, and I'm reassured when he doesn't let go. Our fingers are tightly laced together. With his free hand, he reaches up and traces my birthmark with hesitant tenderness. I reach up and capture his fingers in mine, so that now both of our hands are linked. I pull him to me, and he doesn't resist. I slowly lie back until I am reclining on a patch of overgrown grass, my position one of surrender and request. Justice holds tightly to my hands and hovers over me.

"Cane," he says with pliable regret, "I love you."

He takes my right hand and pries it open. He flattens my palm and presses it against his chest so that I can feel his heart knocking against his ribs. What is he trying to tell me? That I have his heart or that it is the one thing he can't give?

No matter what his answer, no matter the outcome, I'm here with him. I look up into his face, and I don't feel as I usually do, like I've been forced to roam the world alone, the girl with the blood on her hands. Instead I feel purified, like I've been born again. All those times I waited in church, and this is where God has finally come out of his hiding place, beneath the ugly tree.

Love Conquers All

When we kiss, I try to fit everything I feel into it. Love, passion, infatuation, admiration, and devotion. There's more than that. I know there is, but I can't think. Concentrating on all of these things and trying to deliver them by using my lips and tongue leaves me hypoxic. Where has gravity gone?

I find it hard to fix my body and brain in the same place at once. While Justice moves expertly, I do not. Sometimes my motions are clumsy and awkward. Does he notice? Do I make him feel as good as he makes me feel? There are places on my body that I want him to touch so badly that there isn't a word to describe it. Unable to keep pace with what we are doing, I submit to him. No longer the aggressor, Justice takes control. He slides his hands under my shirt, up under my sports bra, and using the pad of his thumb caresses me. I momentarily freeze, both from pleasure and surprise. So *this* is what it feels like.

Our desire is hasty and impetuous. We take turns shedding clothes. I remove his shirt, and he lifts my arms above my head and slowly removes mine. I pull off my sports bra, and he pulls me against him. His warm chest pressed against my own stills my heart and his. He takes his fingertips and draws them up my inner thigh, and I shiver and know what it's like to exist as both liquid and fire. He fits his mouth under my jaw line and kisses my rapid pulse. He pauses, slides both his hands in my hair, and holds his face away from mine. Disappointment and guilt are evident despite his closed eyes, and I dread what will come next.

Behind us, the last of the fireworks comes together at once, and the stimulus of such color, light, and sound, takes Justice away from me. Awakened as if from a trance, he pulls away, sits, and covers his face with his hands.

"I can't do this." He stands and grabs his shirt from the ground. His mannerism is reluctantly dismissive.

"*Because you don't love me enough?*" I ask in furious desperation. If he leaves now, I will cease to exist.

"Because I care about you, and because I have a conscience." He rolls the tip of his finger and his thumb together as if he is manipulating a gum wrapper.

"You're just too young," he adds miserably.

I pick up my shirt and cover my chest. "*Don't do this to me, please,*" I beg.

"I've already done too much. If I stayed—" he shakes his head as a silent, emphatic reprimand of himself. His expression, the crease in his brow, the way his eyes turn down at the corners portrays conflict and uncertainty. "I would never forgive myself."

The smell of sulfur hangs in the air. I swallow it, and the taste coats my mouth and throat.

"What's going to happen?" My voice vibrates with my fear. "You can't leave. I need you."

"You'll be absolutely fine without me, more than fine."

"*This is it? The end,* just like that?"

"I'm not sure."

But he knows what will happen and so do I. His expression hides more than it shows. Only I know what's underneath it; reading between the lines is my curse. He's already gone.

Reaching down, he runs his fingertips the length of my forehead, pausing on the birthmark that has both infuriated and protected me.

"Don't leave me," I whisper and close my eyes. I don't open them until he is gone, until I can no longer hear him running away from me.

Rising shakily, I drop my shirt to the ground and expose myself in the darkness. I stare at Justice's shadow as he disappears into the thick of trees. Although all I want is to chase after him, I stay where I am. There is a hurt that is capable of momentarily stopping the heart, and I press my hand to my naked chest to check to see if I'm alive. There it is, just a fraction of a second later, a hard thump against my hand. I'm alive after all. Frozen in place, I stand with my hand still pressed over my bare breast. After a time, I lose all sense of being connected to my body. Bones, muscles, tendons, and ligaments cease to exist.

What will I do without Justice? Breaking my statuesque pose, I press my body against the ugly tree and wrap my arms around the trunk, trying to hold onto something that won't reject me. The ragged, textured bark presses against my chest, arms, breasts, and stomach, leaving indentations and senseless patterns that will temporarily mark me. I stand holding the tree as I would if it were Justice. I hold tightly until my flesh is pained from the pressure, but still, when I leave there will be no evidence. It will fade. My skin will not be marred no matter how much I want it to be.

The fireworks, now completed, leave behind a screen of smoke that reeks of reckless celebration and independence. Releasing the tree, I sit down carefully and watch the last of the vapors dissipate. I dress reluctantly, feeling the cool cotton against my skin while trying to forget Justice's warm fingertips against my flesh.

The sultry night sits heavily on me and around me, and I need to be cleansed of the heat and of everything else that has happened. I want to swim in the deep, clear pond in the gravel pit. Running down the hill, I make my way through the trees and paths, sprinting faster than I thought possible, the landscape becoming a cloudy blur. I exit the forest preserve, and make my way to the gravel pit.

With each stride I transfer emotion, and my heel strikes wicked and hard, my knees punished with each step. As I think of Justice, I run faster, and as I think about Jelly Roll and all the things she has said and done, I run harder, so that my body is a medium for my emotions. My body weeps sweat, and my chest heaves as I fight to pull in oxygen. I push myself beyond the physical limits of what I think my body is capable of. Have I run a mile in less than five minutes, or is it my anger and grief manipulating time, playing tricks on me?

I arrive at the gravel pit quickly, and instead of stopping I continue to run and shed my clothes at the same time. Skin fully exposed, I dive into the cool water screaming as loudly as I can. After swimming the length of the pond, I turn around and return to the shore. Exhausted and panting for air, I crawl laboriously onto the smooth rocks. I grip handfuls of smooth stones in my hands. My hair hangs on either side of my face, a heavy, wet veil that curtains me from the world. Bowing my head, I let my hair close in around me, shielding me and offering me privacy. Finally, after having pushed myself to my physical limits, I feel the sting in my sinuses, but still no tears.

Why can't I cry? Has God stolen this ability from me? In my ears I hear a phantom roar that is reminiscent of the tornado, a disaster that in many ways was the start and end of my life, and I realize I'm the one making the noise. I bellow and scream until my vocal cords refuse to cooperate.

My grief and sadness collide with disgust and impatience. My wallowing ends abruptly, and then, predictably, I want to slap myself in the face for allowing such self-indulgence. Unfurling myself from the fetal position, I'm met with self-loathing. *Get a grip*, I tell myself firmly. Although it feels like it, it's not the end of the world as I know it.

After dressing, I begin the journey back to the Schaeffer farm, but progress is slow. Because I have no desire to see Justice or Jelly Roll, I walk as if injured. During my beleaguered pace, I contemplate what will happen with Jelly Roll when I return.

Our feud is ridiculous. I'm not sure why I'm investing so much time and energy into despising her. Is it because she knew my parents, that she has just as many connections to my father and mother as I have, maybe even more? If I wasn't living under the same roof as her, this never would have happened. The cause and effect of the tornado makes me dizzy, and I often picture God as a scientist, throwing things at humanity and watching carefully to see how we respond.

With the exception of the cows mooing and the electrical hum of overhead lights, the farm possesses a pervasive silence. Jelly Roll's extended luxury van that resembles a miniature bus, is parked neatly on the concrete pad adjacent to the large garage, but Justice's truck is missing from its usual spot. It doesn't surprise me that he left. If I had the means, I would do the same.

As quietly as I can, I enter through the back door that leads into the family room. I make my way upstairs, tiptoeing and half expecting Jelly Roll to jump out at me with a knife raised over her head. I make it all the way up to the attic without being stopped by anyone. Justice's door is shut, and I stand outside it and press my hands against it, feeling the heat of his presence even though he isn't here.

Deciding I need something tangible that belongs to him, like a shirt, I open the door. He's disappeared from my life, pulled the ultimate vanishing act.

There's barely evidence suggesting that he had been here at all. The dresser drawers, many of which are still open, are empty. The closet hangers are bare. His large stereo that sat on top of the dresser is gone, as are the Sports Illustrated magazines and text books that had littered the night stand.

At the foot of his bed, the garbage can sits, spilling over with newspapers, green gum packages, and foil, but beneath the paper lies something more substantial. Bending over, I pick through what remains and discover the frame I had thrown across the room. I remove the splintered remains, expecting to see just the frame and not the picture, but he left that behind as well.

This is the only photo that I have of Justice, and it's likely all that I will ever have. Cradling the frame in my hands I go back to my room and remove the picture. I fold it in half, using my nails to crease it carefully on both sides. I repeat this until the photo falls apart, until he's no longer holding Nikki.

Since Justice is gone, I no longer have a reason to be here. I pack hastily, stuffing my suitcase with no logic or thought. Clothes are mixed with books, shoes, and hair products. In less than ten minutes, everything I own is a mound that covers the full size bed.

Given that I've been so focused on gathering up my things so that I can leave, I haven't considered what to do next. The prospect of planning seems insurmountable, so I decide to go with what I crave. My body, hot and covered with a dried crust of salt wants to be clean. Standing under the cool stream of water in the shower, I experience a wild and willful clarity that must be the side-effect of a broken heart. I'll go see Grandma Betty and make her wake up, and then I'll find Justice, drive all the way to his hometown if I have to. I'll get both of the people that I love back tonight.

I have to look fantastic for both of them, so I take great care in my appearance. Despite the late hour, I blow dry my hair and put on makeup. Given that I have packed carelessly, it takes time to find an outfit in my heap of belongings. After rifling through two suitcases, I find the perfect outfit to win Justice back, the very same one I had seen in a magazine and made Grandma Betty go out and buy at the mall in Clinton.

When I'm finished with my preparations, I sneak downstairs, fearing that I may encounter Samson who sometimes keeps late hours, something I've learned the hard way, but everyone is safely tucked away in their rooms. It's only when I reach the door that I realize I have no means of transportation.

A scheme quickly develops in my head, forming completely by the time I return to the kitchen. When I see Jelly Roll's keys hanging on the key hook, I know it's more than luck. For a brief second, I consider the rational, moral side of my brain that reminds me that stealing a car is a crime and that this one act could have enormous repercussions that involve me standing in front of a judge and being thrown in a juvenile detention center. Then I tell that moral side to *go to hell*. I'm not going to let legalities get in the way of my plan.

I tiptoe out of the house with the keys in hand. When the van turns over, I cringe, fearing the sound will surely wake Samson or Jelly Roll, and in case it does, I drive away quickly and only turn on the lights after I make it onto County N.

I'm no virgin behind the wheel. I've been driving since I was twelve. On my thirteenth birthday Grandma Betty let me drive all the way to church. Given my frequent excursions and the recent acquisition of my driver's permit this spring, I've gained a confidence that leans toward arrogance when it comes to being behind the wheel.

However, the perspective of the road against black night is terrifying. Gripping the steering wheel, I go under the speed limit and slowly make my way to Clinton. During the trip, my emotions get the better of me, and snot starts pouring from my nose. By the time I arrive at the hospital, I dare a glance in the rearview mirror. My eyes are bloodshot, and my face is puffy and swollen.

I drive cautiously around the parking lot. Maneuvering an extended van is quite different than driving Grandma Betty's Ford Escort. I carefully park close to the building in a spot that's reserved for physicians. If the police come searching, this probably wouldn't be the first place they would look. At any moment I expect to see red and blue lights circling, and I'm shocked at how non-reactive I am as this thought passes.

My fight or flight response takes absolute control of my autonomic nervous system. My insides are iced over, and I'm riding the roller coaster of this natural chemical. My heart pounds so hard I fear it might detach itself and emerge from my chest. Wouldn't that be a sight? It would be like the *Indiana Jones Temple of Doom* scene only no one would have to yank it out. I hop out of the van, and when my feet make contact with the ground, it feels as if my bones have liquefied.

Once inside the revolving doors of Mercy General Hospital, I'm reminded by the front desk woman, who resembles a walking corpse, that it's after midnight and that visiting hours are over. I lie and tell her my Grandma is a nurse here and that I'm bringing her a set of keys; I jingle Jelly Roll's key chain to prove credibility. The woman either believes me or has one foot in the grave and isn't about to stop me. She barely watches as I walk past.

The nurses in the long-term care wing know me well and are sympathetic to my plight. They buzz me inside. Grandma Betty is in a different position, and I know she didn't move on her own. The nurses did it for her to prevent bed sores. I take the chair from against the wall and put it next to her bed and watch her breathing on her own. Why can't she just wake up? Doesn't she have any idea what I'm going through right now? Doesn't she know that I need her?

I stand, put both my hands on Grandma Betty's bony shoulders and shake. "Wake up! Please."

Her lack of response discourages me and incites a fresh batch of snot. Folding my hands, I try to think of something to pray, but the only thing that comes to mind is the creeds that I memorized in Sunday school, the ones that I had to repeat over and over again to Mrs. Steinbach, whose nostrils flared each time I made a mistake.

Prayer takes too long. I want to perform a healing, a miracle that will guarantee her recovery. Why I haven't thought of this before, I don't know, but I lean over her and lower my face to hers. Closing my eyes, I reach up and pull the hair away from my forehead and press it against hers. The cross that has saved me from destruction more than once presses against her skin. I want to transfer all the power to Grandma Betty. I don't deserve or want the protection it has offered me.

"Give it to her, God," I whisper.

For more than a minute I stand with my eyes closed and my forehead flush against hers. Heat is transferred, and I convince myself that when I pull away her pale forehead will bear the same cross as mine, that I'm marking her. Yet, when I do open my eyes, I see nothing, not even a faint imprint.

The nurses pass sympathetic looks back and forth when I emerge with a tissue pressed under my nose. My first plan has failed. Despite my best efforts, Grandma Betty can't be roused from her preternatural slumber. What will become of the rest of my plan? Will Justice resist my best efforts too?

Stepping outside the hospital with keys in hand, I don't see him at first. He stands in the shadows of the van, and when I insert the key into the lock, he steps forward, causing me to jump and drop the keys.

"I thought you might be here," says Samson, his large hands manipulating his baseball hat.

I'm going to be handcuffed and hauled away. "Are the police here?"

He shakes his head, bends over, and picks up the keys. "Nothing like that."

I look past him, to his car.

"Jenny isn't here either," he says, anticipating my next question.

"How did you know?"

"You're fifteen-years-old, Cane. I've been watching your every move. I always know where you're at."

A shaky sigh escapes my lips, and I'm suddenly crippled by an exhaustion that has sprouted roots; it goes all the way from the top of my head out through the bottom of my feet. "So you followed me?"

"I'm not that good. But after the argument you had with Jenny, I knew you would be up to something tonight. I couldn't sleep, and so I went to check on you. You weren't in your room, and all your things were piled on the bed. I went outside and saw the van was gone. So, I went to the only two places I thought you would be. You weren't at your house, so by process of elimination," he pauses and glances at the long-term care wing, "I came here."

"What now?" I hand him the keys. "The police?"

"I'm not going to turn you in. You aren't a criminal." He smiles and rubs his jaw. He puts his hat back on and pulls it low.

"Let's drive home. If you got here, you can surely drive back. I'll follow you, okay?"

I pull my hair away from my face and resist the urge to start braiding. "What about Jenny? Does she know what's going on?"

"If she knew, you would be getting your mug shot right about now." He tosses me the keys. I catch them. "Let's go," he says.

Now that the incentive is gone, that I know I can do nothing to wake Grandma Betty and that I won't have an opportunity to find Justice, I'm physically and emotionally wrecked. If it wasn't for Samson behind me, watching my every move, I would probably have fallen asleep at the wheel.

Even though Samson told me that Jelly Roll has no idea what I've done, when we pull in the driveway, I expect her to be standing next to a squad car, telling them how I stole her van and giving them a detailed description so that they can produce a sketch and hunt me down.

Turns out my imagination is more entertaining than reality. Samson and I are greeted only by Tango, the tabby male farm cat who pilfers food from the house. He brushes up against my leg and then Samson's, weaving in and out in a figure eight pattern.

"Let's go inside," says Samson, in a fatherly tone that hints at a lecture.

We sit at the kitchen table facing each other. It's no court, but given Samson's intimidating presence, I may as well be sitting in front of a judge. I slide the keys in his direction, in a way that is both thankful and apologetic.

"Don't think it's okay to try this again." The mass of keys disappears as he cups his hand around them.

"I didn't think it was okay initially. I was just caught up in what was happening."

"You know who that sounds like?" Samson asks with a smile. "Your dad." He picks at a splinter under his thumbnail and winces. "He jumped right in without considering the consequences."

"I considered them. It's just that what I was doing was more important than what might happen if I got caught."

"You did get caught."

I shrug dejectedly; I don't need a reminder that my plan was thwarted. Although stealing the van was criminal, I can't say I wouldn't do the same thing again, just for the chance that it might have worked.

"Justice is gone," I say it out loud, trying it on for size, seeing if my heart will hurt more if it is vocalized. I rub my fingertips on the side of my nose.

"I know. I asked him to leave. I offered him a management position at one of our stores in Clinton. He left tonight."

"*You asked him?*"

"He didn't need much persuading. I think he planned on going anyway."

I cover my eyes so that I won't have to look at Samson; his betrayal is the final straw.

"Whatever was going on between you two, shouldn't have been going on. You're just too young."

Spare me the lecture, I want to yell. I hold my lips firmly together until they feel like two rubber cords.

"I don't want to see you get hurt."

Too late for that.

"I'm doing what's best for you. I hope you know that. I'm trying to do what your father would have wanted."

I slam my palms down on the table. The sound is jarring and seems more conspicuous given the time of morning and the stillness of the house. "*How can you possibly know what he would want? He's been dead for almost sixteen years. I didn't ask you to be his substitute. I didn't ask for anything. I don't need you to watch over me!*"

Samson rubs his mouth with his hands and takes a deep, cleansing breath, exhaling through his nose. I know that he's trying to find the perfect thing to say to calm me down, only there isn't anything.

I trump his efforts by declaring, "I'm going to bed." In the aftermath of my angry words, it sounds cowardly and conciliatory.

In my room, I face the mound on my bed and am too weary to push it on to the floor. I simply walk down the hall to Justice's room, strip down to my underwear, and crawl into his bed; it's where I want to be anyway. The pillow smells just like him, and I hold it against my naked chest.

Every nerve in my body experiences a pulsating mania, and I'm unable to fall asleep. Feminism aside, I'm a sucker for the handsome prince. I want my happy ending, but it seems I never got the directions on how to get there. Love conquers all, but in this case, the only thing love has conquered is *me*.

Up in Flames

When I come into the kitchen at seven in the morning after three hours of fitful sleep in Justice's bed, I want to be alone, but no such luck. Jelly Roll, wearing her red, white, and blue robe, complete with sparkly red stars, purses her ghostly lips while she measures coffee with a teaspoon and dumps it into a paper coffee filter. Intending to escape without being seen, I turn around and inadvertently step on a squeaky floor board. I stop. Feeling my stress level and body temperature elevate, I take a deep breath to calm myself and turn around to face the enemy.

Jelly Roll glares at me like she's seen me on *America's Most Wanted*. Is it possible Samson told her after all? Maybe John Walsh will show up at the doorstep with a television crew and haul me away in handcuffs. My heart shrivels with fear.

"I saw the Atwoods last night at the fireworks." Jelly Roll pushes a button, and the gurgle of coffee brewing fills the kitchen. "Annette said that you are more than welcome to stay with them," she adds coldly.

"All my things are packed."

"I think it's best if you find someone you know to help you move, a friend or something. Justice is gone, and we can't help you." Jelly Roll picks at the ends of her spiky hair with her fingernails and bends down over a list.

No use harnessing my hatred now.

"I didn't ask you to, did I?" I respond, my voice as nasty as my sentiment.

"Exactly why you're leaving," she says in a sing-song voice that conveys relief, not cheerfulness.

Jelly Roll cinches her robe tighter, causing her ample belly fat to spill over the top and pop out underneath. It occurs to me that her insides may very well be jelly, and if she squeezes herself too tight, it may ooze out of her ears or nose.

When she reaches into the cupboard for a coffee mug, I turn and sprint back upstairs to the attic.

I make Justice's bed and smooth the blankets with excessive precision so that no one would guess that I had burrowed my body in it. Once it's finished, I fight the urge to throw back the covers and crawl in again, to make it my living tomb. Thoughts of Justice make the surface of my brain itch, and I keep reaching up to scratch my forehead, only to realize that the sensation is on the inside.

Is he thinking about me? Should I go find him? What would happen if I did find him? Does he really love me? Why did he leave me last night?

These questions are as good as a flogging, and my posture, usually square and strong, sags under the strain. I return to my room. In the morning light, it's obvious that my attempt at packing was violently hyper, the effort of an insane girl. Everything is so jumbled that I can't even decide on a starting point. How would I even load this into a car? I take everything off the bed and start over.

Once all the clothes are neatly folded and the shoes have found their mates, I separate all the other things that I've held onto: Seventeen and Teen Beat magazines, Bazooka gum wrappers, romance novels, concert tickets, friendship bracelets that were meant for Grandma Betty and Mikayla, and peculiar rocks I collected along the way. What use do I have for this collection of worthless things?

In shameful haste, I yank an empty box from the closet and in oversize capital letters write-*BURN*. Before I have a chance to reconsider or grow sentimental, I scoop up the items by the arm full and dump them into the box. When it's full, I find another. Nothing is spared, and when I finish, I close the flaps of the box, one over the other so that I can't see the contents.

I line up my suitcases and place everything neatly inside, which is so very unlike me. Grandma Betty would be proud if she saw how conscientious I was being. The trivia cards I put in my backpack. Now, I just have to find somewhere else to live, but I'll sort that detail out later.

Thinking that all the kids are still sleeping, I'm surprised to find Jocelyn downstairs in front of the television. It will be impossible to sneak out without her seeing me.

She turns and grins, exposing a mouthful of pop tart. "Cane! Have breakfast with me."

I shrug. "Sure."

"Do you want strawberry Pop Tarts or chocolate?"

"I'll just have cereal."

Jocelyn crumples up the package and rushes into the kitchen, dumping it in the garbage. "That's what I'm going to have too. I don't like Pop Tarts," she says as she chews and swallows a large piece. "What kind of cereal do you want? Fruity Pebbles? Cocoa Puffs? Apple Jacks?"

Those all sound good, but I'm determined to makes this girl see that there are other things in life besides high fructose corn syrup.

"How about we both have plain Cheerios, no sugar on top, and some fruit, okay?"

"Okay!" she says enthusiastically.

"How about you get the bowls and spoons and I'll get the rest of the things out?"

"I can pour the milk for myself," she says confidently, "even though Mom thinks I'm still a baby and I'll spill."

Jocelyn gathers the spoons and bowls while I retrieve the cereal and fruit. "Where's your mom?" I look around cautiously, fearing Jelly Roll may emerge from her room at any second wearing fuchsia lipstick and squeezing herself tight with glittery clothes so that her jellied insides won't ooze.

"She's gone running errands for the business."

Jocelyn studies me carefully as I pour the cereal. "Mom said you're leaving, that you want to go stay with the Atwoods."

"That's what she said?"

"She was mad at you last night. She threw that rooster, and she never throws anything."

Across the room, I spot a red chip of pottery that was overlooked in the cleanup. "I have to leave."

"Why?"

I take a big bite of cereal and chew slowly, considering if I should lie or tell Jocelyn the truth.

"I'm leaving because your mom hates me, and she doesn't want me here anymore. I don't think she wanted me here from the start."

Jocelyn sighs and squeezes her bright blue eyes shut for a moment. "I don't want you to leave."

In between bites, she taps her spoon on the edge of the bowl. "Why does she hate you?" she asks quietly.

I shrug. "Guess that's something you'll have to ask her."

"Why don't you ask her?" suggests Jocelyn innocently.

"I don't see any reason to."

After we finish eating, I deliberately wash the plates with the cleaning sponge—my subtle way of telling Jelly Roll to stick it.

"Watch cartoons with me," Jocelyn grabs my hand and leads me into the living room.

"Why don't we go for a walk instead?"

Jocelyn peeks outside and scratches a mosquito bite on her cheek. "It's too hot outside."

"You stay and watch cartoons. I need to get out of the house today."

"You don't want to stay with me?" she asks glumly.

"It's not that."

"Are we friends?"

I look down and see that she has again written my name on her arm; the fascination she has with me makes me equally fascinated with her. "Absolutely," I smile.

She claps her hands together once. "I knew it."

I sling my backpack over my shoulder. "See you later kiddo."

I have absolutely no idea where to go, so I start walking. I'm determined to stay away from the Schaeffer farm and have no desire to move in with the Atwoods given the current situation with Nate, Annette, and Mikayla, a love triangle with a Jerry Springer spin. Homelessness doesn't really suit me. I spend the better part of the day at the forest preserve beneath the ugly tree feeling sorry for myself and reliving last night with Justice. When I grow weary of that, I hike down the road to the gravel pit for a swim.

Stripping down to my underwear and bra, I glide into the water and float on my back. The spiteful sun makes my skin sizzle, and having neglected to coat myself in sunscreen, I get out of the water feeling woozy from the heat and the burn which is already tender to the touch. I take refuge in the shade and realize just how exhausted I am but refuse to close my eyes, because all I see behind my lids is Justice.

When I'm dry and dressed, I wander down County N, ultimately ending up on Scott Road. With my backpack on, hair straggly and damp, and my skin the color of a red geranium, I fit the bill of homeless girl. When a car passes, I stick out my thumb and attempt to hitchhike, but they don't stop. Even if they had, I'm not sure where I would have asked to go.

I've given up on everything, which goes against my very nature. I pride myself on going to the point of no return and getting things done. I own a Nike shirt that reads, *Winners Never Quit, Quitters Never Win*, and I take this phrase to heart. I even take it beyond that. I've accomplished feats for the pleasure of proving to myself and everyone around me that *anything* is possible.

I've been doing it all my life, accomplishing the impossible. When I was barely a day over three-years-old, Grandma Betty took me to the pool. I remember holding her hand, made slippery from sunscreen, and walking along the edge of the pool on concrete so white it made my eyes sting. The contrasting blue of the water was so spectacular and alluring that I wanted to submerge myself in it. Pulling away from her, I ran to the deep end and despite her vehement protests, I leapt into the water with my arms spread wide. Surfacing, I swam like a fish despite the fact that I had never had a lesson. When the lifeguard jumped in to rescue me, it was more for Grandma Betty's benefit than my own.

Grandma Betty accused me of being just like my father. "Always doing before thinking," she would say, pushing air out her nose in a disbelieving huff.

I made it my mission to show her she worried for nothing. I scaled trees, rode my bike hands-free for miles, and roller skated as fast as my muscles would take me.

I never grew out of this. In seventh grade I claimed that I could run at least ten miles without even training. Peter Hogan, the class clown, said that it was impossible. I told him it was more than possible, that it would be a piece of cake.

To prove my point I invited everyone to the high school track on a Saturday and told them to start counting. Forty laps and two and a half hours later, I had run ten miles, earning the respect of the entire class and sore legs for a week.

Last year in freshmen biology, I made some offhand remark to my friend Jennifer that the text book wasn't that challenging and that I could score one hundred percent on every single test. I said that my trivia knowledge in general was going to make high school a joke. Brittany, of the BOMMB squad, had been listening to our entire conversation and said that there was no way I could ace one test, let alone all of them.

"Just watch me," I said with carefree confidence.

So last year I committed myself to making sure that I knew biology so well that I could teach the course. I practically memorized the book and found every science trivia card that related to biology. The results spoke for themselves. I scored perfect on every test but the last, receiving a ninety-nine percent on the final. By that time, however, I had already discouraged Brittany, and the rest of my class had lost interest. About the only thing my impressive performance earned me was a hyphenated nickname; after maintaining a 4.0 grade point two years in a row and acing every test, I was commonly referred to as *brainiac-freckle-freak*.

Before this summer, I was generally full of myself, not in an arrogant, stuck-up bitch way, but in a confident *I know who I am and can do anything* way. I was so willing to place a bet and show that I could overcome anything. That was before Justice and before the tornado. Now, things have gotten so bad that I just want to throw in the towel.

I stop walking, look up, and realize I've arrived at my house. I push open the back door.

"*I Give Up!*" I shout.

The house is abandoned, and so am I. With chunks of plaster missing, it's easy to see how little substance a house has; the honest and blatant fragility of it makes me shudder. It's no wonder the tornado took advantage. It's a wood skeleton with a circulatory system made of electrical conduit and wire, and all of it is disguised with thick sheets of paper. When they rebuild, will it be stronger than before? They will have to reinforce what's here, won't they?

I think Frank said the contractors would be here at the end of the week to start rebuilding, but I could be wrong. We had this conversation at the hospital, when I first realized what was going on between Grandma Betty and him. I was too distracted by the way his hand found Grandma Betty's while we were talking and the way he moved his fingertips over her delicate, ice-blue veins. Two lovers separated by consciousness.

I didn't care about rebuilding the house at that moment. I just wanted to know when he had started to love Grandma Betty and how I could have missed it. He knew that I wanted to know, could see it in my expression.

When I looked carefully at Grandma Betty's waxen face and then searched Frank's eyes, the color of weak coffee and asked, "How long?"

He answered promptly, "Eight years."

"Oh." *Eight years*! How could I not have known? Am I blind or just so wrapped up in my life I didn't take time to notice?

"Does it upset you?" he asked. "She was always worried about that."

"No," I answered, shrugging one shoulder. Did they sneak around? Did they have date nights when I was spending the night at Mikayla's?

Why did they leave me out of it for so long?

Now that I've had some time to process their relationship, I don't know what to feel. It doesn't make me happy, sad, or jealous, but maybe that's because I can't feel anything other than fear.

What really bothers me, what really upsets me, is that Grandma Betty is not getting better. Despite my vigils, as well as Frank's (I found out he had been coming every day as well, only we had coincidentally missed each other), there hasn't been a shift in her condition. Many nights this summer I've woken from a nightmare that is eerily similar to Rip Van Winkle, in which I become the main character, slip into a coma, and wake up as old as Grandma Betty, my silky, auburn hair in tight, gray curls.

As I roam through the interior of my house and slide my hands over the scarred walls, I think about what I've lost, who I've lost. Will Grandma Betty ever come back to me? Will Justice ever come back to me?

My heart has had all the loss it can take. I've discovered that this organ, after enduring tragedy and stress, dislodges itself and takes up residence elsewhere. My heart is no longer in the left side of my chest beating predictably and comfortably behind a cage of sturdy ribs, but now it has split in two. Half of it has risen to the base of my throat, just below the Adam's apple. I can feel it pushing against my windpipe, making it hard to breath. The heavier half, as dense as an anchor, has sunk to my stomach. It's fat, parasitic, and takes up too much space, stealing my appetite and my ability to move freely.

Despite the thoughts that roar inside my head and threaten to make me insane, my sleep-deprived body demands a reprieve. I plod upstairs and step over the Lively Lavender paint stain that is helplessly streaked and smells of a powerful alcohol based cleaner. Why did Frank even bother cleaning it up when the contractors are probably going to rip everything out and start from scratch? He says with the money from the insurance company and with him doing some of the work, we're going to build a brand new house, something that according to Frank will, "Knock Grandma Betty's socks off!"

Why rebuild? Doesn't it make sense to wait and see if Grandma Betty will wake up? Frank and his optimism can't be stopped. The house is prepped for surgery. I'm pleased to see that for the most part he left my room alone. My bed and dresser are still here. Feeling the need for darkness, craving it, I crawl under my bed, and the space is expansive now that all my silly collections are at the Schaeffer farm waiting to be incinerated.

My eyes close, but my mind is open wide, running as fast as it can.

Justice is around every bend. I see his eyes, a smoldering blue that reduces me to ashes. Even though it was hours ago, I can still feel the contours of his body on mine, his bare skin against mine, our heat infinitely multiplied. All of the words we spoke to each other echo, and I hear them not just once but over and over again. *Please don't leave me.*

I only have to reach a little ways before I can't go any further; my fingertips make contact with the slats of the bed. Rubbing them carefully over the surface, I feel the grain of the dried out wood, wondering if this is what it would feel like to be in a coffin. Will this be Grandma Betty's fate? Will I have to put her in a box in the ground next to everyone else that left me?

If only I could cry, if only I could release all this pain, but tears never come. This part of me is broken as well.

Sleep isn't incremental; it comes with vengeance.

I wake as if drugged to tomb-like darkness and hushed voices. It takes me a moment to orient myself and remember where I am. I try to sit up, but my head slams against the bed slats.

The voices are louder. Who is in the house? I don't need to think on it for long. Given the way my stomach flips and then tightens, I already know who it is. Footsteps, hesitant and heavy, fill up the first floor. Sophomoric laughter follows.

I reach up and tuck my crusty hair behind my ears, evidence that I must have cried in my sleep. Rolling over, I wiggle my upper-body out from under my bed so that I can listen.

"So this is the *brainiac freckle-freak's* house? *This place is a shit hole.*"

Nate's friends laugh.

"*It's not like there was a tornado or anything,*" responds Nate sarcastically. "Dumb ass," he adds for good measure.

"Even so, it must have been one hell of a shit hole before then. What the hell is up with all the colors? It's like a rainbow puked in here."

Snickers follow this comment.

"Dude, why did you bring that here?" Nate asks.

"Thought we could toke up."

"We aren't here to party. Anyway, I'm in deep shit after Samson called my dad and told him that I destroyed her bike. This is pay back. She needs to learn to keep her mouth shout. And I'm not going to get high and screw it up and land myself in more trouble."

Great. Samson followed through with his promise. I never should have opened my fat mouth and told him who wrecked it.

"You wanted to wreck the place, but it's already ruined."

"What about the upstairs?" someone asks.

"Let's check it out."

"What's the point?"

A cardboard box is ripped open, and I can hear hands making contact with aluminum cans. Tabs are ripped off and discarded on the kitchen floor. Someone tosses one in the sink.

One of the boys belches so loud, I jump and scurry back under the bed. Unpredictable, foamy laughter follows.

"*Jesus,* Rick."

"I'm *the king,*" Rick replies proudly, taking the comment not as an insult but as an accolade. "Why did you buy this shit, Nate? Couldn't you have at least sprung for the MGD? I can do much better with quality beer."

"At least I have enough balls to walk into a liquor store and buy. I don't see your pansy ass making any attempts."

Rick laughs. "Good point."

"She here?" one of the other boys asks.

"What do you think Einstein? The place is deserted. She's been living at the Schaeffer farm."

"Let's see what it's like up there," someone suggests.

They trudge upstairs, and I scoot as far back under the bed as I can and press my back against the wall. They have flashlights and the beams make irregular, dizzying patterns against the floor and walls.

It sounds like there are at least four, maybe five, and I know they're all football players. Rick and Nate, the co-captains of the football team, only fraternize with those they deem as equals, preferring barbaric strength to intelligence. If they discover I'm here, what will they do?

I'm strong, but I'm also realistic. My breathing seems loud, and I cover my mouth.

The flinty sound of a lighter swats at the air.

"Christ. There's nothing to destroy. It's worse up here."

A sharp cackle follows, and Rick says, "No better than your house, Ben. Your mom is obsessed with cows, cows all over the damn place."

"Very funny, asshole."

"It's hard to take a shit when you have a heifer staring straight at you."

"Shut the hell up, Rick."

Someone lights another cigarette, and the stench of the smoke makes me queasy.

"We're not going to use the sledge hammers?"

"No," answers Nate. "Let's just get out of here." He takes the steps two at a time.

"Sounds like a plan."

Their footsteps are careless and rushed. When they're finally out of the house I relax, roll away from the wall, and breathe deeply. But, I can't take a clear breath. The smoke lingers. It curls its way around my room and assumes a sinister quality. It isn't the familiar, nicotine odor of cigarettes burning, but a toxic, chemical odor that pinches my lungs.

The smoke coagulates in my room, and instead of scrambling out from under my bed, I watch in fascination as it rises up around me, a living thing without boundaries. Smoke precedes something that sounds like dead leaves crackling. More snaps, crackles, and pops, that would shame a box of Rice Krispies follow.

When I see the light from the fire, a concoction of red and orange, I'm alarmed, but it's a lethargic response, and I have to coax it out of me. It's fascinating how calm I am. Sliding out from my hiding place, I become aware not just of thick smoke, but of the heat and how it paws at me with avarice. Glancing out the window, I realize the oak tree is gone, and I have no safe way to escape this inferno.

Grabbing my backpack, I quickly open it and pull out my damp towel. Bunching it up, I hold it against my nose. Sprinting to the door, I kick it shut and know that eventually this barrier won't exist. Coughing and sputtering, I hold the towel tightly against my lips and my nose. Holding my breath, I momentarily drop the towel and crank open one of my windows then yank off the screen. The air is so fresh that the oxygen feels liquid and crystallizes in my nostrils. I look down, but the distance is too great and I have no desire to leap. I could scream, call for help, but I can't make myself do it.

Turning, I place my back against the wall. Am I really trapped? Is this the end?

I'm going to put God to the test one more time. I've got nothing to lose. Not Grandma Betty and Justice, who are both so far gone there's no point in trying to bring them back.

The house is disappearing, sinking, and I wonder if quicksand and fire are one in the same. They must be, because I can feel the framing giving way. I have just one fantasy, just one hope, and it isn't saving myself, but rather having Justice save me. I want him to be the knight in shining armor who rescues me.

Where is he?

A fit of coughing ensues, and I shrink to the floor, feeling my lungs burn with a fire of their own. I hear a bang against the side of the house as something is put firmly into place. A voice follows the noise.

"*CANE!*"

"I'm here," I say loudly, but the words become a prolonged, agonizing cough. I push the towel against my nose, thinking at this point suffocation would be a merciful end.

The rattle of feet ascending aluminum rungs is muted by the symphony of fire. My walls and door are no longer barriers, but enemies, for the fire has converted them over to its side.

"*Cane, answer me!*"

She grabs onto the sill and sticks her head through the open window. "*Oh, my God. You have to get out of there!*"

Crawling over to her, I reach up with both my hands. She grabs tightly; our fingers mesh together, a perfect fit despite the significant difference in our heights and build. She pulls me up to a kneeling position.

"Lean out the window and breathe some air!"

Following her directions, I stick my head out and take in clean air.

"*Can you get out?*" she asks in a panic. "We have to hurry!"

I nod and cough until I feel like my diaphragm has come loose. She partially descends, and I turn and lower myself out of the window, my legs shaking.

"You can do it, Cane," she encourages. "A few more steps, that's it."

We descend in tandem, and whenever I have doubts that I can't make it to the bottom, I look down at her steady hands. Near the bottom, I lose my footing and slip, and I feel her arms around my waist. She holds all my weight and drags me backward until we are near the road. We collapse together, sitting hard on the grass. I continue to hack, and her hand rests on my back for comfort and assurance.

The fire is a vulture, feasting on what the tornado left behind. In the distance I hear the blare of sirens.

She turns and looks at me.

"Everything's going to be okay," she says with a confidence that grieves me so deeply I want to cry more than anything but can't.

When the emergency teams arrive, I'm placed on a stretcher. They fit a mask over my face, and it's easier to breathe. Through all of this, she never leaves my side. We watch together as Grandma Betty's house, my house, endures a hasty and impassioned cremation.

The firefighters are efficient and determined with their strategies and experience, but they're waging war with a house that is a century old and has no defense mechanisms against fire. The demise is blatantly evident. The men with hoses are merely controlling the speed at which it happens, and I want to tell them they are wasting water and their time.

Let it burn itself out, I want to say. *Let it die. Let it go.*

While it takes more than an hour for the house to be reduced to a charred carcass, it seems like years. The process has been so painful to observe that when I turn to finally look at my friend I wonder if she sees me as an old woman. Has my skin wrinkled and my hair gone gray? Have my freckles become age spots or cancerous lesions?

She slowly lies down on the stretcher next to me, so that our shoulders touch. Space is limited, and half her body hangs off the stretcher so that she must support it with one bent leg. Sliding her hand down next to mine, she wraps her fingers around mine.

"Are you okay?" she whispers.

How can I be okay? I've lost everything, haven't I? Grandma Betty. Justice. My job. My home. My security. My ignorance.

But, what about my best friend? Has she found me? Can you go back to something you thought you permanently left behind?

"I knew you were in trouble. I knew something was going to happen all day. I can't lose you, Cane."

TWIN, I think.

"I'm okay," I say, because it turns out that I haven't lost everything.

Because of the chaos around us, I don't hear the furious footsteps approaching.

"*Cane! Mikayla!* Oh my God! What happened?" Annette bends over the stretcher and grabs onto my hand and Mikayla's. Her eyelashes are clumped together from crying.

"We're okay, mom," assures Mikayla.

Preoccupied, Annette nods and looks over her shoulder, motioning with her hand. Frank approaches in a jog, his face reflecting the embers. In his hand he grips his video camera. Is he recording this too?

Annette glances down at me and pushes the hair off my forehead.

"Oh, Cane. They've been looking everywhere for you." Annette says hoarsely holding the base of her throat with her hand. "It's Grandma Betty."

I turn my head and close my eyes so that I can't see my world going up in flames.

Love Will Keep Us Alive

Last year on the evening of my fifteenth birthday, Grandma Betty and I sat on the top steps of the porch in the velvety August evening, buzzed from birthday cake and ice cream. Grandma Betty, fly swatter in her hand, took aim at mosquitoes and horse flies while I sat observing how lifeless the leaves were on the trees, how the indigo sky appeared frozen, how nothing but the insects seemed inclined to motion.

With all this stillness around me, I was desperate for movement, not the physical kind that I so often craved, but an emotional motion that would propel my life into a lofty stratosphere far from where I sat. Perhaps it had everything to do with my age and hormones, but I wondered what it would be like to fall in love.

Then again, maybe it had something to do with my love of the movie *The Man in the Moon*, a tragic story involving a girl who falls crazy in love with an older boy, a boy who happens to love her older sister. Despite the girl's young age, her life becomes a dramatic adventure, full of passion and angst, and I wanted some of that for myself.

That wasn't the kind of birthday gift you could unwrap. For the second time that day, I put my fingertips against my lips, held them there delicately and wondered what it would be like to be kissed. Unlike most of my peers, I had never played spin-the-bottle or seven minutes in heaven, and thankfully I had never been extended an invitation to one of the BOMMB squad's make-out parties. My utter lack of experience translated into a sense of wonderment and anticipation.

Grandma Betty whacked a fly, missed, and muttered under her breath.

I leaned back until I was propped up on my elbows and had a view of the back of Grandma Betty's curls, damp with sweat.

"Grandma Betty, when did you first fall in love?" I asked wistfully.

She laughed and dropped the fly swatter against the step. "Your age, I guess."

"With who?"

"A young man in our church." Grandma Betty replied, her answer more breath than words. "He was going to be married."

"What?" I rolled my lips together and cast a her look of significant doubt.

"It's the honest truth. I fell in love, but he didn't even know I existed, so I suppose the love affair was more in my head than anything."

"I've never been in love." I kicked a loose piece of cement, and it tumbled down the stairs and into the withered grass.

"Love doesn't solve anything." Grandma Betty pushed at her sleeves, hiking them higher up on her arms. "Sometimes it causes such a ruckus, it's impossible to see your way out of it. Men and women spend more time worrying about love than anything else on earth, and then when they find it, it's a rare thing to get it right. Let's just say it's usually the man who messes things up. Think of all the energy wasted," she exclaimed and softened her adamant statement by turning to face me and cupping my chin in her hand. "Why are you wondering?"

I shrugged and pulled my face away from her hands. "I just am."

"Is there someone you like?"

"No," I responded sharply and dragged the sole of my shoe against the worn edge of the concrete stair. "I just wanted to know."

Grandma Betty placed her hand just under the lapel of her button-up shirt, directly over her heart.

"I know you think about boys. You're fifteen now," she gave me a level stare. "You're going to fall in love, and I think it will be sooner than later. It's a hard lesson, at least the first time around."

"Like I'll ever get the chance," I said with credible disbelief. Who would want to fall in love with me, the freckle faced geek who got straight A's and could run a faster mile than most boys her age?

"Oh, honey," Grandma Betty glanced back at me and shook her head. "You've got to learn to give yourself credit for the beautiful and amazing girl you are."

I cupped my hand over my mouth, rested my elbow on my knee, and looked away. Grandma Betty's compliments were obligatory. I couldn't take them seriously.

A slight breeze stirred, shaking the murky world awake. A fluffy cloud skated an inch or so, and then came to a rest.

Grandma Betty folded her hands in prayer form and rested them against her stomach. "After everything I've gone through Cane, love does become something of a mystery. You can love a person so deeply you somehow forget just how much. It was like that with Grandpa Henry. During a marriage, after a long time of loving someone, you just forget. I mean, you love them, but you aren't necessarily aware of it. It's just a given. You don't know how deep that love runs until they are taken from you, and then you swear you're going to drown in what's left. Love can make you want to die."

Grandma Betty scratched the skin on her forearm. "I shouldn't say that," she sighed impatiently at herself. "I felt that way at first when Grandpa Henry died in my arms. Then, after the shock wore off, after the grief became bearable, I remembered what it was like when he was here, and that love kept me going when all I wanted to do was give up."

"But, isn't there another kind of love?" I asked wistfully. "The kind where you love too much and when that person leaves or dies, you just decide that you have to go with them, that there's no other way?" My recent obsession with Shakespearean love stories skewed my perspective of reality.

When Grandma Betty turned around to look at me, her eyes swimming with sadness that had been there for longer than I had existed, I knew instantly that asking this was a mistake. For I could tell she was thinking of my father and of Uncle William. I was thinking of romantic love, and she was thinking about love for a child. The divide between the two was great, and I understood neither very well, certainly not enough to make dreamy, naïve assumptions.

Cupping my hand over my mouth again, I looked away, for I couldn't bear to see Grandma Betty hurting.

She inhaled forcefully, and then exhaled delicately. Reaching down, she patted my bare foot.

"Honey, the only thing that keeps us alive is love."

Part Three
August 1992

Riding the Wave

Grandma Betty is alive, awake, and no worse for the wear. It's eerie how normal she is, how mentally sharp and physically agile. With the exception of her pale skin, fifteen pound weight loss, and muscle weakness, I equate her coma to a pause button. My Rip Van Winkle dreams don't seem so outrageous anymore.

What really freaks me out is that she actually remembers me being in the hospital room with her and also remembers quite a bit of what I said to her. One of the first things she asked me when we were alone in the room together the night of the fire was, "How's Justice, honey?"

How could she know his name when she had never seen his face?

She said that she remembered his voice and us being there together. She took one look at me, straight in the eyes, and said that she knew I was sick with love. She said if she wasn't mistaken, he was as well.

We haven't had much time to iron out the details on everything that happened while she played Sleeping Beauty. She knew about Justice, both my discovery and acceptance of her relationship with Frank, and also about my reconciliation with Mikayla, the fire, and all of the other gory things that had happened because of the tornado. I would have given her the play-by-play (leaving out certain information), but there simply wasn't enough privacy. Between Frank, a steady stream of visitors, and the medical staff, I couldn't get a moment alone with her.

The doctors were the worst. They had all these questions and ran every test known to mankind. Frank referred to the tests as "the great inquisition," and when everything came back completely normal, they weren't satisfied, just more annoyingly curious. Apparently they couldn't find the medical loophole they were looking for, something that would explain what had happened, and when Grandma Betty was discharged, all those doctors were still scratching their heads.

It isn't just the doctors who find Grandma Betty's recovery captivating. The town is equally fascinated by her miraculous awakening. Because of everything that happened, we've been catapulted to fame. I'm asked about her by everyone I see, and the phone at Frank's house hasn't stopped ringing since the night of the fire. The newspaper and television reporters are suddenly interested in our theatrical tale and the happy ending, which include me nearly perishing in a fire, being rescued by my psychic best friend, and then on the very night that I could have died, discovering that my grandmother had finally awakened from a coma.

Every time a microphone is stuck in my face or a reporter shows up at the door with notepad in hand, I make sure my answers are consistent.

"What were you doing in your house that night?"

The real answer is that I went there to escape everything and to mourn Justice and Grandma Betty, but I don't expose myself to them.

"I'm not sure," I lie. "I just wanted to see my house."

"You said that you don't know how the fire started even though you were there at the time. Can you explain?"

"I had fallen asleep. I was exhausted. I didn't hear anything, and when I woke up, the fire had already started."

"The police suspect vandalism. Do the authorities have any idea how the fire started or who started it?"

"I don't know," I answer glumly.

Truthfully, the police don't seem too interested in finding suspects, probably because the tornado had ruined so much of the house anyway. It was already going to be rebuilt.

I haven't told anyone about what Nate and his friends did. They hadn't intentionally tried to kill me. My theory is that one of them dropped a cigarette on the ground and the chemical stain in the hall caught fire. Besides, the last thing I want to do is go up against Nate and his cronies in a court of law. I have everything back the way I want it, for the most part anyway.

"You weren't able to get out. Who saved you?"

"My best friend, Mikayla."

"It's rumored that there is a connection between the two of you, something deeper than friendship. She said that she knew something bad would happen to you that night, so she went over to your house. Can you tell me more about that?"

"I don't know what to tell you." What can I tell the public about this when I don't even understand it?

"This all happened on the same night that your grandmother woke from

her nearly eight-week coma. How did you react to that?"

Isn't it obvious how I would react? Even though I think their question is beyond ridiculous, I serve up something sweet, "I was thrilled and relieved. I was so glad she finally woke up. I never thought she would."

I don't tell any of them that I believe I actually had a part in saving Grandma Betty's life. What I did the night before she woke up is my secret. After what happened, I believe that my birthmark does have some power after all, or, at the very least, I have pull with the Big Man Upstairs.

While people are fascinated with the story of the fire and Grandma Betty's medical miracle, Frank is completely fascinated by Grandma Betty. Three days after she woke up and the hospital finally released her, he drove us both to his house to live, a plan that neither Grandma Betty nor I protested. With the amount of boxes that were moved into his large house and the care in which he took to make us feel at home (stocking his fridge, buying new linens for all the beds, and repainting the bedrooms some of Grandma Betty's favorite paint colors), it was fairly obvious that this move was premeditated. Permanence is what he had in mind.

We hadn't been in the house for two minutes when he pulled a small, velvet box out of his pocket, got down on one knee in front of both of us, and said that life was too short to put this off for one more second and then asked for Grandma Betty's hand in marriage. She looked at me first, clearly surprised by Frank's impromptu proposal, and I smiled my blessing. She gave hers to Frank with a tremulous and happy, "Yes."

When we sat around Frank's dining room table that first night, a new makeshift family, intoxicated by the happiness of having Grandma Betty back in our lives so that nothing about our new situation felt awkward, I joked that this was the stuff of romance novels.

"Wouldn't Danielle Steel love to get her hands on this story?" I asked with a pompous smirk.

We all laughed, but behind my humor lurked something darker.

Joy is a tidal wave, and the ride started the night of the fire when Frank drove me to the hospital and I hugged Grandma Betty and she hugged me back for the first time in almost two months. Joy can take you on the ride of your life, but what happens when the crest of that wave breaks and you are crushed beneath the weight? The undertow drags you far out to sea, holds you there, and smothers you. The initial relief and overwhelming rapture that I felt have been replaced with a numbness that has matured into a subtle, frayed melancholy.

One of the symptoms is inertness. The ants in my pants that have always plagued me have all but disappeared. Yes, I'm inclined to motion, but it's habitual and premeditated. I run, wander aimlessly on walks, and swim at the gravel pit, but the motion lacks authenticity and spontaneity.

I'm in a conscious coma. I'm on idle, and my engine revs with nowhere to go. I still indulge in my hobbies. I read, memorize trivia cards, and help Frank paint more rooms in his house (Breezy Berry, Rocky River, and Golden Treasure, all colors chosen by Grandma Betty), but inevitably, I end up stopping for no reason and staring into space and thinking about *you-know-who*. Absence doesn't make the heart grow fonder; it breeds obsession.

I'm thinking about Justice right now as I sit at Frank's dining table pushing around a glass of orange juice. I squint at the microwave to read the time. It's early, barely six in the morning. Most kids my age would be settling in for another four or five hours of slumber, but one of the side effects of unrequited love is insomnia. Another is weight loss. I'm becoming a freckled toothpick. It's doubtful that Justice is suffering at all. He's probably back together with Nikki, and maybe they're even engaged again. Maybe she's pregnant with his child. Maybe they've rented a small apartment with a balcony. Get a grip, I tell myself. Even though it feels like six years, it's only been a week.

I hear the shuffle of slippers in the hallway. Grandma Betty appears. Already she has a knitting needle tucked behind an ear. She gives me a worn, sympathetic smile. Standing behind me, she rests her hands on my shoulders, bends, and kisses me on top of my head. "Up early today."

Her voice betrays her ordeal; she still sounds like a hard-core Camel addict.

I shrug sleepily. "Were you knitting?"

She nods. "I want to replace everything that tornado took away." She fills a mug with hot water and then places it in the microwave. "I think it's time I finally go see what's left of the house, and then I want to take a tour of downtown."

"Really?"

"I need to."

"Are you feeling up to it?"

"I have more energy than I know what to do with. I took a very long nap." Grandma Betty smiles at her wry joke. The microwave beeps. She removes her mug and dips her tea bag into it.

"I would like it if you came along."

I make a guttural sound that clearly indicates I have better things to do. "I've seen enough of it already."

She sits down across from me. The intensity of her stare terrifies me. I've been dreading this. My stomach knots, because I know what she is going to ask. I'm surprised she hasn't asked it sooner.

"Where were you that night?"

The question seems to make the room larger, and all I want to do is shrink.

When I don't answer, her eyes tear up in anger and hurt. "I looked all over for you, Cane. I was just about to go outside. I remember that much, but the rest," she stops and makes a scramble motion with her fingers, "I can't remember."

Ashamed, I study the checked pattern on the stained tablecloth. "I'm sorry."

"I know," she sighs shakily.

We both glance out the window. The sun, blood red, has curdled the air.

"I was waiting for him, but he never came." My admission drags my thoughts back to him. Why can't I be satisfied with having Grandma Betty back? Why do I need Justice as well?

Grandma Betty reaches across the table and takes hold of my arm, rotating it until the palest part of my forearm is exposed. I've connected some freckles to make his name. Since I couldn't risk having it fade, I've done it repeatedly, making the skin tender.

"Oh, honey." Her expression is raw with grief.

I yank my arm away and cradle it against me like it's broken. "He doesn't love me," I state with defiant petulance.

Grandma Betty shakes her head. "If you feel this bad about it, chances are, he does."

"Please." I close my eyes. "Don't say that."

Grandma Betty reaches up and takes her knitting needle from its perch behind her ear. She taps it against the table and changes the subject.

"What color do you want me to use for your afghan? I can pick up any color you like."

"I'm sorry I left, Grandma Betty," I blurt. The remorse makes my throat swell. "I never should have gone out."

Grandma Betty places her hand on my forearm and gently rubs her fingertips back and forth across the spot where I've tried to scar my skin with his name. "All I could think about that night was what I would do if I lost you." Tears roll down her face.

The image of her lying limp and unconscious in the wet grass that night comes back to me. Pressing my hands against my face, I bow my head in shame.

She takes a napkin and hands it to me.

"I'm sorry," I say again helplessly and push the napkin under my nostrils.

"I forgive you. We're both okay now, and that's all that matters."

I don't get a chance to tell her that I felt the same way she did that night, that if I had lost her, I wouldn't know what to do, because Frank walks into the kitchen wearing a ridiculous, lopsided grin, his lips sticking slightly to his dentures.

He bends down and gives Grandma Betty a kiss on the cheek, and then does the same to me. I swear, even with aftershave and fresh breath, he still smells like film. Grandma Betty must notice this since she can smell everything. Doesn't it bother her?

"What are you girls talking about this early in the morning?"

Grandma Betty wipes at her cheeks and winks at me.

"Oh, nothing."

Frank rubs his hands together and slips an apron over his head. "How about I make my girls a fancy breakfast?"

My girls. Is there such a thing as an instant family? Apparently there must be, because as soon as Grandma Betty came out of that coma, Frank dashed back to his house with us, threw a ring on Grandma Betty, and *scha-zam*, instant family.

After a hearty breakfast of pancakes, eggs, sausage, and bacon, all prepared by Frank who is an excellent cook and has made spoiling Grandma Betty and me a hobby, Frank invites me to go downtown with them and then to Clinton. He says he wants to buy me a fancy new bike. I decline politely. Smurfette can't be replaced.

When Frank and Grandma Betty leave, I immediately regret not going. My mind has turned into a fickle creature, and now that I have no job (I haven't spoken to the Schaeffers since Grandma Betty woke up, even though Frank and Grandma Betty have) my day has no jumping-off point.

After aimlessly wandering through Frank's enormous Colonial that is filled with antiques, I take a seat on one of the plush chairs in front of the expansive picture window in the living room. The property is situated on top of a hill providing an outstanding view of the countryside. On top of an ornate marble table sits a large pair of binoculars that Frank and Grandma Betty are fond of using. I pick them up and place them against my face, twisting the dials until the scenery comes into focus. I can see for miles. I scan the countryside looking for something interesting, but the deer and wild birds are hiding in this heat.

On one of the roads, about a mile out, I see a van making its way to the house, the same van that I stole approximately seven nights ago. Panic jolts me like an electrical shock. Why is she coming here?

Dropping the binoculars on the table, I pace the room. By the time the van door slams, my hair is separated and braided into two perfect plaits.

When the doorbell rings, I stick my fingers in the braids and work my way down, undoing them and flinging my hair back over my shoulders.

When I open the door, Jelly Roll attempts to smile but at the last second opens her mouth too wide, so that her mouth forms a rectangle. She bypasses a formal greeting by jumping right into conversation. "How are Frank and Grandma Betty?"

"Fine."

"Are they home?"

"No."

She looks satisfied with my answer. "First off," she points her finger at me, "I want you to know that Samson didn't put me up to this. I'm here because I need to clear things up. Things have gotten out of hand. I've never been particularly candid with you before, so I'm just going to get this out in the open right now." Without a gentle pause or hesitation, she blurts, "I don't like you. I'm sure that comes as no surprise to you."

Plenty of people don't like me, but as far as I know, they're all under the age of eighteen and most say it behind my back. No one has ever said it to my face, not even Mikayla who I fought with for years. Reactively, my hands form fists and my toes curl.

"What did I ever do to you?"

Jelly Roll uses her pinkies and wipes at the corner of her mouth, sloughing off dead skin and coagulated lipstick. Her laugh, haughty and choppy, makes my ear drums itch.

"You've never done anything. It has nothing to do with you. You look like your mother, you know. But," she stops and regards my face, then stares at the doorjamb as she finishes, "your personality is your father's."

She says all of this like she's delivering an apology, and I know this is all I'll get. I guessed all along that she hated me because I looked like my mother, but I never considered she might not like me because I reminded her of my father.

"Is that the only reason you came, to tell me what you think of me?"

"I've brought the rest of your things. There were a couple of boxes that Frank didn't get." She turns and waves at Jeremy who sits in the front seat. He opens the door and moves to the back of the van.

"I'm also here to offer you your job back." Jelly Roll crosses her arms and sticks out one of her large hips.

My laugh turns into a confused stammer. "W-What?"

"Our relationship shouldn't interfere with business. You can work for us."

"It's Samson that wants me back. Am I right?" Samson might not have put Jelly Roll up to this trip, but I know the rehiring idea is his.

Jelly Roll pulls on the bottom of her iridescent shirt, a rayon material replete with shiny fishlike scales, and throws back her shoulders.

"Hey," Jeremy says when he comes to the door.

"Hi." I smile awkwardly and step aside so that he can carry the boxes into the entry. He stacks them carefully.

"Thanks," I mumble.

He shrugs. When he leaves for the van to retrieve another, Jelly Roll cranes her head so that she can see inside the house. Frank is probably the only other person in town with a house that comes close to rivaling hers. I can see her mentally comparing it to her own.

Jeremy comes back with an awkward box that's bigger than me. I don't remember leaving anything like it at their house.

"That's not mine," I say, shaking my head.

"It has your name on it. My dad said to make sure I gave it to you."

Jelly Roll looks at the box suspiciously. "What's in there, Jeremy?"

"I don't know."

"Didn't your father say?"

"No."

"Is it a gift from him?" she asks with sugar-coated indignation.

Jeremy shrugs. Exasperated, Jelly Roll sighs and with her ring finger delicately swipes the layer of sweat that has emerged on her upper lip.

When he's finished placing it on the floor in the foyer, Jelly Roll looks at her son and says, "I'll be just a minute."

He half waves and hurries back to the van.

"So, are you coming back or not?"

"Do I have to answer right this minute?"

Jelly Roll raises her jaw slightly, revealing white crevices where the sun can't reach. If someone managed to take a rolling-pin to her body and flatten out the skin, she would be marked like a zebra.

"Not right this minute, but soon." She takes one last look inside, tugs on the bottom of her shirt, and leaves.

In the kitchen I find a big knife and set to work slicing open the mystery package that resembles a coffin and appears to open like one, with all but one side taped. When I'm finished cutting my way through the tape and breaking all the seals, I tentatively lift the lid.

It's hard to describe how it feels when something you love comes back from the dead.

Smurfette

As gift-givers go, Grandma Betty's one of the best. If there was a gift-giving hall of fame, her name would be in the top ten.

The year that I turned five, I spent the better part of the summer and the majority of the autumn whining that I didn't have a tree house like Mikayla. I begged Grandma Betty to hire someone to build one for me. I told her it didn't even have to be in the trees, it could just be on the ground, as long as it had at least two windows, a full size door, and was made of real wood, just like Mikayla's. When Halloween came and went and the first snow started to fall, I finally gave up on my dream. I'm sure this was a relief to Grandma Betty who told me that when it came to wanting something, I could be a horrible nuisance and that sometimes I made her so mad she wanted to spit.

When Christmas morning came that December, I bounded down the stairs and to my amazement discovered a tree house in the living room. I spent most of my Christmas vacation inside my miniature, wooden house with the vibrant red shutters and door. It didn't matter that it wasn't perched high in the trees like Mikayla's, because it was just as big and belonged to me.

At the time, I credited Santa, but a couple of years later when I discovered the fat guy with the white beard was a myth, I knew the elves had nothing to do with my beloved wooden house. It was all Grandma Betty's doing.

When I was nine, I found something new to obsess over. Cabbage Patch Dolls. It was a virtual Cabbage Patch daycare at school, as the girls in my class would parade around with their dolls, which always had cute outfits and fashionable names. The only girl who didn't own one, besides me, was Violet, the girl who had an aversion to bathing and smelled so unlike a flower that her name made no sense at all. Thankfully, Mikayla had four of them and often lent one to me, sparing me embarrassment.

Grandma Betty thought the whole Cabbage Patch craze was laughable and pathetic seeing as how she thought their faces looked weird. She also couldn't believe how much chaos those dolls incited, and when Christmas time came and mothers were fighting over them in stores, she said it was just horrible what the world was coming to. She was so opposed to buying the overpriced dolls that I thought I would never get one. As it turns out, I was wrong.

On my birthday that August, I woke up to Grandma Betty yelling surprise. When I managed to rub the sleep out of my eyes, I discovered not one, but two Cabbage Patch boxes perched on the end of my bed. Completely stunned, I was mute for the entire day. Grandma Betty said that the last time I was that quiet I had been crawling around in diapers.

Two years later, for my twelfth birthday, Grandma Betty outdid herself again. That was the year that I started to show an interest in trivia. I spent hours at the library looking things up in the encyclopedias and writing them down. In a few months time, I had filled an entire notebook with miscellaneous facts that I had learned. Grandma Betty was impressed with my commitment, and on the morning of my birthday when I came downstairs, I discovered an entire set of encyclopedias. She had found a way to bring the library to me!

Much to Grandma Betty's delight, I carried the set of books upstairs to my room right away and spent the entire morning opening each book and reading sporadic articles on topics ranging from Bengal tigers to rare diseases. It wasn't just the reading and facts that I loved, but the way each of those books felt in my hands, the way the spines creaked when I opened them, and the texture of the paper, cool and slick, beneath my fingertips.

I've been spoiled by Grandma Betty and have constantly received things that I adored and loved. Yet, the best gift wasn't given to me by her. It was given to me before I was even born.

Just after the fourth of July, weeks shy of my birth, when my mom's stomach had miles of stretch marks, my father brought home two gifts for his unborn children.

Grandma Betty and my mother, who were busy canning strawberry jam and red up to their elbows, laughed as my father walked through the back door with two children's bikes.

"Aren't they amazing?" He ran his hand over the frame of the bright blue bike, the one that would belong to me. "Just perfect. Red for our son, blue for our girl."

"Alex! Oh my gosh!" My mom sat heavily on a chair and sandwiched her belly with her arms. "Why not two stuffed animals or two blankets? That would have been simpler."

Grandma Betty pulled the pen out from behind her ear to write the date on some masking tape. She pressed it against the lid of the Mason jar, smoothing it out with her thumb. "They don't even have training wheels, and even bikes with training wheels are years off."

My father straddled the blue bike and sat gingerly on the flowered banana seat. "You guys don't have any vision. This is the future we are talking about. These bikes have longevity. This is something that will last years. They'll outgrow stuffed animals and blankets in no time at all."

"Don't be so quick to wish them grown. It goes too fast as it is," warned Grandma Betty.

My mother placed the tips of her swollen toes against the wheel and moved it back and forth. "They are adorable. I've never seen such shiny bikes, and I love the blue one! The flowers on the seat are so sweet. Our baby girl is going to love it."

"See, Mom," my father raised his eyebrows in an 'I told you so' fashion, "They'll love these bikes. They'll never want to get rid of them."

Grandma Betty wiped her sticky hands on a wet washcloth. "Just wait until they're teenagers-they'll be itching to get rid of them."

"No way," my father stood and put the kickstand down. "They'll keep these bikes forever."

My father was wrong about this. Lessons come hard and fast. People don't have permanence and neither do the things they own.

Grandma Betty learned this time and again, which is why I think she was quick to give away my brother's bike soon after the funerals. She said having that bike around was like being haunted by the ghosts of the past, present, and future. I've always treasured my bike, but those first few years when I was riding it, I would catch Grandma Betty looking at me on my bike and her eyes would follow the empty space right next to me. I could tell she was thinking about the red bike that should have been alongside me. Even though I loved Smurfette more than anything, I sometimes hated her. She was survivor's guilt incarnate.

Until Death Do Us Part

    The wedding was pieced together in less than three weeks. I'm still adjusting to the idea that Grandma Betty is getting married, and here I am, maid of honor, standing in front of Grace Lutheran Church holding a simple bouquet of lilies that were cut early this morning. Grandma Betty told me that if I lock my knees, I might faint, but, I'm having a hard time balancing on the high-heels, so I ignore her advice and press my knobby knees together.

    I prepare myself for a long, tedious service, where it is possible that I won't faint but quite possibly pass out from sheer boredom. Pastor Fry, who is infamous for his long-winded sermons that he delivers every Sunday and at funerals and weddings, pulls a fast one and barely speaks at all. He's probably in a rush to make sure that Frank and Grandma Betty are man and wife so that they don't have to live in sin one second longer. Before I know it, the vows have been spoken, the rings exchanged, and Frank and Grandma, now husband and wife, lean into each other and kiss.

    They're happy, and I'm happy for them, but I'm also mortified that they're lip-locked in front of family and friends. I've never actually seen them touch, let alone kiss. They even sleep in separate rooms, although I'm sure that ends tonight. I can't even imagine how grossed out I will be if I hear any sounds coming from their room. Just thinking about them having sex or even touching like Justice and I touched horrifies me. Their kiss seems to last longer than the whole ceremony, and I stare at the bright flower petals I'm holding, feeling my face ignite from my chin all the way to my scalp.

    Finally, they finish, and I breathe a hefty sigh of relief. The small gathering of family and friends continues to applaud, and my skin takes its time getting back to normal. When Grandma Betty turns toward me, I hand her bouquet back, and she gives me a quick peck on the cheek before linking arms with Frank. They walk down the steps together. Frank's eldest son, Ray, a military man with a sharp haircut and stiff lip, waits until his father and Grandma Betty are no longer visible before escorting me back down the aisle. Mikayla, sitting in the front row next to her mother and father, tilts her head back toward Frank and Grandma Betty and rolls her eyes in sympathy. I swallow a laugh; it's nice to have her on my side again. I've only just begun to realize how much I've missed her. Annette holds a hand to the base of her throat and smiles uncomfortably. Every time we look at each other, we're both thinking about the thing that no one else knows.

At the back of the church Grandma Betty, Frank, Ray, and I form a reception line. I've never given so many hugs at one time, and with everyone throwing their arms around me, I almost lose my balance. I slip off the ridiculous high heels and give each of my Achilles' tendons a good rub with the back of my hand; I wish Grandma Betty would have just let me wear my white Keds.

When Mikayla reaches the receiving line she leans in and whispers in my ear. "They were totally making out. *Disgusting!*"

"Tell me about it," I lament.

"You look amazing! You going to wear that to prom in the spring? You *totally* should."

"Maybe."

My navy dress hugs my upper body and flares out slightly just below my hips, but the heels are throwing me for a loop and so is my hair, which is piled up strategically on top of my head. With the hundred of bobby pins pushed against my scalp, I feel like a voodoo doll.

"You look stunning, Cane," says Annette, who stands just behind her daughter. "I just can't believe how grown up you look. You didn't do your hair by yourself, did you?" She reaches out and gently pushes at a loose, strand tucking it behind my ear.

At her touch, I flinch and then try to smooth my reaction with a smile. "No. Grandma Betty and I drove to Clinton this morning to have our hair and makeup done."

Annette's skin has a grayish cast to it. "You look amazing. If you'll excuse me." Her hand returns to her throat, and she turns and heads for the bathroom.

Mikayla links arms with me and pulls me off to the side. "You know how Frank and Grandma Betty are making out? Well, that's *nothing*. I'm about to be *publicly humiliated*."

My heart squeezes hard and gives my ribs a good whack. My saliva disappears.

"Why?"

"I'll talk to you at the reception." She raises her eyebrows and dramatically flips her blonde hair over her shoulder. "I've got plenty to tell you." She steps away from me and gives an upside down wave.

I'm more terrified than intrigued by what Mikayla may tell me, but I don't have time to dwell on it, because Samson and Jocelyn are next in line.

"Hi, Cane!" Jocelyn shouts. "Do you like my dress? It's blue, just like yours!" She twirls dramatically, making the fabric flare.

"I love it."

Samson holds his hands together awkwardly, his fingers tapping against each other. "Hi, Cane."

"Hi." Thank God Jelly Roll isn't with them.

"I heard Jenny Ryanne came to see you a couple weeks back. Any decision about the offer? We would love to have you back."

"We miss you!" Jocelyn chimes in. "I want you to come over and go swimming. Can you? Please?" she whines.

"Sure," I say hastily to appease her. I glance at Samson. "I'm not sure about working, though. Cross-country practice starts up on Monday."

"There's a job waiting when you want it." He puts his hands in his back pockets and regards me. "You look very pretty, so much like your mother."

"Thanks," I mumble gratefully and hastily change the subject. "Hey, I got your present. The bike is amazing. I've been meaning to call and thank you, but this week has been really busy. It must have taken you forever to fix it."

"Bike?" he asks, momentarily confused. "Oh," he says and shakes his head. "So that's what was in there. That makes sense."

"It wasn't from you?" I ask.

"No, not from me." He places his hands on Jocelyn's shoulders to stop her from doing another pirouette. He bends down, "That's enough, honey."

Jocelyn tucks her neck in like a turtle and pouts. "Does your dress do that, Cane?"

"I'm not sure. I haven't tried." I address Samson again. "Who was it from?"

Samson lowers his gaze before answering. "I think you already know the answer to that," he says deliberately. "He said to make sure you got it. I'll see you at the reception. Maybe you could save a dance for me?"

"What about me, Daddy?" Jocelyn pulls on Samson's blazer.

"Yes, you too."

"We need to take some pictures," Grandma Betty takes my hand.

How can I think about pictures when I just found out that Justice is the one who put Smurfette back together again?

After a series of predictable poses, we're on our way to the reception. Grandma Betty and Frank sit in the front of his car and behave oddly, like a pair of teenagers. They giggle, talk, and hold hands. I can only hope that once this day is over, they'll settle down and act like normal adults.

Ray and I sit in the back seat, and since we are separated by more than a generation, we obviously have *nothing* to say to each other. Even if I wanted to make small talk, something I'm no expert at, I couldn't because I can't relax around him. It's the military outfit and attitude; Ray's a hard-core marine. It makes me nervous, and I find that I stand at attention, and even sit at attention, when I'm around him.

The reception is at Frank's house (our house, but I still can't quite get used to saying that). He has a beautiful yard that's filled with immaculate and lush gardens, making it an ideal setting for a wedding reception. A rented white tent was set up this morning, and now it's filled with tables, music, and a lively crowd of guests who want nothing more than to celebrate.

When we walk through the tent opening, there's an explosion of applause and loud, obnoxious whistles, the kind that involve two fingers. I blush yet again, my skin a perfect match for the cabernet that sits on the tables. Mikayla would be better suited for the maid of honor gig; I had suggested it, but Grandma Betty thought I was joking.

Mikayla, who sits near the rear of the tent, gives me a small wave, as does Jocelyn who sits the next table over, only Jocelyn's waving more with her body than with her hand. She already has a Coke in hand; I wish Samson was more aware of his daughter's weight problem and sugar intake.

Once we're seated at the head table, I turn to Grandma Betty and tell her about Smurfette. "The bike was from Justice."

"Oh, yes. I know," she smiles and winks at Frank who is standing behind me talking to Ray.

"What?" I shake my head in confusion. "How did you know?"

She's too distracted to answer because the DJ is asking everyone to have a seat so that the best man and maid-of-honor can toast the newlyweds.

The guests quiet and take their seats, and the tent fills with the sound of silverware clinking against wine glasses. Frank and Grandma Betty oblige the crowd and lean in for a kiss. This is going to be a *long* night.

After the kiss, Ray stands, and places his hand on his father's shoulder before he begins.

Oh, crap. I'm next, and I can't even remember what I wanted to say. Useless facts are easy to memorize, but remembering a speech is an entirely different beast. I should have written down what I wanted to say. Ray will probably talk for a few minutes, so I'm sure I have plenty of time to rehearse in my head.

Ray holds the microphone with a stiff fist. "Thank you all for coming. I have to say that I never expected my father to find someone as special as my mom, but he has. I couldn't be happier for the two of you. Let's raise our glasses."

Not already. He can't be finished. What the hell am I going to say?

"Congratulations. Eat, drink, and be merry."

Eat, drink, and be merry? Lame, but who am I to judge? In less than three seconds, I'm going to make an absolute fool of myself. If my hair wasn't strapped to the top of my head, you can bet I would be braiding away. Instead, I've twisted the cloth napkin in my lap so tightly that it's no wider than a pencil.

Everyone looks at me, and as I stand up, the back of my high heel catches on the rung of the chair. I teeter, but thankfully don't fall on my face. Although, I do feel a preemptive blush coming on.

I look at Grandma Betty, who smiles at me sweetly. She said I didn't have to do this, but I had insisted, told her it was tradition and that I would be fine.

When Ray hands me the microphone, it feels slippery in my hands.

"Thank you for coming," I croak and then clear my throat. Everyone smiles reassuringly, but I can feel the uncomfortable prickle of sweat in my armpits. Trying to ignore the likelihood that my nice navy dress will have crescent-moon sweat rings, I forge ahead.

"I love Grandma Betty, but that goes without saying. The night of the tornado, I almost lost-" I stop, because my sinuses are burning and my throat's closing. I almost think I could cry. I can actually feel water in my eyes, but I won't let it happen now. When I take a deep shaky breath, Grandma Betty places her hand on my lower back. I continue with breathless nervousness, "Frank was there through everything. I know he's been an important part of Grandma Betty's life for a long time, and now I'm glad he is part of mine. Please raise your glasses."

I'm almost to the finish line. "A long life of love and happiness for Grandma Betty and Frank."

Everyone murmurs congratulations and then drinks. I raise my champagne flute, but it never quite reaches my lips, because I see *him*. He's here. He's standing in the back of the tent. In a matter of seconds, I go from amazement, to absolute joy, and then to blistering anger.

"That was wonderful, honey." Grandma Betty slips her cool fingers into my sweaty palm.

Even as I sit down, somewhat shakily, my eyes never leave Justice's. He watches me as carefully as I watch him.

"He's here," I whisper in shock and rub my forearm in response. His name has finally faded from my skin, but the scarring is below the surface.

Grandma Betty follows my line of vision. Her smile is one of relieved joy.

"Oh, that's good, I'm glad he could make it."

"Did you invite him?" I ask incredulously while still watching Justice, who has left his position at the tent entrance and sat down next to Samson.

"I did."

"Why?"

Grandma Betty reaches over and touches my cheek. "Because I knew it would make your night."

"But, this is your night."

"I'm not happy unless you are. I wanted you to have a guest at the wedding, so I called Samson and then got in touch with Justice."

"He wanted to come?" My greatest fear is that she bribed him with something.

"He said he would be honored."

"Why didn't you tell me?"

She tucks a gray curl behind her ear. "I love surprises."

I look over at Justice again, who happens to be wearing a dark suit that coordinates perfectly with my deep blue dress. Knowing Grandma Betty, she told him what color I would be wearing.

Due to my excitement and anticipation, I can't eat a thing. My stomach does the hula dance, so I forgo the dinner and sneak a few sips of champagne, but the bubbles only make the feeling in my gut worse.

When the dinner dishes have been cleared by the caterers, I thread through the crowd, sidetracked occasionally with well-wishers and finally arrive at Mikayla's table. I squat down next to her, trying to avoid eye contact with Mitch, who has just arrived, and with Annette, who has been looking at me strangely all evening. Does she think I'm going to spill the beans? If I was, I certainly wouldn't pick Grandma Betty's wedding as my venue.

I rest my elbow on the table and lean conspiratorially close to Mikayla. "He's here," I say in an octave lower than my normal voice, conveying the message with my tone and then my eyes. I've told her everything about Justice.

"Seriously? Where?"

"Samson's table," I say quietly.

She sneaks a peek and smiles with friendly wickedness. "He's here to rob the cradle." She raises her eyebrows several times and laughs.

"Whatever. He's only here because Grandma Betty invited him."

"I don't think she would have invited him if she knew *everything*."

When I told Grandma Betty about Justice, I omitted the intimate details. Not so sure she would be supportive if she knew that her granddaughter had been half-naked with an older man.

"What did you want to talk to me about?" I ask.

Mikayla glances covertly at her parents to make sure they are occupied and then places her hand on the back of my neck and yanks me toward her until my ear is right against her mouth.

"My mom is pregnant," she whispers dramatically.

My eyes widen in horror.

Mikayla releases me. "Disgusting, right?"

"Seriously." But, it's disgusting on a level that Mikayla knows nothing about. It's not that far of a mental stretch to figure out that there's a good chance that the baby inside of Annette belongs to Mustang Moron, especially considering Mitch has been away for almost the entire summer.

I'm trying to think of what to say to her when she steps on the tips of my toes and presses hard.

"Ow," I squirm and pull my foot away from her. "What?"

She opens her eyes wide and smiles at someone behind me.

"Hi, Justice," she says slickly, pushing her hair back from her face and at the same time grabbing my wrist.

"Hi."

His voice is deeper, sexier than I remember.

My heart beats fast in response. I stand up slowly and turn.

"Hey." I don't know if I should hug him, which is what I want to do, or offer a handshake, which seems like an incredibly stupid gesture given our history, so I do neither. My arms are locked across my chest, and I can barely make eye contact with him.

Mikayla nudges my back and cranes her neck around me so that she has a view of both of us. "Why don't you two go dance?" she suggests.

He regards the dance floor, hopelessly empty thanks to the tacky Kenny G background music.

"Why don't we save the dancing for later," he suggests. "Would you like to go for a walk with me?"

Mikayla raises her brows imperceptibly and smiles with the corner of her mouth. I shoot her a *wish me luck* look.

"Sure," I agree.

He walks behind me, and I'm acutely aware of his eyes on me and how my heart beats so wildly in my chest I actually feel like its motion could propel me off the ground.

As we exit the tent, I expect everyone to notice, especially Samson who knows more of what has transpired between us than Grandma Betty and has strictly forbidden it to go further, but no one takes a second glance.

When we are far from the din of the crowd, he finally says something.

"How have you been?" he asks tentatively.

"Just peachy," I quip sarcastically. "And you?" Instead of answering, he goes into Mr. Mute mode, and I roll my eyes. That is so like him. Negotiating the grass with heels is impossible, so I step out of my shoes, leaving them on the stone walkway. I feel more at ease, more like myself now that the pads of my feet are against solid, warm ground. We continue walking, making our way around the front of Frank's house to the backyard. I glance down between us and watch his hand, wishing he would reach out and take mine. I don't have enough courage to take his, not after he's already rejected me.

He hasn't yet answered my question, and I feel like we are dragging it between us. Does he hurt as much as I do? Does he know that he has run away with my heart and that I want it back? No. That's not what I really want; I just want his in return.

We slow down and then stop completely. I turn my face to his, prepared to verbally assault him and let him know where I stand. I'm going to tell him what an ass he is and how he's broken my heart, but when his blue eyes meet mine, I feel like gravity isn't working anymore. The amazing phenomenon of getting lost in a person's eyes doesn't seem that far-fetched when Justice is involved. I can't look away and neither can he.

Our bodies fold in toward each other until we stand facing each other so closely I'm reminded that Grandma Betty and Frank stood just like this at the altar. My eyes fall from his, and it isn't because I'm nervous or defeated. I'm merely trying to think of what I need to do to keep him by my side and in my life.

"You are so-" he stops and looks at some indistinct point on the horizon.

"It's an amazing night," he finishes.

I wonder if he was about to tell me that I'm amazing or beautiful, but he couldn't bring himself to say it.

He is right, though, it's a perfect evening and not just because we're here together. The sun is just about to slip away, and the moon has already turned on. The world around us buzzes as it prepares to tuck itself in for the night. The leaves on the trees whisper lazily. The crickets do a sound test, and the birds are indistinct shadows indulging in chaotic laps across the sky.

Something hums between Justice and me as well, and when he reaches out and takes one of my hands, I feel it being transferred between us in waves. Briefly, I close my eyes, and the world ripples beneath my feet.

"Do you think I'm amazing?" I ask. I want his approval and love more than anything else in the world.

"You are more than that."

His praise is sincere, but I can sense a resistance within him.

"Did you like the gift?" he asks.

"I loved it. My father bought me that bike before I was even born."

"I could tell that it meant something to you." His fingers squeeze mine and he says, "I'm so glad about Grandma Betty. Everything turned out the way that it should have."

His broad statement stirs the ashes of my anger. "*How can you say that? What about us?*"

"The situation got way out of hand."

"Why do you have to put it that way?" I ask indignantly. "We," I point to him and then myself, "aren't a *situation*, are we? I thought we were more than that."

"We are. You know that. I know that."

He sighs quietly and turns sideways, his expression gets complicated. He gazes out at the landscape. The skyline turns inky as the last strip of tangerine light fades.

"You still see me as a child, don't you?"

"You're fifteen."

"Actually, fifteen is just a technicality at this point. I'm sixteen in a matter of days."

"Cane," he shakes his head and lowers his chin to his chest. His eyebrows are scrunched together in consternation.

Just the way he speaks my name shatters my heart into irregular pieces. I can feel them floating around in my bloodstream and getting caught in the back of my eyes. There's a good chance that at the end of all of this, the dam behind my eyelids will finally break and flood the entire county. Can Savage survive two natural disasters in one summer?

"Maybe it wasn't such a good idea for me to come," he says repentantly. "This is just going to make it harder. On both of us."

Is he going to leave again? Is this it? As my heart slips lower, my legs follow, and I find myself slowly sinking, allowing gravity to pull me to the ground. Kneeling before him, I rest my hands on the front of my thighs. I expect him to walk away, but to my surprise, he kneels on the grass in front of me. Our eyes meet.

In the background there are sounds of applause and music, but I am not tied to any of it. I don't want to return to the celebration; I want to stay here with him and let the night collapse itself around, below, and above us.

"I love you," I say easily, believing that those words can mend everything together and secretly knowing that it isn't enough right now.

Reaching forward, I splay my hand and press it over his heart just like he had done to me on the grass beneath the ugly tree. Through his crisp, white dress shirt I can feel the rapid push of his heart against my palm. He moves his hand up to mine and gently takes hold of my wrist.

Words aren't exchanged. No promises are made or sealed with a kiss, but I swear we are both thinking *until death do us part.*

September 1992

Beggars Can't Be Choosers

Mikayla hasn't been a great conversationalist lately. I don't blame her. Nate dumped her, probably because he's terrified of what I know and what I might do. He's got a lot hanging over his head, and I'm the one who could drop the guillotine just like that. Not only is she dealing with her broken heart, but she's dealing with the idea of her mother giving birth. That is a hapless situation I know more about than I should. The secret I'm keeping could blow everything wide open. Sometimes I feel like I'm walking around with a grenade in my hand, and I'm constantly making sure that I don't pull the pin with the words that come out of my mouth.

Needless to say whenever Nate's name comes up, which is frequently since Mikayla has decided she wants to win him back, I tell her it's absolutely out of the question because he's a complete moron. Then, I scramble for another subject. Almost one hundred percent of the time, it's Justice.

He's all that I think about, and now that I have him on film, he's all that I watch. As a surprise for Grandma Betty, Frank had the wedding reception taped and then professionally edited. When I saw it for the first time and discovered there were quite a few shots of Justice, I was hooked. So, guess what I'm doing at two in the morning when I can't sleep? I'm watching the wedding tape.

My favorite scene is the one of Justice and me dancing. In the low lighting, our profiles are grainy, but that doesn't matter because I can see Justice's arms around me and his hands against my lower back. The scene lasts for less than ten seconds, but I have turned that time into hours with the pause and rewind button. I've watched it so often that I've memorized every nuance of our movement. I could recreate it blindfolded.

No doubt this makes me a complete geek, but I'll admit that there have been a few nights that I've snuck out of the house and stood in the spot where Justice and I danced. For the record, it actually makes me feel worse, because I'm not sure when or *if* I will ever get the chance to dance with him again. It's a reality I prefer not to consider.

I'm not naïve, and I don't plan on modeling my hopes and dreams after Disney animation. I don't *need* a guy to sweep me off my feet, but does it make me a weirdo if I *want* that? *Happily ever after* would be ideal, but I have a tendency to get carried away with the fantasy and go all vapid and lightheaded when I think about it. Mikayla assures me that it's only a matter of time before Justice and I end up together. She said that she watched us at the wedding and that she's never had a guy look at her the way that Justice looks at me.

Even though he's only said it once, I do believe Justice loves me. After all, he's the one that suggested we write letters to each other. I'm not pleased with the arrangement of four letters a month, since it may be a ploy to get me off his case, but I have to take what I can get. He may be breaking my heart in increments, but that remains to be seen. I wanted to go full steam ahead, but I didn't press the issue for obvious reasons, one being that I'm not in a favorable negotiating position. Even though I finally have a driver's license, I'm still hopelessly younger than him.

I'm not head-over-heels in love with the idea of *just* letters; I think it's archaic. Grandma Betty, however, thinks it's a fantastic idea. It's no wonder, because I think when she met Justice face-to-face at the wedding, she took some time to do the math. A little more than five fingers are all that's between us, but the physical differences make it worse. Damn Justice's muscles and facial hair. If only he was slightly scrawnier, maybe it wouldn't be so noticeable. Grandma Betty was more accepting of the idea when she was unconscious and hadn't yet met him in person.

She wouldn't support me dating a twenty-one-year old. If I tried, I would be locked in my room and forced to wear a chastity belt. Even Justice doesn't support us dating. I should be wearing a t-shirt that says, "I had a summer romance, and all I got was a lousy letter." Only I haven't even gotten one of those yet.

I'm not convinced Justice will hold up his end of the bargain. As for me, I've already broken the rules. I've written him every day since the wedding, but I haven't sent all the letters just yet. I plan on doing that this morning. Hopefully, there will be a letter waiting for me. If there isn't, I'm going to have to break another rule and call him. What's he going to do, *arrest me*? I'm the one who's jailbait.

Keeping my mind off Justice isn't easy, but I have distractions. I've been busy running cross-country, studying, and my social life, thanks to Mikayla, has been remarkable. My popularity has soared, but I've clipped my own wings by not getting too involved. It's amazing how members of the BOMMB squad clamor for my attention and talk to me constantly. Do they notice that I don't bother talking to them all that much? Is that what makes me more appealing, my careless attitude towards them and my status? The guys (the ones without the pocket protectors and body odor) have also taken notice that I exist and that my name is Cane, not brainiac-freckle-freak. I've had several run-ins with Nate, and because he knows that I hold all the cards, he's been sweet as pie. That's not to say he doesn't still despise me.

If Nate saw me right now, he might consider another hit and run. Despite the fact that I now own a brand new royal blue Chevy Cavalier, a sixteenth birthday present from Frank that upset Grandma Betty (Frank didn't tell her about it) and also made Mikayla and all my other friends drool with jealousy, I'm pedaling out to the Schaeffer farm on Smurfette. I've been so wrapped up in the freedom of having a license and in the glory of owning my own car that Smurfette hasn't seen the light of day in weeks.

With only a quarter mile left to go, I'm having second thoughts about the plan that I've concocted. Will I regret my decision? Would my father be upset if he knew what I was going to do? Would Justice be upset about it? After all, he had taken all that time to restore her; he told me he had called several bike places just to get all the right parts. Knowing that the two men I love most have had a hand in preserving this bike, I should feel attached to it, but I don't, not anymore.

As I approach the Schaeffer driveway, my second thoughts dry up. I've moved forward, and I need to part with things that belong in the past.

Unfortunately, the first person I see is Jelly Roll, who has her arm stuck in the mailbox at the corner of the driveway. She pulls out the envelopes and flips through them. Predictably, she sports a sparkly outfit. The spandex orange shirt, with black shiny trim is horribly tight; her breasts are squashed and her midriff looks like rolls of Playdough. The pants, sporting the reverse color scheme, are at least looser, but not loose enough to let her thighs breathe. She looks like an enormous, misshapen gourd.

As she pushes the mailbox shut and slams the plastic flag back into a horizontal position with the corner of a magazine, she spots me.

"What are you doing here?" she asks loudly in surprise and suspicion. "You want your job back, is that it? You could probably talk to Samson about that. I think he's in his office."

"I came to see Jocelyn."

Jelly Roll makes a noise that sounds like air escaping a bike tire and shakes her head as if she has long hair. She plants her hands on her hips. The mail she carries juts out at an odd angle from her body.

"She wanted to go swimming with you before school started. You were with her all summer. Naturally, she grew attached to you. You should have figured that out and spent more time with her."

"I know."

Jelly Roll stalks down the driveway toward the back of the house, and I follow silently in her path. When we arrive at the iron fence that surrounds the pool and the back entrance, I get off Smurfette and carefully position her. I take hold of one of the posts adjacent to the gate and brace myself for the rest of Jelly Roll's lecture.

"You didn't hold up your end of the bargain," she reminds me sharply. "She asks about you constantly."

"I haven't had time." The excuse is lame, but I haven't wanted to come here for obvious reasons.

"What do you want with her anyway?"

"To give her something."

"You can't just waltz in and out of her life."

Despite the fact that I can't stand Jelly Roll, she has a point. "I don't plan on doing that. I'm already a part of it."

Jelly Roll sniffs and adjusts the orange spandex around her middle exposing a roll of white fat. "I think she's in the family room. You wait here while I get her."

She slams the gate, and in the process nearly pinches my fingertips. Somehow, with her evil radar, she knows that I'm glaring at her. She stops and turns around, eyeing me suspiciously.

"Don't break her heart, Cane. I mean that."

I won't break her heart, but I'm considering kicking your ass. Life would be so much more entertaining without censorship. I bite the tip of my tongue and nod graciously. While I'm waiting, Samson comes out of the large barn. He waves and walks over.

"Good to see you, Cane."

"You too."

"Glad you stopped by."

I nod and watch the back door, hoping Jocelyn will come out so I can get out of here. Not that I really have a tenable reason, but I'm kind of pissed at Samson. I've tried to analyze it, but as much as I can figure, I'm simply angry at him for being married to Jelly Roll. How can he stay with that shrew of a woman? How can he stay with someone who hates me so much?

There's that, and then there's also the fact that he busted me and Justice. What would have happened if he hadn't?

Samson props his boot up against the fence. "How's Betty getting along? Her and Frank happy?"

"She's fine. They're fine."

More than fine. I'm nauseated by all the kissing and hugging that goes on in the house. It's a painfully embarrassing experience to witness your grandma making out.

"It's amazing what she's been through. The reporters still hounding you guys or has it eased up?"

"It's better, but *Women's Day* magazine called and they want to do an article about the whole thing. I'm not sure Grandma Betty is going to go for it. She's tired of telling everyone what happened." And so was I for that matter.

I've repeated it so many times at school, for both teachers and classmates, that it now has a folk tale spin to it. Occasionally, I embellish just to see people's reactions when I tell them that I was actually lifted up in the air by the tornado and carried for over a mile. Or, sometimes, I go with the Wizard of Oz version and tell them that our entire house was lifted off the ground and ended up in a cornfield. If you can believe it, the one about me traveling inside the tornado was an easier sell.

"What have you been up to?"

"School. Cross-country."

"Your dad was a fantastic runner."

"That's what Grandma Betty always says."

"I saw in the paper that you ran a six minute mile the other week. That's pretty impressive. From the sounds of it, looks like the team is a sure thing for state. You guys might even take the title." Samson holds on to the rim of his hat with both hands and pulls it a fraction lower. "I would like to come watch you sometime and bring Jocelyn if that's okay. She wants to be a runner like you."

Holding a grudge against a man like this is impossible. He's too nice. I know why my father loved him. "Sure, that would be cool."

"You have a home meet next Saturday?"

"Yeah."

"We'll be there."

Samson drags his boot off the fence and onto the concrete. "How's Justice?" he asks with fatherly wariness.

"Fine, I guess."

"We talked a bit at the reception, but we didn't have much of a chance to catch up." Samson looks pointedly at me. "You two disappeared for awhile," he says in a tone that lectures.

"Nothing happened," I say defensively.

Samson lowers his chin to his chest, but his eyes stay locked on me. I look away, because it isn't completely the truth. Things never got overtly physical (even though I wanted them too), but it was emotionally heady. The blush that creeps up my neck and stains every part of my light skin suggests something more lascivious, and I rush to minimize. "We're just going to write letters to each other," I say, sounding every bit the sullen teenager that I am.

"I love my nephew, but I don't think you two should be together, at least not now. Letters are a good idea."

"I guess."

No, they're not. Letters suck. It's a miserable arrangement, but beggars can't be choosers, right?

The screen door is thrown open and slammed shut; Jocelyn barrels toward the fence. Samson opens the gate for his daughter.

"Cane! You came to see me!"

"I have a present for you."

"You do?" Jocelyn throws herself against me and winds her arms around my middle. Her breath smells of stale Coke and Little Debbie treats. If this girl is ever going to get healthy, I'm going to have to spend more time with her.

"I came to give you this." I take a step back and do my best Vanna White impression, and it's not great considering I've spent years watching *Wheel of Fortune*. I should be much better at it.

"You're giving me your bike!" squeals Jocelyn.

Samson's eyes widen. "You really want to part with it?"

"I can drive now, so I don't really need it anymore. I thought Jocelyn would like it."

"I love it!" proclaims Jocelyn who jumps up and down and claps her hands.

"Take it for a ride, then." I take the handle bars and wheel it toward her.

She snatches it from me and takes off. Samson and I watch her zip around the concrete driveway and head around one of the barns.

"I'm surprised that you're letting that bike go, considering the history and who gave it to you."

"Justice didn't really give it to me."

Samson folds his hands in prayer form and leans back against the fence, propping his heel against the bottom rung. "I'm not talking about Justice. I know who gave you that bike," he says quietly and then smiles at his daughter who races by and calls a greeting.

"Look at me, guys! This bike is so cool!" Then she's gone again, this time circling the largest barn and then heading out through the large manicured yard, zooming around trees and bushes.

I put up my hand, intending to wave, but my arm juts up too far so that it looks as if I want to ask a question. I do want to ask Samson something. How did he know that my father gave me this bike? I would say something, but my throat is clogged with a lump so big it would scare a gallon of Drano away.

Samson clears his throat and wipes at his jaw with the back of his hand. He looks down at me briefly, and it's a struggle to keep my face free of emotion.

"She has a bike, so if you change your mind," he suggests casually.

"No. It's hers to keep," I say firmly. "I should get going."

"Sure. We'll see you at the meet next weekend."

"Yeah, see you then." I turn and high tail it out of there in a feverish sprint.

About halfway back to Frank's house, I'm astounded to discover that my cheeks are wet and the top of my shirt is soaked. I'm upset, but I don't think my snot could make this big of a mess. Is my nose running? Am I bleeding? Has something happened?

Trembling, I raise my hands up and put them on my face. *I'm actually crying*. I'm bawling like an infant. It's so intense that I have to stop running. Years without shedding one tear, and now my face is molting! *What the hell is wrong with me? Is this about the bike?*

Snot streams out my nose and my eyes spurt water faster than Old Faithful. I'm convinced that this is a nervous breakdown in its infancy. Something inside of me has finally snapped, and the bike must have set it off. After everything that's happened this summer, I've finally lost it.

I duck into a corn field off County N and crouch to the ground, grabbing two fistfuls of dry dirt. The cornstalks hover over me, offering both protection and judgment. They talk amongst themselves; their conversations grow increasingly passionate as a light breeze becomes a gust of wind. I can't decide if they're trying to tell me something or if they're simply arguing amongst themselves. When the wind ceases, there's a sudden onset of uncomfortable silence; apparently, they have nothing more to say to each other or to me.

Squatting in a field and grabbing dirt screams crazy chick, and even if I am having a nervous breakdown, which is entirely possible, I don't want to project that kind of image. I force myself to stand up and start walking, although, admittedly it's more of a stagger since I'm still weeping profusely.

I haven't taken time to replay the entire summer. Can you blame me? Sure, I love to hit the rewind button on things that I want to see, like Justice and me dancing, but I avoid the memories of all the horrible things. I plod my way through them until they're over, and then, for me, it's finished, or at least I thought so until now.

In real life, the kind of life where tornadoes whiz over my head and destroy my house and almost kills the person I love the most; the kind of life with messed up, possibly unrequited love; the kind of life where someone attempts to run me over because I know a secret; the kind of life where I nearly perish in a fire; in *real life* there isn't a spot where *The End* pops up and the credits role. A delightful, satisfactory resolution that makes me smile and sigh with contentment eludes me. Even when ordeals end, they aren't really over. Where is the *justice* in that?

I've tried not to think about all the gory details, and now I'm paying for it. I've carried all these things along with me, pushed them down, and now they've gone all psychotic Jack-in-the-Box on me. They've popped back up and are shaking their fists at me, demanding my attention.

I'm still crying, and it seems that I won't be stopping any time soon. I stumble through the cornfield, nearly blind because my hair, sweaty and wet, hangs in my eyes. I half-heartedly push it out of my face, but it falls right back. If I had scissors right now, I swear I would hack all of it off, right to the scalp.

The thought of a pointed object appeals to me. Bloodletting comes to mind. I want to take scissors to everything and everyone around me. Nate and Annette would be first; how could they have been so incredibly stupid? Haven't they heard of birth control? Jelly Roll would be next on my list.

Is this what losing it feels like?

I stumble and almost fall when the ground takes a sharp dip downward, and the rush of adrenaline temporarily slows my tears. It occurs to me that I must have walked quite a ways. In the maze of corn, I can see only the polished, azure September sky and desiccated crops. I've lost all sense of direction, although it's debatable whether I had any in the first place. I've been so engrossed in my meltdown, it would be impossible to find my way back to the road. With an angry screech that borders on hysteria, I hack my way through the rest of the field, arms swinging madly in both sorrow and anger, which I'm beginning to think are inseparable emotions. You can't have one without the other.

My arm and legs are sufficiently scraped and scratched from my impromptu and irrational voyage. I'm tempted to rest here, to lay on the damp, cool soil and wait for night to spread itself over me. I only entertain this thought for a brief second, because somewhere behind me I can hear the persistent, diesel rumble of farm equipment. Death by combine isn't something I relish, and so I gather speed and run.

The field ends abruptly, and after being surrounded on all sides by bars of dried corn, the open air feels like a jailbreak. In front of me, not more than a few hundred yards, is the stream that borders the forest preserve. I plod through the overgrown grass, waist-high weeds, and cattails. Folding my upper body forward and picking up one leg and then the other, I slip through the cracked, split rail fence that smells of moss, age, and sun. The stream, although wide, trickles lamely; the summer drought has taken its toll.

On the sandy shores of the stream I see a remnant of the fireworks celebration, a bottle rocket stick, once red, that the sun has bleached to faint pink. Unsurprisingly, my thoughts track back to that night with Justice, and my eyes scan the countryside and locate the hill and the tree. How many times have I found myself here when I had no intention of coming? My kinship with the tree is deeply rooted in the past and the night that we both share.

I sprint down the sandy shores, through the shallow stream and then cross over the broken down railroad tracks that are no longer used. Out of breath, I reach the top of the hill and I rest; I press my palms against the ugly tree, allowing it to support my weight.

When I can finally breathe normally I turn and sit, with my back pressed against the base of the trunk. Unbelievably, I'm still crying. I must be making up for lost time. I don't know if it's the shift in perspective or because I'm at the place where I always feel things make better sense, but it occurs to me that I'm grieving. Giving away Smurfette, giving away a piece of my childhood, set something in motion. I couldn't stop it even if I wanted to.

In grief, there is a broad, flat sense of isolation, and all of my five senses are involved in the process, which is why it makes sense that I don't hear her approach. Although, part of me knew that she would find me, that she would sense something was wrong. Ever since the fire, the connection between us has strengthened.

Mikayla hasn't seen me cry since we were toddlers. Embarrassed, I can't look at her. She must understand, because she sits on the opposite side of the tree.

When she's settled, she says, "I knew you would be here, don't ask me how. Just did."

When are the tears going to stop anyway? I swipe at my cheeks with my hands, leaving streaks of dirt. "It's all caught up to me. Just, just...," I pause and try to take a normal breath, but it's still comes out wobbly. "Everything," I finish weakly.

"You going to be okay?" she asks.

"I will be." I wipe my face again, this time using my shirt. "You always see me at my best."

She sneaks a peek around the tree and angles her body toward me. "You look one hundred percent better than my mom, who is almost always puking or crying since she and my dad are still fighting. I don't know what the hell is going on between them. I thought this new baby thing would make them both happy. You've been around enough to see what's going on, what do you think?"

"I don't know," I respond miserably and then deliberately look away from her.

Every time this subject comes up, I'm waging an internal moral battle. *Tell my best friend that her mother is most likely pregnant with Nate's baby or don't tell.* Can you hurt someone by trying to protect them?

Mikalya scoots around the tree, so that now we sit side-by-side. She stretches out her long legs and pries off each of her white Keds with her perfect toes. "Whatever. All I know is that something weird is going on."

It's frightening to think that in six months the stork could be the one to give it all away. If that baby comes out with alligator eyes and a cocky smile, it won't be that hard to solve the equation.

"Smurfette is gone," I say casually, even though I can feel the density of the words inside my stomach. "I gave her to Jocelyn."

"No way." Mikayla shakes her head in disbelief. "I honestly thought you would never get rid of that thing. Why?"

I rake my hands through my tangled hair. Opening my eyes wide, I stare at Mikayla, doing my best to imitate Norman Bates. *"We all go a little mad sometimes."*

Mikayla rolls her eyes. "So true. But, I have something that will cheer you up. No, scratch that. Actually, something that will make everything better." My lips pucker and curl at the edges, revealing my doubt.

Mikayla raises her eyebrows in response. "Don't you know that I have my ways?" She reaches into the back pocket of her jean shorts and produces an envelope. "Stopped by your house earlier. Saw this on the counter. Grandma Betty said to take it since I would probably see you before you got home."

My heart picks up speed and pounds so hard I can feel the pressure in my teeth. Did he actually send me a letter before I sent him one?

"Open it!" she demands. "God, I've been waiting all afternoon to give it to you."

I take it from her and slide my finger under the top, slowly breaking the seal. The sound of the paper ripping sets off a fear in the pit of my stomach; this could be the official end. *Dear Cane, I've decided it's best if we stay friends.* Am I prepared for that?

Instead of paper, Justice has written on a napkin, one that he saved from Grandma Betty's wedding.

Dear Cane,

Letters were my idea, weren't they? What was I thinking? Just letters? I have a plan for us, but it may take some time. Can you wait about two years?

My heart swells to twice its size; my smile starts on the inside and moves to my face.

"So?" Mikayla asks expectantly. "What did he say?"

I line up the corners of the napkin, crease it, and press it to my chin where it absorbs what remains of my tears. "Exactly what I wanted to hear."

October 1992
Epilogue

The summer kicked the bucket almost a month ago, and from my vantage point up on the hill the rate at which the leaves are dropping suggests that autumn may expire sooner than I would like. Yet today, the sun sits at its zenith and infuses the air with unseasonable warmth, making me nostalgic for the turbulent months that took me on the ride of my life.

I've settled into my new existence just fine. Living with Frank and Grandma Betty is the closest I've ever had to a family unit. It's odd that Mikayla is actually jealous of my small family when I've spent so many years being jealous of hers. Not that I can blame her; the situation with Annette and Mitch has gone from bad to worse. Mikayla lives with constant volatility, and I recognize a tailspin when I see one. I don't have much confidence that they'll be able to pull out of it. As Annette's middle grows larger, the secret she carries eats up space in their house, dominating everything. The birth of that child could be the death of that family. I only hope that Annette gets wise and tries her hardest to put things back together again. I'm not sure how she should go about doing that, but that's her problem.

As for the part I play in the drama, keeping my mouth shut doesn't mean I'm culpable for anything. When I finally broke down and told Grandma Betty the story, and even shared it with Justice, both of them reassured me that I didn't have a hand in what Annette did, and so I can't right her wrongs or police her actions. Logically, I know this, but I still struggle with it, because my best friend's heart is on the chopping block.

Certain chapters in my life are finished, and surprisingly, I'm not freaking out. When I drive by my old house on Scott Road that's finally finished being rebuilt and see the *For Sale* sign in the front yard, I don't feel a pang of melancholy, nor do I feel compelled to sneak in and take a look. Maybe it's because I'm perfectly content in Frank's house. Grandma Betty always says it's the people that make a home, not the house.

I have a new appreciation for letting things go and moving on. Now that Samson and Jocelyn have become permanent fixtures in my life (they've come to almost all of my cross-country meets much to the dismay of Jelly Roll), I see Smurfette on a regular basis since Jocelyn feels it's absolutely necessary to take her everywhere. Hard to believe I don't get misty-eyed when I see that bike. However, I am prone to tearing up when Samson tells me stories about my father, like how he and my dad used to camp on this very hill when they were kids. My connection to this place makes more sense to me now.

While I've mastered the art of letting go of things (I finally burned those boxes that I had packed up this summer), I can't say the same for people. No matter what happens I will never let go of Justice. Grandma Betty says that first loves can be tricky; what she's implying is that it won't last forever. I don't try to explain what I know to be true. Justice and I are meant to be together. Love can't be defined or quarantined. It's infinite. It's abstract. What Justice and I have belongs only to us.

Because I've learned that talking about Justice usually means lectures from Grandma Betty, Frank, and Samson, I'm not an open book when it comes to the subject. That's not to say he doesn't dominate my thoughts, but I've had to put limits on that since I have a tendency to fixate. I only let myself think about him during certain times of the day, like when I run, which is probably why I'm running about thirty miles a week. I want to see what's at the end of the road for us, but I have to have faith in what I feel and in the truth.

Truth is a thorny thing. In the past, I've carelessly twisted it, put a spin on it, and because of my recklessness, I made myself bleed. The birthmark on my forehead wasn't God being vindictive or His way of telling me that I had done something wrong. He put it there to remind me of all the love I have in my life. He marked me on purpose, just like He marked this tree that I love. My past is ugly and beautiful, and my future, nothing but risky, defiant hope.